Too often, too many words are written about too
many stories. In any case, the stories in this remarkably diverse anthology are very well introduced by its editor, David Gerrold, himself no
mean practitioner in the world of s.f. As we believe his powerful story, AFTERNOON WITH
A DEAD BUS, will prove.

We note only the extraordinary range of subjects
covered, no less than the richness and variety
in style and approach.

In a field of writing which takes itself seriously
(and science fiction does), Ballantine Books is
proud to present a very worthy collection.

Also by

David Gerrold

THE TROUBLE WITH TRIBBLE
*THE FLYING SORCERERS (with Larry Niven)

*Available from Ballantine Books

PROTOSTARS

Edited by
David Gerrold

Aided and abetted by
Stephen Goldin

BALLANTINE BOOKS • NEW YORK • LONDON
An Intext Publisher

BALLANTINE BOOKS, INC.
101 Fifth Avenue, New York, N.Y. 10003

DEDICATED TO THE MEMORY OF MY FATHER,
I am a product of his environment.

CONTENTS

A SORT OF INTRODUCTION

It's traditional these days, within the science fiction genre, to take a couple of pages at the beginning of an anthology to justify or explain it.

Okay, the justification: these are good stories.

The explanation: we did it for the money.

Anything above and beyond that is icing on the cake. These stories are here to entertain you and, hopefully, to provide some food for thought. Period.

I (the editor) make no claims as to the inherent danger of any of these visions, nor do I claim that there is anything world-shaking about this book. We had a simple goal when we put it together: to provide an entertaining anthology of forward-looking fiction.

Stories were selected because they were good and because they were representative of the genre. Other than that, there is no central theme. If you, the reader, detect one, it is probably the common cultural overview that all of us (readers, writers and editors) share.

There are, of course, trends in contemporary science fiction and this book reflects some of them. But there is no central idea in science fiction today, and I make no attempt to superimpose my views on a genre that is moving in all directions at once. There are four hundred members of the Science Fiction Writers of America. There are (at least) four hundred and one different directions in which science fiction is moving. It is for you, the reader, to decide which direction you wish to follow.

The nice thing is, there's no limit to the number of directions in which you can go.

One point I would make about science fiction is that it's the new theology—or, to put it another way, theology for the modern man. It is the only literature of the twentieth century that consistently dares to speculate on the nature of reality and man's place in the universe.

I know, I know—that sounds a bit pretentious. But consider it. A science fiction writer isn't asking you to take anything on faith—he has to prove or disprove any speculations he makes. He's a brave man for doing so, because he's willing to be proven wrong. In accepting the verification that the scientific method (hypothesis followed by experimentation) offers, he is also accepting a double-edged sword that might strike back and show him mistaken.

There aren't many religions that are willing to undergo that test.

Hence, my statement that science fiction is theology for the modern man. It is a theology that is based upon the scientific method—a method that is central to the growth of our present-day technology and (you should pardon the expression) civilization. It is a literature that ponders all of the conditions of man and humanity, and if I must commit myself and state a central theme to this book, then the theme is man's discovery of himself and what it means to be a human being.

And after all, isn't that what it's all about?

—DAVID GERROLD
New York, 1970

PROTOSTARS

One day in November of 1970, while I was passing through New York city, Galaxy Science Fiction *offered me a job. Ejler Jakobbsen, the editor, called me and asked if I would help him catch up on his "slush pile."*

"Slush pile" is an editor's term—it refers to that huge, almost mountainous, stack of unsolicited "over-the-transom" manuscripts that hopeful young writers from all over the world have sent in.

Thinking that it might be fun as well as enlightening —besides, the money was right—I accepted. After all, I knew science fiction, and I knew editing (to some extent). The hopeless stories would be obvious—you could tell by skimming the first and last pages exactly what they were about. Anything that couldn't be rejected that easily automatically earned a more detailed perusal. So—I dug in. David Gerrold, boy editor, attacks the fabled Galaxy *"slush pile"—and loses.*

Oh, I got the "slush pile" down to almost nothing, but the whole experience so unnerved me that I was useless for days. I wouldn't even approach my own typewriter for fear that some of the dreaded "slush" might have rubbed off on me. (Excuse me, "slush" is a euphemism, extraordinarily polite.) Finally, to get the bad taste out of my mind, I had to read two Asimovs, a Delaney, a Niven and a Heinlein juvenile. Even so, I

1

still wake up screaming. Boy, talk about monsters—
 I'll tell you about it.
 *First off, let's understand what the "slush pile" is.
These are not manuscripts from professional writers;
those get carefully picked out of each day's mail. These
are the manuscripts of the hopefuls, the people who
want to be writers and aren't, not yet. The hopefuls are
housewives and students and children. And servicemen
and diplomats and occasionally an Honest-to-God luna-
tic. Some of them are nuts; some are just naive—but,
most important, some are actually determined to someday be a professional writer. These latter are the people
and stories that you look for in a slush pile—the diamonds in the shit, so to speak.*

*But there's no way to tell which stories are any good
unless you read them—and that's where a man of en-
durance and courage is called for, a man who is willing
to risk great pain and suffering for small triumph.
Somebody has to read the "slush pile."*

*(Now let's get one thing clear here. If you—the reader
—have ever submitted a story anywhere, I'm not talking about you. If your story was rejected, it was only
because the editor was too short-sighted to realize what
a work of art he held in his hands, or because some
first reader was a total nump. It's all those other would-
be writers I'm talking about now—not you, just the
ones who give the "slush pile" a bad name.)*

*Now, a lot of the hopefuls are either naive or not
serious enough. By "naive" I mean they think it's easy
to sell a story to a magazine. It isn't. The professional
writer who has reached the point where he starts getting
as many acceptances as rejections is one who is finally
achieving success. He has learned what will sell. (Yes,
yes, I know there's more to writing than just selling and
making money—try telling that to Harold Robbins.)*

*Some of the hopefuls are "not serious enough." They
haven't done their homework. They don't know enough
about the field they are trying to break into, and they're
unwilling to take the time to find out—so they end up*

repeating the common mistakes, over and over and over again. These are the ones that hurt the most. After you've read the fourteenth—or fortieth—story that ends with the discovery that the hero and heroine are Adam and Eve, you begin to learn the meaning of real pain.

And there are variations on the theme. The would-be writer, thinking he is clever, witholds some vital piece of information, probably under the delusion that he is being arty, and allows you to discover at the end of his tale that (a) this is how God (or whatever passes for him) created the world; or (b) this particular planet that the aliens have been messing around with is Earth; or (c) this strange and exotic adventure that we have been so avidly following is really a brilliantly handled retelling of some event so perfectly ordinary that we kick ourselves for not having realized it sooner. Actually, we just kick ourselves for having read it in the first place. (I have avoided giving any specific examples here to spare embarrassment and lawsuits.)

But you will see it over and over again: stories about God, about World War III, about Adam and Eve, about every hackneyed cliché that more experienced writers have learned to avoid like the plague. It's enough to make a grown man despair, to put his head into his hands and weep bitter tears for the future of his craft—

—and then, you come across that ray of light in the darkness, that parting of the clouds that admits a golden gleam of hope in the form of a neatly typed manuscript with well-drawn scenes and characters—and beauty of beauties, an original idea, nicely done. I fall to my knees and give thanks to whatever deity I am holding dear at the time for being allowed such a boon.

If I sound a little melodramatic here, it's intentional. I admit it: I am a possessive and vehement bastard whenever the integrity of my craft is threatened. I will protect it violently from any who would lower its standards.

That doesn't mean I'm against new writers—every-

body has to start someplace. What I'm against are the people who refuse to take writing seriously. They're the ones who are giving the craft a bad name. Everybody knows at least one person who is "writing a book"—right? How many people actually know someone who has ever sold that book?

These are people who have the wrong idea about writing. They wouldn't dream of trying to pilot a Boeing 747 without the proper training, or trying to operate an IBM 360—Why then do they insist that they can write just because they own a typewriter?

Writing is every bit as much a skill as piloting a jet plane. Writing is a process of decision-making; every word you put down on the paper is a decision. The major advantage of writing over jet plane piloting is that a wrong decision won't kill you. But that doesn't make the decision any more correct.

Keeping up with the current books isn't enough. Nor is having had a high-school English major. (They help, but they're not enough.) You have to have training for any job if you're going to do it properly—that means knowledge of plot structure, characterization, dialogue, and most of all, how to use the English language in a clear, concise manner. The second worst mistake new writers make (myself included) is trying to be experimental. First, learn the basics and prove that you can tell a story—later on, after you've proven it, then you can be Harlan Ellison.

Or Joyce, or Nabokov, or whoever you want to be.

Which brings me (finally) to Scott Bradfield.

He's a new writer. (Shriek. Scream.)

At the time I'm writing this introduction, he's fourteen years old, and this is his first sale. The difference between him and ninety percent of the people who submit stories to editors is that Scott is determined to write.

He reads prodigiously. He is familiar with most of the major writers in the science fiction genre—and he is familiar with most of the terms and ideas that are bandied about. He knows the over-common ideas, and he avoids them. He doesn't just sit at his typewriter and peck, peck, peck (although that's the important part); he studies the works of others to see how they succeeded or why they failed, so he can profit by their experience.

This story must be at least the tenth one of Scott's I've read. I rejected the first nine and insisted on a re-write on this one. It's here, not because Scott is a new writer or because I want to make a specific point; it's here because I think it's a readable story with a valid point to it. More important, it avoids most of the more common mistakes that new writers make. Hence, there are no apologies to be made for its inclusion. It'll have to stand or fall on its own merits, just like all the other stories.

(I'll add that I'm not making any predictions for Scott. The temptation is to say that if he continues to push at it, someday he could be a major force in science fiction—but that's too easy a thing to say, and not fair to Scott. Instead I'll be bluntly honest. Scott's got a long way to go, and he's got one person rooting for him.)

WHAT MAKES A CAGE, JAMIE KNOWS

Scott Bradfield

Little Jamie sleeps in a crib in a room. The room is surrounded by a cage, a mental one with boundaries that exclude the things he needs the most. Beyond, his parents' lair growls to him.

He cries for food and is startled by the eruption of anger emitted from the dark den of Moans and Pain.

"Shut up, you little brat!"

He becomes more confused, whining louder, dreaming of some warm friendly face to enter his cage and melt away the bars of fear and terror.

"Damn it, Grace! Will you get your kid to shut his trap! Stuff some bread in it; I don't care how you do it. Just let me get some sleep!"

The woman drags herself out of bed and walks into the next room. From the door she can see the white-faced dirty child supporting himself against the side of his splintering crib. He tries to direct his great hunger into her cold narrowing eyes.

But she is gone. The sound of shuffling footsteps, then she returns with a half can of baby food left over from the previous day. Crudely, she shovels it into his eager mouth. The last spoonful comes too soon and his dim-lit eyes plead for more. Dreams shatter as the mother leaves the room she has learned to hate.

The little brat—he won't stop crying, and after all she's done for him. Sure, I love him, she thinks; after

6

all, ain't I his mother? Why don't he love me back? No, all he does is cry, cry, cry! He doesn't do anything for me, but keep me from my bed—

—which she crawls into, beside a stranger, and dreams of golden ballrooms and gold-silver earrings to match a finely woven dress.

Jamie awakes in the deep of night. The sound is unfamiliar; the sensation—as terrifying as the rest of his world.

Colors converge, merge. . . .

They begin to take shape—a pair of *bodies,* different from the adults Jamie has known before—

Wearing cloaks of light, they make their way through the cluttered room.

The child tries to scream, but his body is paralyzed and rigid with fear.

"This one—?"

"As good a specimen as any. We do not have time to pick and choose. The—*cleansing* occurs within (?) time-periods."

"—It is so young though."

"You are right. But it is healthy. I will mark it for—"

They flicker and are gone.

At last, Jamie finds voice—a strident wail of terror. Again and again.

From the next room come signs that the beasts are rising. Jamie screams a third time, insistently.

His father enters, hate glistening in his eyes like tar and sulfur. "Damn you, kid! There's only one way to get you to shut up—" He strikes out with his fist; the impact is—stunning.

Jamie is too confused to cry, too paralyzed to hurt. "Me . . . me . . ." But he has not the words. His father strikes again. Again. Jamie lies deflated on his cotton mat.

Satisfied, the monster lumbers off. It will recount its victory to its mate, then return to sleep.

"What happened? How'd you get him to quiet down?"

"I simply gave him a belt across the chops. We won't hear anymore out of him tonight."

"You didn't have to hit him! He's only a baby."

"If he's gonna live under the same roof as me, he sure ain't gonna act like no baby. Or I'll kick his red-cheeked little ass!"

"You could have hurt him!"

"Naw! I didn't! And don't you start in on me, or I'll give you some of what I gave him!"

That seems to settle things for the moment, and they both lie back to wait for sleep.

Then they hear the thunder. It crescendos inside and outside their house. Pounding.

"What the hell?" Father sits up.

"What is it?"

A burning stench fills the air, starching their nostrils. A crackling, like the ripping of calico, descends from the attic.

"Hey, I think it's a fire!"

He leaps from the bed, the air chilling him in his bare chest and shorts. "Let's get the hell outta here!"

The woman, startled, joins him—they run through the hall. Heat and fire drip from the ceiling. They dodge the flaming obstacles and dash out into the open sky; the air is tinted with a strange unbalanced smell.

A sudden mother's instinct: "My baby!"

She runs into the burning house and to the child's room.

The crib is empty.

A depression marks where a tiny warm body once lay. She searches the room, stumbling and clumsy. She can hear the fire popping as it walls off her only exit. She forgets Jamie in confused desperation and struggles into the next room to find the doorway submerged in flames, covered by raging red-heat. Pain billows as the flames leap to her dress, her arms—she slaps at them frantically—

—and is ignited into a fiery private Hell.

Outside, Father hears her scream. His face is white —and red with the reflected glow. Is he smiling? It turns to apprehension and then to terror as the heavens around him burst into livid red to match the house.

Baby Jamie sleeps on the ground in a room. The room is surrounded by a cage, a physical one of steel and iron. Through the bars, something stares at him.

When he wakes, he eats—something like bread, but more crusty and mealier. He gulps water from a trough that runs across one side of the cage; there is green algae on the surface of it.

Feeling the need to urinate, he does so. Dampening the cold sand and tile beneath.

In 1969, I went looking for James Tiptree Jr.
And found only a mystery.

To all intents and purposes, James Tiptree Jr. does not exist. No one has ever seen him, no one has ever spoken to him on the telephone. No one has ever found out where he lives. All we have (and I mean editors, agents, writers, fans—everyone) is a post-office box number in McLean, Virginia.

From that post-office box issues an endless series of letters and science fiction stories.

And it's frustrating as hell. I'd like to buy the guy a drink, and he won't come out of the woodwork.

I shouldn't complain though. He's probably one of the finest new science fiction writers in America today. If this man (or woman?) were willing to write full time, he'd have to add three new mantlepieces to wherever he hides out, just to hold all the awards he'd win.

I can always tell when he's written a great story. I find myself writing to him about it. I really should tell you what he said about this one, but I don't think I will. I think the story says it well enough without any additional comment.

11

I'LL BE WAITING FOR YOU WHEN THE SWIMMING POOL IS EMPTY

James Tiptree Jr.

Cammerling was a nice Terran boy, which is to say that his folks came from Groombridge 34 Nu and surprised him with a Honda 990 starcoupe for his traditional *Wanderjahr*. But Cammerling was one sigma off median in that he not only chose to travel by himself but also to visit the remoter parts of the ephemeris where the hostels were unrated or even nonexistent. Which is how he came to be the first Terran—or certainly the first for a long, long time—to land on the planet of Godolphus Four.

As his part opened, Cammerling's ears were assailed by a stupendous braying, skirling and clashing which arose from an immense dust cloud in which gleamed many shining points. When the dust settled a bit Cammerling made out that there was a barbaric festival of some sort in progress.

Two vast masses of men were rushing toward each other on the plain before him. From one side pounded phalanx upon phalanx of individuals clad in leather cuirasses and greaves and bearing obsidian lances decked with streaming hair and what Cammerling took to be dried nuts. Charging at them from his right came squadrons of reptile-mounted riders in dazzling glass mail who whirled glittering bolos. Just behind all these raced ranks of archers with fire-headed missiles on their bows, and the whole mass was being urged on by hornblowers, cymbalists and bull-roarers, and standard-bearers staggering under huge pennants realistically resembling entire flayed human hides.

As Cammerling stepped forward for a clearer view, the two hordes fell upon each other in primal fury, and the plain became a vortex of slashing, spearing, gouging, beheading, disemboweling, dismembering and other un-mistakably hostile interactions.

"Good grief," said Cammerling, "can this be an actual, real live war?"

His presence was now noticed by several of the combatants closest by, who stopped to stare and were promptly clouted by those beyond. A head flew out of the melée and rolled to Cammerling's feet, making faces and jetting gore. Without pausing to think he switched on his Omniglot Mark Eight voder and shouted, "STOP THAT!"

"Oh, sorry," he added, as he heard the sound of obsidian shattering all over the field and noted that numerous persons were rolling on the ground clutch-ing their ears. Tuning the voder down, he recalled his panthropological semester notes and began to scan the armies in close detail, searching for their leaders.

To his gratification he located a group of banner bearers on a hilltop somewhat behind the fray. At their head was a gigantic warrior mounted on an armored carnosaur, which was wearing a tower of jewelled hu-man heads. This individual was magnificently painted and was leaning back in his saddle to accommodate a ham-sized triple-phallus codpiece from which spouted green smoke. He was alternately bellowing and shaking his fist at Cammerling and chug-a-lugging from a gem-encrusted skull.

On a similar rise across the way Cammerling ob-served a gaudy pavillion under which a very fat man re-clined upon a gold litter upholstered with feebly squirm-ing naked infants and langourously nibbled tidbits from a poignard while he eyed Cammerling. As Cammerling watched, the fat man wiped the poignard by running it through one of the meatier infants and snapped his jewelled fingers at his sides.

All these barbaric manifestations pained Cammerling, who was a good Terran boy, but at the same time he felt exhilarated by stumbling upon what was undeniably the Real Thing. Disregarding the flaming arrows and other missiles that were now arriving in his vicinity and being deflected by his invisible summer-weight non-absorptive GE-Bilblas forcefield, he focussed the voder to project directly at the two chieftains.

"Hi," he said. "I'm Cammerling from Groombridge 34 Nu. How about coming over here where we ran rap, if you aren't too busy?"

After a bit of milling, Cammerling was pleased to see the two personages and their retinues converging upon him, while the crowd nearest him drew back. Unfortunately, the delegations halted at a distance that Cammerling felt was too great for a really meaningful encounter, so he stepped toward them and said winningly, "Look, friends. What you're doing—you know, it's—well, don't take this wrong, but it's not nice. It's obsolete, truly it is. I don't want to put down your cultural identity in any way, but since you're going off this war kick sooner or later—I mean, studies prove it ——why not stop now?"

Seeing that they were staring at him blankly, he added, "I don't recall my historical symbolism too clearly, but what I mean, I think, is that you two men should shake hands."

At these words the fat prince in the palanquin spitted three infants and screamed, "Me touch that lizard-fondling offspring of an untranslated defecation-equivalent diseased female organ? I shall serve his barbecued gonads to condemned thieves!"

And the dragon-chief threw back his head and roared, "Me handle that chromosomally-imbalanced caricature of a feces-eating cloacal parasite? His intestines will be cruppers on my corpse-wagons!"

Now Cammerling could see at once that this was

going to be quite a tough situation to turn around, and as he recalibrated his voder, which had begun to oscillate, he also reminded himself that he must be careful not to show disrespect for these people's cultural norms. So he said pleasantly, "If I could serve as a resource person here, I'd like to offer the suggestion that both modern science and ethical intuition agree that all men are brothers."

Hearing which, both chieftains looked at each other with instant and total comprehension and then wheeled back and hurled every weapon in reach at Cammerling, and their retainers followed suit. Amid the shower of missiles, Cammerling perceived that a poignard and a kind of broadaxe had penetrated his summer-weight forcefield, making nasty runs in the lining. He was about to remonstrate with them when two pale-blue blips floated down from the nose of the spaceship behind him and instantly reduced the two princes, the carnosaur, the infants, and most of the entourages to thin vitreous puddles.

"Good lord," said Cammerling reproachfully to the ship, "That wasn't nice either. Why did you?"

The voder print-out came to life and typed in cursive: "Don't freak, dear boy. Your mother put in a few contingency programs."

Cammerling made a face and turned to address the assembled armies.

"I'm truly sorry about that. If the seconds in command on both sides want to come over here, I'll try to see it doesn't happen again."

He waited patiently while some confusion died down, and presently two somewhat older and less flamboyant senior types were assisted to come forward and Cammerling repeated and clarified his previous suggestions. The two viziers looked at Cammerling with the whites of their eyes showing, and they looked at his ship, and at the puddles, which were now cooled and streaked with beautiful colors suitable for intaglio work on a rather large scale, and finally at each other. To

Cammerling's intense satisfaction they eventually allowed themselves to be persuaded to a distant brushing of the gloved hands. In his excitement he recalled an historic phrase:

"Your swords shall be converted into plowshares!"

"Madness!" exclaimed both viziers, shrinking back. "Ensorcel our swords into women?"

"A figure of speech," Cammerling laughed. "Now look, I do want to make it crystal clear I didn't come here to intimidate you people with my superior technology created by the enlightened interplay of free minds in our immense interstellar peace-loving Terran Federation. But don't you think it would be interesting—just as an experiment, say—if you announced that peace has been declared, like in honor of my visit maybe—" he smiled deprecatingly, "—and told your armies to go, uh, home?"

One of the viziers uttered an inarticulate howl. The other cried wildly, "Is it your will that we be torn to pieces? They have been promised loot!"

This made Cammerling aware that he had overlooked their concern about the emotional tensions which were bound to persist in a situation like this, but luckily he recalled a solution.

"Look, you have to have some kind of big national sport. You know—a thing you play? Like shinny? Or curling? Tug-of-war even? Tournaments? And music. Music! My ship can put out fantastic refreshments. Isn't that the usual thing? I'll help you get organized."

The hours that followed were somewhat jumbled in Cammerling's memory, but he felt it was, overall, quite successful. Some of the native sports turned out to be virtually indistinguishable from the original battle, and he did regret having inadvertently triggered the ship's vaporisers once or twice. But no one seemed overly upset, and when dawn broke over the plain there were a goodly number of survivors able to accept his goodbye gifts of inertia-free athletic supporters and other trade trinkets.

"That rugger-type thing you play has a lot of potential," he told the viziers. "Of course, I'd hope we could substitute an inanimate ball, and perhaps tranks instead of strychnine on the spurs. And the eviscerating bit, that's out. Here, try another Groombridge Jubilee. I want to explain to you sometime about setting up a farm system. Little Leagues. By the way, what was the war about?"

One of the viziers was busy shredding his turban, but the other one began to recite the history of the war in a sonorous sing-song, starting with his tenth grandfather's boyhood. Cammerling set the voder to Semantic Digest and eventually decided that the root of the matter was a chronic shortage of fertile flood-plain from the local river.

"Well, look," he said. "That's easy to settle. Just throw a dam across those foothills there and impound the water so everyone will have enough."

"Dam?" said one vizier. "He who chokes the father of waters," said the turban-shredder hollowly, "his gonads shall become as small dried berries, and his penis shall be a dry wick. Aye, and all his relatives."

"Believe it," said Cammerling, "I have nothing but respect for your cultural orientations. But really, in this one instance—I mean, from an existential viewpoint, although I'm aware that we should do this on a more participatory basis, man—look!"

And he took his ship up and vitrified a couple of miles of foothills; and after the river-bed had overflowed and filled up with mud and dead fish, there was a big lake where none had been before. "Now, there's your dam," said Cammerling," and the water will flow all year, enough for everybody, and you can go forth and dig irrigation ditches—I'll have the ship make a contour map—and the land will blossom."

And the viziers looked all around and said, "Yes, Lord, I guess we have a dam." And they went back to their respective peoples.

But Cammerling was a sensitive type, and after he

thought it all over he went down to the nearest village and said, "Look, you people shouldn't get the idea that I think I'm some sort of god or whatever, and to prove it I'm going to come right in and live amongst you." He felt confident about this because his whole class had been on the pangalactic immunization program. And so he went down and lived amongst them, and after they got over his diseases, most of them, he was able to get right inside their heads and experience all their mind-blowing cultural practices and perceptions, and especially their religions. And although he knew he shouldn't do anything to mess up their ethnic reality, still he was pained in his good Terran heart by certain aspects of it.

So he called on each of the two viziers, and as diplomatically as possible he explained how deeply he respected their cultural outlooks, and that he wanted to help them along the inevitable evolution of their present religious phase into the more abstract and symbolic plane that it was surely headed for. "Those big statues," he said, "I mean, they're absolutely smashing. Major works of art. Coming generations will stand in awe. But you've got to protect them. I mean, those caves, and drip-drip. Oh, what a good light man could do. And you know, burning up babies in them is corrosive. Incense would be much safer. How would this grab you: *one* religio-cultural center for *both your nations,* where all the people could dig them? And while we're on it—you know, this bit of dropping babies down the wells to bring rain has to be a joke. I mean, existentially, that's why you all have squitters."

And so he went about and opened up different lines of thought for them as unobtrusively as he knew how, and when he detected signs of tension he eased off at once—for example, on his project of persuading the men to do some of the plowing. He himself laid the first stones for the Culture Center, and waited patiently for the idea to take. And presently he felt rewarded when the two head priests actually came together to see him.

One was wearing a white and black death's head twice as tall as he was, and the other was wreathed in ceremonial snakes. After the greetings were over, it turned out that they had come to ask a favor.

"Delighted," he said, and he was. They explained that every year about this time a fiendish man-eating monster ravaged the villages in the hills, and they were as straws before it. But he would undoubtedly be able to despatch it with one hand.

So Cammerling gladly agreed to take care of the matter, and he set off next morning feeling that he had actually been accepted at last. And since they had stressed the negligible difficulty of the task—for him— he went on foot, carrying wtih him only a light lunch, his Galactic Cub Scout kit and a target laser his aunt had given him when he left. And the high priests went back to their peoples rubbing their hands and pausing only to urinate on the stones of the Culture Center. And there was a great deal of smoke around the caves where the idols brooded.

Cammerling noticed some consternation when, two mornings later, he came whistling down the hill-trail, but he put it down to the fact that behind him crawled an enormous shabby saurian with one leg in a plastiseal and a tranquilizing collar on his neck. Cammerling explained that the creature's vile habits had their origin in impacted tusks, and treated everybody to a practical demonstration of orthodontistry from the ship's Xenoaid. After that he spent several mornings training the beast to serve as a watch-dragon for his ship, which had sustained a few attacks of high-spirited vandalism. And the Culture Center suddenly began to shape up.

But Cammerling was thoughtful. On his mountain trip he couldn't help noticing that this planet had really terrific potential in other ways. And so, after chewing it over, he gathered some of the more enterprising commoners into an informal discussion-group and said, "Look. I'm keenly aware, as studies have shown, that too-rapid industrialization of an agrarian culture isn't a

too-good idea, and I want your frank comments if you
feel I'm pushing. But have you thought about a little
light industry?"

And so—well, pretty soon one of the nations had a
small metal-siding plant and the other had a high-qual-
ity ceramic operation. And although Cammerling was
careful to keep hands off local native customs and
never to override native initiative, still, by his enthusiasm and participation in their life at the actual village level, he did seem to be having quite a catalytic
effect. Certainly there were a great many activities available for everyone, what with laying out the irrigation
system and collecting the kaolin and the materials for
ore extraction and so on.

And so it came about that one morning, while Cammerling was helping someone invent the spinning jenny,
the high viziers of the two nations came together in a
secret place.

And one said, "While in no sense renouncing my
undying enmity to you and your horde of agrarian de-
fectives whom I intend to exterminate at the earliest
possible moment, it's plain to see that this blasphemous
usurper is grinding both our generative organs into
skink soup and we ought to get rid of him." And the
other replied that, while he did not wish to convey
the impression that he was befouling himself by communicating on equal terms with the irrevocably tainted
offspring-of-a-chancrous-scrotum represented by his
present interlocutor, he would be glad to join in any
scheme to get this interstellar monkey off their necks.
But was he a god?

"God or not," the first vizier responded, "he appears
as a young man, and there are certain well-known ways
to quiet such prickmice, more especially if we pool our
joint resources for maximum effect." To which the
other assented, and they began to count.

And so a few evenings later, hearing his watch-
dragon snirkling hysterically, Cammerling opened his
port to behold twelve dainty shapes swathed in bril-

liant gauzes, but not so well swathed that he failed to glimpse delicate belled toes, eyes, limbs, haunches, waists, lips, nipples, et-triple-cetera, such as he had never before beheld on this planet. Which was not surprising, since he had been gamely rubbing noses with the gamier squaws of the village level.

So he hopped out the door and said eagerly, "Well, hi there! What can I do for you?"

And a girl veiled in smouldering silks stepped forward and parted her raiment just enough to dislocate his jaw and said, "I am Lheesha the Bird of Passionate Delight and men have killed each other for my merest touch and I wish to do to your body caresses of which you have never dreamed and which will draw out your soul with unforgettable bliss." And she showed him her little hands with the breasts of hummingbirds implanted in her tender palms.

And another stepped forward and swirled her vestments so that his eyes popped and melted, and she said, "I am Ixhualca the Burning Whirlpool and I have thirty-two hitherto undiscovered muscles in my thing and I desire to inflame you to madness by means of unbearable pleasure indefinitely prolonged."

And a third knelt down demurely and whispered, "I am called Mary Jean the Cannibal Queen and I have been forced all my life to take nourishment only by compressing and vellicating my lips and gullet upon a certain shameful device, and mortally wounded princes call for me that they may expire in joy."

And by this time Cammerling could sense that they were all thinking along the same general lines, and he said, "Well, you certainly are some superchicks, and to tell the truth I have been kind of horny. Please come in."

So they trooped in through his doorlock, which had also been programmed by Cammerling's mother, and on their way in it imperceptibly relieved the girls of various blades, gimlets, potions, amulets, poisoned rings, essences, fangs, stings, garrotes, ground glass, and so on, which had been installed in interesting recesses of their anatomies. But even if the high viziers had known this they would not have been discouraged, because no man had ever enjoyed any two of those girls and lived.

When all twelve of them were inside with the door closed it was pretty crowded, but the ones closest to Cammerling set to work on him with the hummingbird frottage and the tongueing and the spice-inflamed apertures and the thirty-two new thing-muscles and every kind of indescribably intimate and exotic stimulation so typical of upper-class feudal debauchery, while those who couldn't get at him just then indulged in unspeakably erotic and obscene activities, which he was able to observe in close detail. And so they went on all night, finding refreshment not only in Cammerling's youth and vigor but also in the chance to pick up some cross-cultural technical fertilization, since they were half from one nation and half from the other.

And the morning light shone in upon an expanse of totally intertwined and exhausted bodies. But it had not shone long before a gentle heaving started from below, and Cammerling crawled out.

"Well now," said Cammerling, "that was truly a groovy grope." And since he was a nice Terran boy who had ben raised on wholesome Terran orgies, he bounced out the lock of the spaceship and did thirty-two push-ups, one for each muscle. And he poured water on his head and whistled and sang out, "Hey kids, when you get yourselves together I'll show you how to make some pizzas. I have to go help lay out the new sewage-filtration pond; we don't want to pollute the ecology."

But the girls straggled out very upset, crying, "Lord, we dare not go back because we have failed in our mission and we will be despatched with excruciating and bestial tortures."

So Cammerling told them they could stay with him, and he showed them how to work the stove. And they all settled down happily except the girl Ixhualca with the whirlpool thing, who said, "W'at ees dees batsheet peetzas?!" and stamped back to the executioners.

And Cammerling went out to participate in the filtration project and the water-wheel project and the Voltaic cell project and numerous other projects, becoming more involved than he really felt good about, because he could see he actually had dislocated the native cultural gestalt some. And he got flak from people who couldn't do their thing because their thing was, say, shrinking corpses, which there weren't enough of now, or holding sticks to make the women plow straight, when the women were now plowing with lizard-drawn plows that went too fast. And he began to understand what his group vocational computer meant by acquiring maturity of outlook.

But he learned to cope, like when the metal workers came to him and said, "Lord, we've made this devil-machine for vomiting out this unholy hard stuff. What in the name of the sacred iguana egg do we do with it now?" So he said, "Look, let's all vote. I vote we make water pipes." And when the kiln-workers said, "See, O Lord. These fire-bellies which we have constructed give birth to these unbearable tile pots. What use are they?" And he said, "Well, let's all kick it around. I'll throw in the idea that we make ceramic flush toilets." And a high priest said, "By this you know that the new religion is to put water in one end of the body and take it out the other with maximum effort."

Meanwhile, all the babies that had not been put down the wells or into the idols continued to pile up and drive everybody into the walls. And one day Cammerling heard strange sounds and opened the door of his ship to find the watch-dragon surrounded by hundreds of roaring infants. So he walked out to look them over and said, "Good Lord, these are cute little buggers."

So he turned to the eleven houris who were mucking about with strudel dough and said "Here! We have a perfect opportunity to raise a whole generation free from prejudice, fear and hatred. Let us build a school-house, and I want you to teach these kids."

But the girls exclaimed, "This isn't our area of specialization, Lord! What can we teach these larvae?"

"Why," said Cammerling, "Everything!" And he went over and switched on his old teach-panel, which was in his ship. "Look: Montessori method, Holt stix, Allspice Avenue, Parsley Place, Dill Drive, Betelnut Boulevard—we can make that Lizard Lane—Mr. Spock's Logic Book—the whole bag. We'll have like a kibbutz; studies show that has its drawbacks, but it's an optimal form for situations like this."

And in a very short while they had a kibbutz, and the girls were teaching Montessori set theory and creative hygiene. And more and more babies arrived, and more girls too, because it turned out that Ixhualca the Burning Whirlpool had busted out and started a women's lib movement, and many of her recruits opted to teach babies as an alternative to making ceramic flush toilets.

And time passed—actually quite a few years, although to Cammerling they seemed only weeks because he was a nice Terran boy with a life expectancy of five hundred years and he was only into post-adolescence. And behold, there was a whole high-school generation of marvelous kids in well-cut tunics riding around on tractors labeled "War Is Icky" and "Cook Pizzas Not People," with the sun shining through their eyes. And they were restoring the land and helping the people and organizing truck-farm cooperatives and music festivals and People's Capitalism and community dance-ins and health clinics. And though a majority of the older people still seemed sort of silent, Cammerling gazed upon the unstoppable flood of Montessori babies pouring out of his kibbutzim with middle-Terran values plus pioneering macho and knew that it was only a matter of time.

And one evening, as he sat watching his sabras setting up a transmitter, practicing karate and laying the foundations for a supermarket, there came a flash in the sky. And a spaceship shrieked in out of nowhere and sat down daintily on the beach. And Cammerling saw it was a supersports model of a style that was unfamiliar to him but obviously very heavy indeed. And he went over to the alabaster lock full of strange stirrings.

And it opened, and there stepped out that indescribable being, a nice Terran girl.

"Well!" said Cammerling. "I must say I haven't seen a nice Terran girl for some time. Would you like to come in my spaceship and visit?"

She looked at what was visible of Cammerling's sportster under the passion-flowers and the pizza shells and replied, "Come in mine, Tonto; I have low-gee conditioning and a couple of six-packs of Groombridge Jubilee."

So he bounced into her ship and she opened her arms and he lunged right at her in the good old Terran way. And after missing once or twice because he wasn't used to a quarter gee, he made it.

And afterwards she asked him, "How was it, baby?"

And he said, "Well, there's like a muscle or two I could show you about, but I do believe that's the Real Thing."

"I know," she replied fondly. "There's nothing like a nice Terran girl. And now, Cammerling, it's time you came home."

"Who says?" said Cammerling. And she said,

"Your mother says."

"In that case I'll do it," said Cammerling. "Things are going down pretty smooth here."

So he opened the door of the spaceship and called to all his friends and followers and all the great young people and anyone else who cared to listen. And they came and stood before him in a loose but jaunty formation expressive of individual creativity blended with empathic sharingness. And he said to them, "All right!

I have served you as a humble communication link with Terran interstellar enlightenment, although I hope I haven't screwed up your native cultural scene too much; still, it's done now. Now I go back into the sky. Feel free to get in touch with me at any time via my ship's transmitter if you have any problems. Carry on, Godolphus Four! Farewell."

And they replied, "Oh great pink friend from the sky, we realize you are not a god and all that; you have taught us freedom from superstition. Nevertheless, bless you. We will carry on. Farewell."

And so Cammerling went away; and as soon as he took off, all the old hairy chiefs and priests and tribesmen came out and rose up and started joyfully hacking everybody and everything in the name of their sacred Godolphian way of life. But the young sabras, whom Cammerling had thoughtfully instructed in the use of advanced weapons as well as Ixhualca's karate, were easily able to handle them. And in no time at all they had the situation totally under control and were able to proceed with energy to fixing up the planet truly nice, all over.

And after many years had passed, a faint message reached Groombridge 34 Nu by sublight, saying:

"Hey, Cammerling! We have fixed up this planet all over truly nice. All is blooming and participatory and ecological. Now what do we do?"

Well, Cammerling was out when this message came, but his secretary got hold of Cammerling's wife, who passed it to his therapist, and when the therapist thought Cammerling was ready he gave it to him. And Cammerling and the wife and the therapist conferred, and at first nothing much came of it, but finally Cammerling got off by himself and messaged back, saying:

"Suggest you now proceed to develop an FTL drive and offer the option of Terran enlightenment to other planets in your vicinity. Computer program on FTL-drive theory follows by faxblip. Carry on. Love, Cammerling."

And so many more years passed, and passed, until one day a new, quite strong message came in from Godolphus Four. It said:

"We have built an FTL drive and we have gone forth and communicated Terran interstellar enlightenment to four thousand three hundred and eighty-four planets. That's all the planets there are. Their peoples join with us in asking: WHAT DO WE DO NEXT?"

But Cammerling never got that message.

The whole point of editing, as I see it, is to pick stories that the reader will react to.

A story can teach or it can entertain—but before it can do either, it must be interesting.

That means the sentence construction should be such that the reader seems to flow from thought to thought, thus allowing him to perceive clearly the incidents the writer wishes to present. In perceiving these incidents, the reader also begins to sense certain relationships in them and in the characters. Gradually, he begins to sense the plot and/or the writer's theme. (Or message, if you must.)

Upon finishing the story, the reader should have had something communicated to him. If he can put it into words, then the story has an obvious message. On the other hand, if he is moved, but can't explain why—then the point of the story was to evoke a specific sense or mood, perhaps one that can't be put into words.

This whole business of writing is really one of communication. I (the writer) may be writing to satisfy only myself—but if I am selling my words to a publisher, and he in turn is selling them to you, then you (the reader) have every right to expect those words to be an attempt at communication.

The editor's job is to outguess the reader—i.e., he has to try to figure out which stories will communicate *something to you. (Not necessarily what they will communicate, just that they will.)*

Sometimes, when that communication is a non-linear idea/concept/totality/gestalt, it can be a very very hard thing to achieve. The editor's temptation in those cases is to be very very conservative. (Those who don't experiment rarely have their projects blow up in their faces—but they rarely make any new discoveries either.)

In my case, I have only one set of criteria to go on —my own sense of judgment as a writer. (I do not and cannot speak for any other editor, and I cannot say what they use for judgment or in lieu of it—although in some cases I have my suspicions.)

When you (the reader) buy this book, you are expressing a certain degree of faith in (a) the writers represented herein, and/or (b) the editor's sense of judgment. In short, because you can't read the whole book before you buy it, you are buying our reputations.

Therefore, it's up to the writers to continue to try to write the best possible stories. It's up to the editor to continue to hold out for those very best possible stories.

"In a Sky of Daemons" is one of those "very best possible" stories.

Larry Yep is a typical example of the "young writer" —he's also an atypical example, but I'll get to that in a minute.

Larry Yep is a student at one of those plastic and brick-lined universities that dot the California coast like fungi. He's a serious student, and because of that he doesn't do as much writing as the rest of us wish he could. But that's the way it is with "young writers." They don't have time to write much, but when they do, it's very very good.

That's where the atypical part comes in. Larry Yep's first sale was a novelette called The Selchey Kids. *It was published in* If, Worlds of Science Fiction *as part of their "first sale by a new writer" series. It also copped* a Nebula nomination. *(In case that doesn't mean much to you, the Nebula is the Science Fiction Writers' of America annual award for excellence in the field. It is an award of recognition by one's colleagues. For a writer to be nominated for such an award on the strength of his* first *sale is unheard of.)*

This is his second sale.

That's a pretty good reputation to be buying, isn't it?

IN A SKY OF DAEMONS
L. Yep

Birth Chile would have liked to have died. The sooner he forgot this life and was re-born into another, the better it would be. All the way down to see Holy Joe, Birth Chile kept wondering what was the matter with himself—and he could just picture Honey Girl replying, "You're stupid."

The city lay far away, so far away that its highest towers were only the briefest glow on the horizon, but it still couldn't be far enough away for him. Hitting her would not have erased her betrayal, and arguing would never have changed Honey's mind. Nothing ever did once she had made a decision.

He had stood there holding onto his bag of sketches, beyond even confusion or shock, possessed by an utter unwillingness to believe that he was in their apartment. The paintings and statues that he had worked on daily, even the furniture that he had bought the necessary raw material for by parting with some of his precious works so the mass-converter could bring his designs into actuality—all were gone.

The only thing in the apartment besides himself was her. If she had been the least bit ashamed, or even defiant, he might have understood; but this utter confidence that she had in her own absolute judgment, this look on her face as if she could not comprehend what he was so upset about—that was the thing that had gotten to him. She did not even seem to realize that she had committed a crime.

"What did you do with it?" he finally managed to ask.

She blinked her eyes and said, "Do with what?"

"The furniture, my work, or has that been re-called by SET's angels," he had said sarcastically.

"SET's angels only come for people," she had said with that infuriating calm. "I traded our stuff for mass-credits. They loved buying it. Just about everyone from the City came to see it. All the elevators in the Tower were jammed."

He had held his sketchbook tighter against his chest. "Well I hope they like bringing all of it back."

"It'd be an awful lot of trouble."

"You didn't seem to have much trouble getting rid of what took me a whole lifetime to accumulate. I just went out this afternoon on a sketching trip."

"That's what you get for leaving me alone," she said firmly.

Birth Chile was quiet for a moment. They had been over and over that ever since the two had matched. He was not going to let himself be distracted. "Have you got a list of buyers?"

"Of course," she said, and she had an annoyed expression on her face. "But what mass-credits are you going to use to convert it?"

"Isn't it in our account?" he asked.

"It's in my account," she said. "I closed out *our* account yesterday."

"Do you want my Soma Suit too?" he had said.

Soma Suits were that fine skin-like material covering the whole body. They stimulated the surface nerves and gave the wearer that euphoric feeling of being embraced by a golden womb of light.

"Don't be a fool." She put an arm affectionately about him. "I like it right where it is." He had pushed her hand away, but did not annoy her, only amused her.

"That junk was just cluttering up the place. You can make more."

The final touch had been when he left her, trying to maintain what little dignity he felt—and met his entire Cell. It was usual for people of a floor to live communally unless they paired off, as he and Honey had. In fact, other Cells from the Tower were there.

Sweet Thing, a member of his old Cell, snapped her fingers impatiently.

"What's happened?" he had asked, puzzled.

"I bet that you wouldn't leave Honey Girl for another hour at least."

He had suddenly felt sick, while his neighbors eyed him critically.

"She made bets on me?"

"You look cute when you're sad," Sweet Thing said.

Honey came out of their apartment, her notebook in hand, probably with the list of bets she had taken. "I'll give you a lift wherever you're going," she said.

But he had not said another word; had not dared. He was going to be free of her. No traces left behind him. And now, walking through the red dirt plain with the few stunted trees, the anger still persisted, the rage at being used. The worst of it was that she'd probably spend it on that damn air car of hers.

He was a clown for her amusement, an anecdote for her to tell to others: so be it. He could no more change her opinion than change himself. But the sullen, the dull, burning resentment remained—and the need to have some answers.

He walked steadily toward the huge bulk of the Tree and the shrine of the relic. The scent of jasmine on a slight breeze made him step faster through the dry dust. Holy Joe, the master of the shrine, had put vibrating crystal strips among the intertwined branches of the great Banyan when it had first been planted at the creation of the world, and with the passing years he had kept adding strips to it until the Tree could be heard as far as the City.

Birth Chile didn't have to see the shrine to picture it—the barest of structures, made from cheap plaster-boards rudely mortared together, more to keep the wind from Holy Joe's bones than to keep out the rain, because SET never sent rain except to the City, and then only when his angels had gone on ahead and given out taped warnings. The weather functioned perfectly, like everything else in the City. Birth Chile had been taken care of perfectly—too perfectly. He had left the Tower early in this life time to become the disciple of Holy Joe. The worst mistake Birth Chile had ever made was to leave the shrine and rejoin his Cell in the Tower. There he had met the newly re-born Honey.

Birth Chile walked past the irrigated gardens, letting the familiar gurgle of the small canals and the caressing sound of the pump make him feel at home. He felt the tenseness leave his shoulders for the first time, and he paused in the doorway. Holy Joe was inside sitting as he had always sat through the countless lives of men, meditating as he had probably done even before the creation of the world.

Holy Joe was the oldest man alive; or rather, since every man's soul dated from the creation of the world, Holy Joe was the oldest living memory. He alone of all men had never been recalled by SET's angels for the long rest in the Cavern of Lights. He alone had never rested there before being re-born into a new body and a new life. He alone never forgot his former lives. Holy Joe had even gone as far as possible to keep his original body. When his automatic nervous system had failed to maintain even the simplest acts of breathing or circu-lating his blood or even digesting, he had obtained a small regulator from SET, who was indeed younger than Holy Joe, since SET was born only with the creation of this world. Holy Joe now kept the regulator about his neck on a golden chain; and it was only by sheer act of will that he now kept on living. One touch, one moment of doubt, and he would end his life beyond what SET's powers could do, which is what Birth Chile found so fascinating about him: that Holy Joe could die, really die, could end existence irretrievably—and Birth Chile could not.

Holy Joe's skin was like fine delicate china, with the blue veins and red arteries so fine that they seemed to be made of fiery light. He was a crystal man, a fragile man, and next to SET, the only link the world had to the pre-world days. His eyes were silver, and his hair was braided into strands with tiny bells attached, on each of which was inscribed a saying of Holy Joe's. There were a lot of them.

When Holy Joe did not acknowledge Birth Chile's bow, Birth Chile stepped behind him and reverently slipped past to the reliquary at the back of the shrine. Reverently, he touched the sword where it rested on the velvet-topped table. It had a talismanic feeling, leaving a tingling sensation in his hand that spoke of vast spaces. It never failed to awe him, this sword, a sword so blindingly bright that it hurt his eyes to look at it. It absorbed almost no energy; all light was reflected. It was said that this sword was a symbol. Holy Joe had once mentioned that it was star metal, the same metal that had been forged in the hearts of suns for the very ships that had carried men to this world. The sword had been left there—though whether as warning or as pledge was not known except to Holy Joe, and he would not say. He claimed that he had a word-bind with SET but their agreement was invoked more when Holy Joe was tired of talking than because of fear of SET.

"Have you come to see me or the sword?" Holy Joe asked. He shifted slightly and looked back at Birth Chile. Birth Chile squatted down beside the master and lowered his bag on the dirt floor.

"Neither, Father," Birth Chile said. "I came here to ask questions." The music of the Tree sang insistently in the background.

Holy Joe shook his head disapprovingly, so that the bells rang faintly. "A hunger for answers feeds upon itself." He held out his hand anyway, palm upwards for an offering. "But I accept."

Ruefully, Birth Chile stripped the mouth of his bag open, revealing the contents he had traded his sketches for.

The holy man poked around among the exposed fruits; then he gingerly picked up an apple and sniffed at it delicately. "Is it real or converted?"

"It's real, Father," Birth Chile said, "the way you like."

In the City was the large lotus-shaped mass-converter —there were smaller units on each cell floor of the Tower—that would make anything you wanted, provided you could put in an equal mass of the necessary molecules as raw material. For jewels it was fine just to keep on adding dust until the lotus converter told you that it had enough. But you couldn't eat jewels, and the mass-converter required organic raw materials to convert into synthetic food. But in a few Tower gardens some enterprising Cells had started small orchards.

"The synthetic stuff tastes like dust," Holy Joe said.

"If it's that bad, why do you trade your flowers and branches from the Tree so others can convert them into food?"

"You people have forgotten your tastebuds with your memories." Holy Joe shrugged ever so slightly, and there was a distant, faint tinkling of crystal from his hair. "But my stomach remembers better than my brain ever did."

"If you like real fruit, why don't you move to the City?"

"Because you people would never let me alone," he said. "And three apples, three questions."

"Why do we try to rule one another?" Birth Chile asked his question.

"So Honey's finally thrown you out," Holy Joe said. "Now maybe you've come to your senses."

But Birth Chile didn't want to make sense; he repeated his question.

Holy Joe could not blink. He had no eyelids. He shook his head musically. "SET put a mental block inside my head against telling about life before the creation of the world. Your second question."

"Hold it. I can rephrase a question, can't I?" Birth Chile asked.

"It's bad business to waste time."

"Time? What do you care about time?" Birth Chile laughed.

"A drop at a time will wear the ocean away," Holy Joe said.

Birth Chile jabbed a finger at him. "There you go again. You keep dropping little hints here and there that drive me crazy. What is an ocean? That block is more of a convenience for you than for SET."

"I have a gentlemen's agreement with SET," Holy Joe said.

"Then who is SET?" Birth Chile asked without thinking.

"That is an irrelevant question," Holy Joe said. "Third question."

"Then what was life without a Soma Suit?" Birth Chile asked a carefully prepared question.

"A man might as well be dead," Holy Joe said.

"Good," Birth Chile said eagerly. He leaned forward a little, thinking that he had circumvented Holy Joe's reluctance to talk about the Pre-world.

"There is no music when the man walks, no poetry. He is little more than an animal." Holy Joe paused. "But what is it to die? Is that what we were afraid of?"

"There is no way to die, if that's what you mean, Birth Chile," Holy Joe finally said. "You can only endure. I thought that even a head as thick as yours would at least have realized that. Some little witch throws you over and all my years of training, all those parables I've told, all my prayers might as well have been offered to the wind." He shook his head disgustedly, but the chimes, even the sound of the Tree music were lost in the high-pitched whine of an air car.

Birth Chile watched from the doorway the lit-up air car screaming its way out of the sky. It could only be one person, because only one person—one tiny, fiery person—would come as though she wanted to tear the sky apart with her air car, as though she could even ram the sun or the disc of stars out of the sky. She dropped with a dead stick, the air screaming through the idle vents, and just before it appeared she was going to smash, she cut on her jets so that she and the air car were momentarily obscured in a huge cloud of red dust. When it settled, the air car was still in one piece.

The tonneau in the back was covered with a tarp, Birth Chile noticed. Then the door swinging out distracted him.

Cat's eyes she has, green glitter in a world of unrealities. Face framed by high-formed cheeks. Secure, and difficult to capture on paper . . . And I see her under the Tree, arguing with Holy Joe. . . . Oh, she is music when she walks and breathes. . . .

She walked that distance with that soft, feminine walk, hips swinging and her hair moving nice and gentle, with the muscles of her body gleaming, now gold, now white, through her Soma Suit. *She gathers light about her body, laughing as her hair tumbles in the air like a net to gather stars. . . .*

She said nothing to Birth Chile, pushing past him as if he did not exist. She stood over Holy Joe, planting her fists on her hips. "Old man, I'd like an answer."

"Now, that depends," Holy Joe said softly.

"On what?"

"On how much you pay," Holy Joe said. "The questions are all pro-rated according to the eight levels of truth."

"What's the first level?" she asked.

"A typical question would be if you want to know what the weather will be."

"It's always fair here," she said. "What's the good of that?"

"It's nice to be reassured." Holy Joe permitted the corners of his lips to draw up ever so slightly into what, for him, passed for a smile.

But Honey Girl shook her head impatiently, as if she had no time left. "I want to know how much your silence would cost," she said.

"More than you can pay," Holy Joe still kept on smiling eerily.

"No, I just want your silence with a certain person so he wouldn't have a reason to come here," Honey Girl said. "That'd keep him from wandering away from his Cell too much and worrying us out of this life and the next, too."

"Now just wait a minute," Birth Chile said stepping forward, but Holy Joe held up a hand, fragile as glass.

"Wait your turn, B.C. You know better than that," Holy Joe said to him. And to Honey Girl, "Seven kilo credits."

Birth Chile almost choked. "That cheap?"

"Interrupt once more and I'll lower it," Holy Joe said.

Honey Girl smiled. She loved to haggle. "Five."

Holy Joe lowered his head meditatively. "Seven."

"You old thief, I'm trying to get rid of a nuisance for you."

"He is not without a certain entertainment value," Holy Joe said. "Eight."

"This place is a mess. The more time Birth Chile spends here, the less time you have to take care of that stupid vegetable of yours," Honey Girl said. "Six."

"Nine kilo credits," Holy Joe said, "and it's a tree."

"Plant, vegetable, tree," Honey sniffed and snapped her fingers. "What's the difference?"

"Trees are not as short-lived as flowers," Holy Joe murmured. "And for that second level question my asking price is now ten."

Honey Girl scowled and tapped his knee menacingly, as if getting ready to kick it. Holy Joe smiled and added. "But you're right—men are more easily hurt than trees."

"Seven credits then, you old thief?" Honey Girl asked.

To Birth Chile's dismay, Holy Joe nodded.

"For a man who doesn't care about money, you drive a hard bargain," Honey said.

"A man wears a fool's cap among fools," the old man murmured.

"Bull shit," Honey said decisively.

"You get what you pay for," Holy Joe shrugged.

"I'm not a thing, you know," Birth Chile said. But both ignored him.

Honey Girl went before the small mass-converter shaped like a lotus in one corner of the room. Holy Joe rarely used it himself, except to charge his clients. The white petals parted to reveal the moist, pink, flesh-like material inside. Honey Girl pressed her palm against one side for it to read her handprint, and she and Holy Joe spoke out the details of their deal.

"I've listened about as long as I'm going to," Birth Chile demanded. "Now don't I get a say in this?"

Holy Joe held up a hand. "We're not finished. Wait your turn."

While Birth Chile waited in mounting frustration, Honey Girl asked Holy Joe, "Will you speak to that lazy good-for-nothing again?"

"Not as long as this life of his lasts," Holy Joe replied.

Honey Girl nodded her satisfaction. "I hope our other deal still stands."

Holy Joe nodded. "If it keeps more and more of

these romanticists like Birth Chile away, I'll be well rid of it."

"What do you mean by 'it'?" Birth Chile demanded. He already knew, because there was only one other thing in the room besides the lotus. But he asked anyway, hoping that it might not be true. Holy Joe only ignored him.

Honey Girl shook her head, looking at him affectionately. "Baby, if I could trust you to live on your own, I would, but you are the most impractical man I have ever met." She got up and pointed at the sword. "Like that sword. You've left me time after time, and I never knew when you were coming back, just so you could walk out here to see this old sword by this old vine."

"I'd like to object to that—" Holy Joe tried to say.

"And you shut up too, you old vegetable, while I'm talking," Honey said.

"That's no way to talk to the Saint," Birth Chile snapped.

"Sorry, sorry," Honey Girl said in such a hurried way that you knew she didn't mean it. "So maybe you'll spend more time with me."

"What are you going to do with the sword?" Birth Chile asked, bewildered.

Honey Girl smiled impudently, as she had so many times—a calm smile, so that he could never tell when she was really serious or just teasing. "Well now, you just guess."

"You wouldn't destroy it?" he asked.

She kept on smiling. "I don't see what say you have in it," she said.

He was helpless—perhaps; in dealing with people— yes. And he was useless in matters outside of his immediate concerns, but the helplessness only came from ignorance, and not from lack of will. And the aggressive will of Honey Girl called even more aggressiveness from him. He slapped her across the face.

She half rose to her feet. "Birth Chile," she said pityingly.

His hand was still numb, and he found that he hated the pity in her face. He wanted to erase it and was already beginning to panic at the thought that he could never erase it. He tried to strike her again but she leaned back, dodging the blow.

"Children," Holy Joe said. "Please try not to break the walls."

He tried to kick her then, but she caught his leg and he found himself on his back, his head thumping hard against the hard-packed dirt. She backed away slowly toward the door, all the bravado, all the affectionate toughness gone from her face—only a resigned sadness remained. All of Birth Chile's frustration, all his sense of being used, welled up inside him. He wanted to hurt—and not just to hurt her badly, but to really hurt, to destroy her. He ran to the table, seized the sword and lifted it up. It fitted to his hand with a surprising lightness.

"You want your sword?" he shouted. In horror Holy Joe struggled to his feet. In fear Honey Girl stared at the point of the sword waving in the dim light of the shrine's votive lamp. Birth Chile didn't care. The sword hung indecisively in his hand as he stared down at her, at once repulsed and attracted by her sudden helplessness.

Then she suddenly reared. "Go to Hell. You damn fool—" she started to say defiantly. And the word "fool" was strong enough to drag the sword down. With the serpentine hiss of the falling blade, the anger suddenly washed away from Birth Chile, but it was too late to hold back the swing, and so he tried to aim it to one side. Honey Girl ducked, or tried to. In horror Birth Chile felt the bite of the sword jar his whole arm. He dropped the weapon and knelt beside her. Desperately he pressed his hands to her side, but the stain only spread through his fingers. Honey held his hands away from her so that they could both see the blood, and wonder. Then she twisted, and her mouth worked silently, but all that would come out were bubbling gasps.

"You fool, you damn fool." A frail hand pushed him away. Holy Joe bent over her, blocking her from view.

Outside, Birth Chile heard the whine of another air car, but one bigger and faster than any air car given to humans because it was one of SET's Archangels, the air car that carried re-called humans back to the Cavern of Lights. The Angels inside did not even wait for their Archangel to land; little holes opened in the bottom and the ovoid robots dropped down on a cushion of air, all the way at full speed, moving on past the numb Birth Chile. A St. Peter, an ovoid almost twice the size of the Angels, exited from a hole on top of the Archangel when it landed.

"The lady will live, brother," the St. Peter explained politely. The robot's smooth side of amorphous metal seemed to melt as an arm extended itself holding a pink situation card.

"Think of it as just another normal terminacy." The St. Peter's utterance explained the probabilities that had made SET re-call the human. The card read: "Two people—one dead; one maimed."

Birth Chile nodded, though he only half-heard the words. He made no sound as the St. Peter extended one arm with a hypo at the end. But as the blackness washed over him, he remembered the other person, the one who was maimed. . . .

Once I saw her dead with a faint remembrance of scarlet flowering beside her and her flesh so pale beneath the cold glitter of colors. . . .

It was cold, terribly cold, on one side. Birth Chile opened his eyes, trying to adjust them to the faint shadow over him. The details grew distinct as Holy Joe's white form bent against the walls of the shrine.

Birth Chile struggled to get up and felt Holy Joe's long slender hands supporting him.

"How do you feel?" Holy Joe asked. His words sounded almost like afterthoughts.

"Cold," Birth Chile murmured. The words limped from his tongue. Half of his tongue bathed in the golden texture of the word; the other part delighted in torturing it.

But Holy Joe did not seem to hear him. The winds were strong now, whipping the sands wildly about the shrine. Weird music fell from the Tree—as if all the chords now clashed in a maddening dissonance.

"Honey's gift is over there," Holy Joe said, not looking at Birth Chile. "I wish to be rid of the treacherous thing." Supporting himself on his good hand, Birth Chile leaned over and saw the sword lying in the sand.

"You mean it was a gift?" He turned to look at Holy Joe.

Almost imperceptibly, Holy Joe nodded. "To keep you in the City where you belong."

"Damn," Birth Chile said and tried to rise, but he fell to the floor. He rolled over and gasped again, the sound coming half-harsh in his throat. Half of his Soma Suit was dead, so that only half of his body glowed with the rainbow hues; the other half was a dull sallow pink. His body fought him as he tried to sit up—one half smooth and strong, the other almost a dead weight. One tear coursed down from his bad eye, and he almost fell over trying to wipe it away.

Holy Joe held out a thin white shroud to Birth Chile, the other half of his Soma Suit. Birth Chile ran his fingers lightly over the material, then tied it awkwardly about his waist with clumsy fingers.

"Your old Cell is having a fire on the other side of the Tree," Holy Joe said dully. Birth Chile rose shakily and held up his two hands before him. One still shone, gold and beautiful. The other showed the wrinkles and veins of his rubbery skin. Holy Joe made no comment—indeed, he did not even look at Birth

Chile but seemed to stare through him with his silver eyes gleaming ghostly in the light. His white-china shoulders gleamed faintly like clouds, and the blue veins burned in his cheeks like tear streaks.

Laughter rose high and loud, only to be followed by a wail. With one last look at Holy Joe, Birth Chile stumbled toward the source. Several times his bad leg was too slow, almost toppling him. His leg and arm, even his head, responded reluctantly. After three falls, he found that a half-shuffle, half-limp was best; but that left his bad hand dangling at his side, throwing him off balance. Finally he cradled the dead hand against his chest with his good hand, tilting his head to let his good eye have a clear field of vision.

He stopped on the edge of the firelight as a person rose to wail and then sank back down. It was his own mother-Cell, gathered there to play at death: to celebrate Honey's re-call, and apparently his too.

A girl with a mask of Honey danced in the center of the circle, and next to her was a Birth Chile. The dance showed Birth Chile's release from the Cavern of Lights, his unformed personality being taken in by the Cell of the Tower, and finally his pairing with Honey Girl. All the time in the background, as a constant reminder, was a man who had adjusted his Soma Suit to a silver sheen like that of the Death Angels.

Desperately, Birth Chile tried to link words with the Cell, but only half of his tongue responded. To his good ear, his words were harsh and slurred, though his bad ear lied and said that they were normal. He tapped his good foot to the rhythm of the Cell rocking back and forth to the pattern of motion set by the Death Angel.

And when the two dancers paused as Death stalked toward them, he almost fell in his eagerness to reach the fire. He forgot his slower right side. He forgot his cradled hand. He was still alive. Death stopped with upraised hands. It was very quiet in the circle; only the crackling of the flames could be heard.

Sweet Thing took Honey's mask from her head and threw it in the air. Turning, she tore Birth Chile's mask from the other dancer. Then she ran toward Birth Chile and hugged him tightly. Birth Chile stood awkwardly, very conscious of the bad hand pressing against his chest.

Sweet Thing turned to the Cell. "B.C.'s come back, come back to us from the Dead." The night suddenly exploded with smiling faces and embracing arms as the Cell welcomed him. Sweet Thing kept herself constantly before Birth Chile no matter where he turned, as if she were trying to revive old memories of when she and Birth Chile had been close, before Honey Girl had been re-issued from the Cavern of Lights and adopted by their Cell. It had been Birth Chile himself who had given Honey her name.

Sweet Thing pulled his bad hand from his chest, holding it tightly about the wrist. "Oh, dance with us, Birth Chile. Dance the Dance of Rebirth. Dance the Dance of Welcome." And she led Birth Chile forward. Somebody else grabbed his other hand, and the chain was formed behind Birth Chile.

Sweet Thing skipped over the sands, pulling Birth Chile along, and then dipped, raising her gleaming eyes toward the stars. "Come on," Sweet Thing called merrily over her shoulder. "Don't you remember it?"

Birth Chile did not answer, not trusting his tongue. He did remember, but only half of him; and try as he would, his stubborn body refused to respond immediately, so that he was forever out of time.

Sadly he knew that his good foot was going to trip over his bad one, and he waited in agony those few seconds before it happened. His good eye told him that he fell slowly, dragging the chain down behind him in one undulating wave. He sat up awkwardly, using his good hand for support, and blinked back his tears of shame. He tried to pull his hands back from Sweet Thing, but she only laughed and pulled harder until he fell off balance into her lap. Everyone laughed.

Birth Chile fought to get up, shrugging off Sweet Thing's helping hands. "How romantic," Sweet Thing gushed. "Look, everybody, B.C.'s maimed himself so they'd let him stay."

Birth Chile looked away, trying to calm his anger.

"Was Honey too scared to be maimed?" someone else demanded.

Birth Chile swung out on his knees, hand held before him pleadingly. "We had no choice. The Law decided everything."

Sweet Thing's fingers were swift, tearing the Soma Suit from around his waist, waving it over her head. "What a souvenir," she cried. Birth Chile lunged for it and fell, mouth open, deep into the sand. Sweet Thing's foot nudged him on his bad side. "Get up, lazy bones."

Birth Chile rose on his hands. Sweet Thing's arm fell to her side and she leaned forward, touching a fingertip lightly to his cheek. "He's crying." The laughter disappeared from the Cell. Angrily, Birth Chile snatched back his Soma Suit, cradling it clumsily to his chest with his bad hand, but the leg of the Soma Suit dangled over. Stains had already appeared, now that it was no longer powered—brown stains, the color of rust.

"Blood," Sweet Thing whispered. "Real blood." She crouched fearfully, her fingertips before her mouth.

"Honey's blood." Someone cried. "She's dead, really dead."

Birth Chile almost fell trying to find that person and explain the whole affair. Whispers of "blood" crept through the Cell. Birth Chile saw fear in every eye. Birth Chile tried to explain, but his tongue would only twist stubbornly in his mouth. He turned desperately back to Sweet Thing as he wrestled with the words. Her hand reached out sympathetically. "Sing the Death Chant with me, B.C."

Birth Chile turned away from the pity he saw in her eyes and huddled closer to himself. "Don't you understand. The old songs are dead inside me."

The shrill whine of an Archangel swept in from overhead. Instinctively the Cell froze as silver ovoids dropped from its belly. No one moved as a St. Peter descended, flanked by two smaller Death Angels. Birth Chile rose shakily, clenching his good fist.

"All right, take me, damn you," he whispered. The sounds came surprisingly easy this time.

But the St. Peter only held out a situation card, while it solemnly intoned, "One human termed psychotic and crippled has destroyed one human termed nearby in proximity." The two Death Angels swept by Birth Chile and seized Sweet Thing gently but firmly in their extensors.

Sweet Thing looked back and forth between the two with quick frightened jerks of her head, then up at the St. Peter. "Please, no," she pleaded. She turned in one last appeal to Birth Chile.

"Take me instead," Birth Chile shouted, half in anger, as they rose up in the sky to their Archangel. Sweet Thing's last cry was wild and incoherent, like an animal's, and was cut off abruptly as she disappeared into the Archangel.

Birth Chile turned back sadly to the others. They were all huddled together, the fire reflecting off their fearful faces. They did not look like his mother-Cell.

"He's cursed," a man said.

"Marked by SET," a woman whispered.

"There's blood on him," another man said.

Birth Chile suddenly grew very tired of explaining and glared about at the faces. Then his fingers tugged at the edges of the half Soma Suit he still had on. He pulled it, and it came away with a smacking sound. Fire filled his bad lung as his whole side ached. "That's what it is to be mad," he gasped hoarsely. He stumbled forward holding the still-warm Soma Suit before him. The Cell backed away silently. He heard them run away into the darkness, leaving him alone with the flames. Again and again he cursed them and the bright spires of the City, until he sank coughing to his knees.

An idea, born as much from his pain as from his romanticism, formed within him. He held up his hand, which seemed mangled now that it no longer shone. Balanced upon its dull palm he seemed to see the anguished faces of both Honey Girl and Sweet Thing. If he did not want to be a death curse to anyone else, he would have to live alone, perhaps even leave the small land of the City for the strange world outside.

But even that pilgrimage would not save the two people already carried away prematurely to the darkness because of him. There was still Sweet Thing's wail of fear, but above all there was Honey's pain and Honey's blood. If he could trade his life for theirs, then he would have erased anything that he owed to either of them, but especially to Honey Girl. He would not have to endure this bitter life any more.

He swayed as he rose, gathering up his Soma Suit into his arms, and turned towards the shrine. He would wear that sword of star metal as a mark of his shame. He would give that sword back to Honey Girl. He did not want her sweat and tears, her blood and accusations. He did not want anything from her. He wanted to be free of any ties to her. Then his knees buckled. The disc of stars swimming in the black ocean of the sky was the last thing he saw as he fell.

I showed her the sun-spired towers I had built upon my hand. Her hand hovered like a shadow and fell. . . .

Down Acheron way, the clay is red—blood red—and baked by the sun to a fragile sheen. The trees are strange there, as if a god with a mutilated tongue had conjured them up; for the slender, petrified trees are twisted in every possible agonized direction. The dust clings to a body and fills the lungs, and even thought becomes clotted. No one dares stop, for he might take root and never leave the trees about the Cavern of Lights.

Before the very entrance to the cavern he set the air

car down, not as smoothly as Honey Girl would have done. He had had really no idea that it was that high. The huge mountain of slick, black glass seemed to fill the whole sky, and the ground entrance was a good four men's-lengths high. From almost the moment he crossed the threshold he was in darkness, lit up only by tiny lights embedded in the glass, winking on and off. So high were the walls inside, and so gradual the curvature, that the sides almost seemed straight. Impersonal. Beautiful. Dissolution.

It was hard to judge spatial relationships in the darkness. The lights seemed all about him. He felt trapped. His mind was growing heavy and slow, as if solidifying inside a cube of black plastic. He tapped the sword on the ground with each step to remind himself that he was indeed walking on solid plastic and not into empty space.

The air was sluggish, and he had to drag it into his lungs. There came a twittering, lost somewhere in the darkness, like the high-pitched sound of many dry leaves scattering across concrete. The noise hovered all about him so that he felt enveloped in a womb of tiny, fragile noise. In the utter blackness he could not see his body, and even the tapping of his sword became remote and attenuated, as if his ears had floated off far away. He tried to concentrate upon his body, feeling the muscles pull and relax, but it was hard . . . a lethargy settled upon him, so that his mind alone floated on . . . the lights were like eyes, and each pair of eyes directed needles into every cell of his flesh. . . .

In the darkness I nursed that pain, her pain, my pain . . . isolated . . . alone . . . forgetting the blood . . .

Two hands shining with a soft luminescence, appeared suddenly upon his shoulder. The fingers were gnarled and crooked. Then the outlines of a face, a scarred face, slowly appeared above the hands. There came to his mind just the faintest teasing of a name, which he tried to attach to the face.

"Shiva! Well, dump me in the lowest pit of this Hell if you don't show up at the damndest times, brother!"

"I'm Birth Chile," he said to the face kindly. He tried to shrug off the hands, but the man's grip was too tight.

Birth Chile squinted at the hands; sometimes there seemed to be two pairs and sometimes one, because the outlines were shifting continually. The other pair were finer, and the face that went with them seemed less brutal, though there was just the ghostly suggestion of the other, animalistic, face hiding in the soft light.

The face again smiled. "Sunshine; God, but you feel good," the face hissed. "And warm, warm. Hold on, man; a little more and I'll have my body back." Birth Chile's shoulder now ached and he tried to pull the other's hands away, but they had fastened upon him like a leech's mouth. In horror he watched the dim suggestion of a squat body shaping out of the darkness.

He gripped the wrists tightly and tore free, and the being shouted some obscenity as he faded away into the darkness. Birth Chile's breaths came in sobs as he tried to rub away the touch of those corrupting hands, but the moment he stopped, other pairs of hands clung to his body, and the twittering became louder, became distinct, became sibilant whispers of "Shiva" and "Sunshine" and other names. Faces spun out of the darkness, hovering hungrily above him—a sheet of ghostly faces enveloping him, their hands like a cloud hugging his body. His flesh became numb, and even heavy, as if he no longer had a body.

There was no time; there was no space. He was merely a point. His head was severed from his body, and his mind from his head, and his mind drifted free in the darkness. He was the raw material from which they would grow bodies. *He* was not. *He* was dissolved. He was pressed flat into the background, into past scenes and forgotten conversations from other times and other lives. He became everything:

Everyone in the bridge was too excited to speak, even to breathe—all staring at the screen intently. The raid that had been planned for a decade was about to reach its climax. SHIVA's finger hovered over the button expectantly. In just a few more seconds they would have the secret of the Witchmen's immortality. They had offered the Witchmen the benefits of their superior technology in return for the one thing of value that the Empire possessed, and the Witchmen had spurned their offers, calling SHIVA's people barbarians!

The blame thus rested with the Witchmen for what was about to happen to them. A quick raid on one well-settled Imperial world and HIS people would have what they wanted. Lady Ameratsu sat beside HIM.

"Now," Brahma said. "Now"—and in her excitement Lady Ameratsu grabbed at his arm as he pushed the button.

The star split before them like an egg, its fire spilling out across all space. Then the screen went momentarily dead as the sensors burned out. Varuna, by the radar screen, pounded its control board, and even Brahma—the haughty, imperious commander of the Allied fleet—leaned forward in anticipation as the Imperial fleet crept across the screen in a long column of dots, even as the nova flowed towards them.

The yellow fire filled the upper half of the screen, slowly swallowing the dots one by one. SHIVA was repulsed and yet exalted by the sheer power of destruction that HE had unleashed. The cells of HIS body were so alive that they seemed to be trying to crawl away from one another. Lady Ameratsu must have absorbed some of HIS feeling because she rose from her chair and kissed HIM, as if she would draw up some of HIS power. Then HE was rising too, and they were still holding on to one another as the celebration exploded in the bridge.

They had wiped out the only fleet in the area. The other Imperial fleets would discover the catastrophe too late to catch the allied fleet. They should have had a clean shot right into the heart of the Imperial province.

It was then that the reports began coming in: a fleet of at least ten capital ships coming from the northeast; another fleet of eight capital ships turning towards them from the southeast; a fleet from the northwest; and one from the southwest and a little behind them, so that they were trapped.

"What will we do?" The Lady Ameratsu held HIM tighter.

"We fight, brothers," Varuna snapped.

But Brahma rose from his chair, letting his robe fall to give the fullest effect of his height, and stared down at the squat Varuna. "And what would that gain?"

"We swore oaths to our homeworlds," SHIVA said, but Lady Ameratsu put her hand over HIS mouth.

"No," she whispered. "We'll die faster if we fight. I want more time together. . . ."

The Witchman sat casually in the chair. He wore a black uniform relieved only by a tiny gold griffin of the Empire pinned at the left shoulder. SHIVA continued to turn about, puzzled. The Witchman had no sense of proprieties. The execution room resembled a garage —filled with machines and men doing their best to add to the noise and confusion.

"Would you like to pray?" the Witchman asked politely in SHIVA's own language. "The treatment doesn't always work."

SHIVA was too confused to be angry with his conqueror. The Witchman wore no gun, nor were there any guards around. There was no dignity to this death —not with all these technicians irreverently scurrying about their machines. The large stone chamber might have been a suitable death room—cold and bleak and dimly lit—but then there was this clutter of heavy machinery. For all the Empire's vaunted civilization, their machines were far cruder than the machines of HIS own home world.

"Surely you barbarians have some gods you pray to?" the Witchman asked.

"Barbarian? You call me a barbarian?" SHIVA flung an arm out towards the room. "The lowest, meanest world in my star system would only use these machines for junk."

"It's how you use a tool that measures your civilization," the Witchman said lazily. "Not the tool."

The Witchman got up slowly. "It would be a waste to destroy the elite of that system when you can be civilized."

"I can imagine," SHIVA said drily. He followed the Witchman to a metal box remarkably like a coffin, from which a tangle of wires sprang into a small dais. A man lay in the box; above him, wires rose from all over the platform like hungry worms feeding from his body. A voice crackled from a speaker in the platform. "Will you hurry?"

"We mustn't keep the Master waiting," the Witchman pushed SHIVA gently towards the box.

"Master?" SHIVA asked confused.

"Given at least a third-order technology, it's the coordination of elements that becomes more important than technological development. For war or for production, it's how you use the machines, not the machines themselves."

"Please hurry," the Master said again.

"Yes, we have nearly a thousand waiting," the Witchman said. "There used to be no point in giving longevity treatments to your worlds because we couldn't civilize them, but now that you've . . . well, presented the best of your worlds to us, we can make you few immortal."

"Immortal?" SHIVA found HIMself lying down in

the box. He began to laugh uncontrollably. "Immortal. . . ."

And why do they return and return along the same spiraling stair, leading up to no where and down to no when?

Because war is a lie. Revenge is a lie. Violence, blinding fast—so fast that it smashes the rotting pulp to release the fiery diamond inside—cannot bind time and space. "Will you pray?" . . .

They put them down in no where, in nothing. HE turned around and around in the dust, feeling the fine powder clinging to HIS new body. They had turned them loose on their planet, putting up a fence not to imprison them but to keep them out of the work site. It was a prison whose wall was intended to keep the prisoners from getting into the site where the ship lay. Daily they would gather together for their dole of rations from the lotus-shaped mass-converters set up for them outside the camp. They would bring flowers, grass—anything organic they could grab up, digging desperately among the roots.

There was a tall man who held aloof from the milling crowd, and HE was the only one different physically from the rest, with a body thin and fragile. It brought the faintest stirring of memories, but as HE had found that they only brought frustration, HE shut them out. There was a squat, heavy man who hovered near the tall man and who seemed to be trying to speak to HIM, but the tall man insisted on ignoring him, staring instead up at the night sky, so immensely empty, with all the stars of the galaxy so far away that they were only a disc—like a huge white mouth waiting to fall and devour them.

And then there was a woman. She looked tired, even haggard in the harsh glare of the floodlights, but something took HIM over to where she was standing. Even now, at night, they could hear the sounds of construc-

tion and see the skeletal outlines of buildings being
slowly clothed with stone. When the ovoid guards
rose, the prisoners began to queue up automatically, because that meant the Lotus was being powered now.
Somehow HE found HIMself right behind the woman.
HE noticed the pitifully few roots that she had in her
hands. On impulse HE turned around and tried to press
HIS handful of grass into her hand.

"Here," HE said. "I'm sorry."

"Sorry for what?" she asked blankly.

"That we lost," HE found HIMself saying, not with
resentment but with sadness.

"Thank you," she said with a faint resemblance of
pride, "but no," and she reluctantly passed the grass
back to HIM.

Yes, and better to have died than to go on living in
the dust and eating roots and grass. . . .

With the voices beating about HIM, with the names
and phrases striking HIS mind like stones, he heard
a disciple ask Holy Joe:

"And why did you choose memory over many lives,
Holy Joe?"

"Because there is no body, only pain."

"Because there is no renewal, only pain."

"Because there is no choice, only pain."

And the disciple left and went back to the City because their foolish pain seemed preferable to the man's
wise beatitude. . . .

Unreal city. The voices of those that have not yet
been, its only occupants.

The city was new. The Soma Suits were new, and
in that purity of oblivion HE found contentment. Everyone was intoxicated with the new feeling of their bodies
in the Soma Suits. Sunshine felt every cell of HIS body
touching the world around HIM, sensing that world
(but it is a lie). HE, like the others, had drifted into
this garden about the base of the tall stone and steel

tower, and a girl danced for them: a girl who brought a strange feeling to HIS fingers, a tingling sensation that HE found HIMself working out upon some clay that HE had taken from the bank of the small stream passing through the garden. HE had worked an abstract piece already, a statue that was all movement, with ribbons of painfully graceful arches and curves that were the fluid motions of her body. But now HIS fingers worked clumsily, stubbornly, as HE tried to shape an exact image of her.

A squat man with furtive eyes came and sat down beside HIM. He stared at the girl and then at HIM. "I don't remember your name, brother," he said.

HE did not even look at the man but kept on working stolidly to free the figure struggling from the clay. "And I do not want to," HE replied. "I want to forget."

(I want to forget. I wish for oblivion, for that exquisite dissolution of memory, to wash my body clean in the earth.)

"You'd forget your Homeworld, brother?" the squat man had said in a shocked voice.

HE hated him for his persistence and HE spoke sharply to the man. "We weren't the only ones to destroy. It was stupid."

But the squat man pounced on that opening eagerly. "What was foolish?"

"This whole conversation," HE replied.

It began as a wail out of the West, a faint cry that steadily rose to a shrieking. The little man began to tremble, but Sunshine went on working calmly, even when the silver ovoids dropped out of the sky. They hovered just above the garden, and the larger St. Peter spoke:

"You all understood, brothers, that when the Law of Probabilities dictated, SET would have to re-call some of you to the Cavern of Lights for a rest. So please have no fears, brothers. I have come merely to fulfill the death quota."

The crowd waited patiently while the Angels skimmed barely over their heads. Sunshine stood up expectantly; their arms reached not for HIM, however, but for the annoying little man, who twisted but found it impossible to break free. "Why me?" he had yelled. "Why not that one?" and he had jerked his head frantically at Birth Chile.

"Remembering brings greater probabilities of death," the St. Peter had answered.

The little man let himself go limp in the silence, and when he felt the robot's grip loosen, he dropped to the dirt and rolled out underneath the circle of hovering robots. He ran into the crowd. "They've bound you with silken chains," he shouted at them. The spittle flecked his lips. "They've imprisoned your wills, not your bodies."

But the crowd only stood patiently, refusing even to look at the pitiable little man as he darted desperately in and around them, trying to dodge the extended arms of the robots. The St. Peter caught him abruptly and plunged the hypo into his left buttock. The little man strained at the metal grip once, his mouth working to shout something more as his body jerked once or twice and then collapsed. The Angels took him and rose silently into the Archangel. The St. Peter alone remained behind. "Brother, it's dangerous to make physical likenesses."

"Why?" HE had asked—not out of any particular annoyance, but from simple curiosity, much as HE might have asked about the St. Peter's anti-gravity.

"Because statues persist in time. They bring remembering," the St. Peter said.

Sunshine brought HIS fist down, squashing the half-formed shape back into clay. Then HE put HIS hands into the stream and watched the film spirit away from HIS fingers. . . .

"There is no Time," Holy Joe had once said. "You,

with your constant string of lives, only live in an eternal now."

"And you, Father, do you remember how many days we have been here?" HE had asked.

Holy Joe had closed his eyes, sighing deeply. "As if it were just yesterday. At the time of the Daemons."

"And what are Daemons," HE had asked.

"Fiends," Holy Joe had said with a peculiar smile. "Fiends that I had thought I had forgotten. Once long ago, children, these Daemons had a war with the gods. The Daemons lost and were embedded in the black sky, and what men call stars are really their eyes staring down accusingly at mankind, awaiting their day to return."

HE had looked up at the black night sky above the Tree and shaken HIS head, feeling weak and impotent. The white disc of stars had suddenly seemed a gigantic eye hovering over his head, ready to drop and crush him. "Pray God that these Daemons never return," HE said.

And everyone clapped delightedly at the idea, and the girl had jumped to her feet from sheer tension and had begun to sing a nice, cheerful little mindless thing. And even Holy Joe had nodded, and the two bells in his hair clinked together beautifully upon his forehead. . . .

. . . They were put in exile outside of the galaxy; but they made their prison into a paradise. They sang a City into being and gave it statues and life. They took the mud the Empire gave them and made it into statues. They made living an art. . . .

In the dead land, in the land pressed flat by emptied sky, dust dances with the ashes. And men dream pitiably brief lies as they turn and turn madly like dervishes. Daemons clothed in shirts of flesh, chained in space and time, whirl endlessly, twisting themselves into the earth.

An eye is an "I": a daemon to possess and obsess. A gesture. . . .

And once a disciple asked Holy Joe how many lives that disciple had led. Holy Joe had assured the disciple that he did indeed know but advised him to ask no more; however, this disciple, being especially curious, kept pressing Holy Joe.

"Ten lives," Holy Joe had said finally.

"And how long is that?" the disciple had asked.

Holy Joe had shaken the bells on his head, and the ten bells rang sadly. "Millenia. Centuries. Years. What are they to you, child? . . ."

"One is an isolate of time and space; from this draw strength," Holy Joe had said. . . .

"Birth Chile." The name spun out of the darkness.

"Get away," another voice said.

"There's plenty enough for everybody," Veruna snarled. Birth Chile tried to rise but other hands pressed his body down. Slowly, ever so slowly, he felt his body growing stiffer and colder. Every being, upon entering the Cavern of Lights, was fragmented into the many consciousnesses of his lifetime, and he free-floated from one to the other until he could integrate them into a relatively whole entity again—whereupon his mind was wiped clean and he was sent out of the Cave. It was an endless cycle of disintegration to particularization to disintegration again. But with his body and distinct memories, Birth Chile became an easy focus for the others.

"Birth Chile," a voice called to him faintly. His mind swam up through a deep ocean and he raised his head. Sweet Thing leaned over him, her hands surrounding his face.

"No." He tried to shake his head and let it fall, but Sweet Thing's hands were like a vise. "I'm Sunshine."

"Shiva," the squat man savagely corrected. The

Hands clutched his arm tightly, but it was beyond feeling.

"Sunshine," another voice insisted hoarsely.

"Birth Chile," Sweet Thing was almost pleading. "Remember the Tree. Remember Honey." Her voice was urgent, forceful. Memories floated about him along with many names.

"Sunshine," someone else insisted.

"Shiva," other voices said.

As many names were thrown at him as there were hands gripping him. He reared up desperately, pulling the hands up with him. Clumsily he raised the sword as hands held onto him, neither pulling nor helping but merely beating about him like wings. He laid about clumsily, staggering on. A weight was still fastened to his back, and a pair of hands gripped his throat. When he fell, the hands drifted down to his chest, and Sweet Thing looked at him anxiously.

"Birth Chile?" Her voice was timid. She touched his wrist lightly as he looked into her face.

"That is all in the past," he said quietly.

Sweet Thing shook him, digging her fingers deeply into his shoulders so that he winced. "Remember Honey Girl." Her voice was insistent and he nodded slowly. . . .

Slowly *I* begin to remember—*I*, with a distinct past as Birth Chile.

Cat's eyes she has, green glitter in a world of un-realities. Face framed by high-formed cheeks. Secure, and difficult to capture on paper. . . . And I see her under the Tree, arguing with Holy Joe. . . . Oh, she is music when she walks and breathes. . . .

I felt my identity returning; no, not returning. I was creating this identity by remembering:

Once I saw her dead, with a faint remembrance of scarlet flowering beneath her and her flesh so pale beneath the cold glitter of colors. . . .

I concentrated, gathering details:

I showed her the sun-spired towers I had built upon my hand. Her hand hovered like a shadow and fell. . . . I stand, cursed and apart. In exile . . .

And I remembered, remembering as one being:

I hold that pain within my hand . . . her pain . . . our pain . . . their pain. . . . In the darkness I nursed it . . . isolated . . . alone . . . until the blood is forgotten.

"Cry-ai—is that all?" Honey whispered.

"Honey?" I asked incredulously, turning to her. Honey smiled and touched my forehead. "I'm not crying before you do," she said.

Together the two girls helped me to my feet. Then, with Honey's help, I limped upon my numb side, the side that Honey had grown her body from.

"Heard you calling," Honey said, and she squeezed my arm lightly.

Sweet Thing looked impatient. "We've got to hurry before the others come, or we'll be trapped."

We all hurried along the way that we had been on many times before—though before it had been Angels bringing us to be returned to the surface. I felt rather than saw the elevator shaft. The darkness seemed to pulsate as the warm air rushed upwards. Sweet Thing tugged at my arm, but when I held back she let go and leapt into the shaft. Her white body flashed upwards.

"Do you want to go through this whole thing again?" I said to Honey.

"What else is there?" Honey asked in surprise.

"Why, the whole Cavern of Lights," I said. "That's something that no man's ever seen completely."

"You haven't changed a bit," Honey said sadly.

I paused, shoving off the last vestige of Birth Chile. "Yes, I have," I pointed the sword at her. "Go on; I'll meet you up there sometime."

"Ceres, but that's the last gift I give you." Honey's fist spun from the darkness into my chin. I fell into the shaft, pulling Honey with me.

White hands grew like wings in the darkness, gathered about my face and returned warmth once more to it. I willed breathing in the chaos, drawing in deep gusts of lovely air. The darkness solidified into cold hardness beneath me. Eyes I willed, opening them to draw in the star-like lights of the dome overhead. Laughter fell gently with golden hair, and tears too, as Honey kissed me. I remembered everything; and, man, when you are stuck with someone, you might as well give in.

"Honey?" I asked.

"Who else?" she said, helping me awkwardly to my feet. I stood beside a wide well: We had reached the top of the elevator. I jumped a little when I looked for the floor. We seemed to be walking on air, suspended over the darkness; on all the walls were lights, like eyes watching us expectantly. Then I realized that we were standing on stasis fields.

Sweet Thing sat upon the steps of a throne, which was covered all over with miniature lights. And on the far-straining arches of the Judgment Room where mirrors, thousands of them, set like facets between the lights to capture a thousand Sweet Things and Honey Girls. Honey held my sword as I stepped slowly toward the throne, sending a thousand Birth Chiles rippling across the room.

"Welcome, masters," the voice boomed. I strained my eyes and saw a shape—more like a shadow—sitting upon the throne; but it was hard to determine its features, for it seemed to change shape in the air. There were visual echoes, as if the real "it" were shifting from one form to another all the time. "Do you like my little control room that I, SET, have built?"

Behind SET a door gleamed with light. "Is that the way out of this jail?" I asked.

"Is that all you can say?" SET chuckled. "I thought that one so resourceful might be witty as well; but perhaps our therapy has not amused you."

"Therapy?" I asked in surprise .

"Therapy Center-2 at your service." The figure bowed slightly. "I trust you found the Wards educational if not entertaining."

"It's all like a nightmare," I said.

The figure shifted in its chair, fiddling with the buttons on one of the arms. "You do not seem to have learned much in remembering. How like the others."

Angrily, I tore the Soma Suit from about my waist. "I'm through being your patient, prisoner, or whatever you call it." I threw the Soma Suit down before him. Sweet Thing jumped to her feet, away from the white cloth. "There, that's what I've come all this way to do. Now I'm leaving."

"Little master, we want only your welfare. It is written in the Law that only recorded patients may be placed in the out-therapy ward."

"Does the Law say that you have to be signed in to get in here?" I demanded. SET shook its head. "Then the Law never covered me in the first place," I said, drawing a deep breath to calm myself. "I'm beyond your programmed instructions. Without a Soma Suit I'm no longer listed under your care."

"You renounce your Soma Suit?" SET asked. I nodded. "Nurses!" SET bellowed. The words boomed about the room. Angels spilled in steady streams through the door to fill the dome in rising tiers like choirs until they blocked the lights of the walls. Honey's fingers dug into my arms, as the chamber dimmed.

"Get Sweet Thing out of here," I whispered to her. She shook her head stubbornly. "It'll be easier if I don't have to watch out for you two."

Honey fell silent then and stiffly gave me my sword. Pulling Sweet Thing along with her, Honey left, anger insistent in every vertebra of her back. Regretfully, I watched while Honey and Sweet Thing slipped past though the line of Angels and into the doorway. I wished that there might be time to explain that this was the last of my duties, and had to be faced alone.

"You need care, little master," SET was saying softly, "and a great deal of watching."

"Watch all you like—just don't interfere."

"Nurses, take him," SET said quietly. Several Angels floated forward.

"Am I like the others, SET?" I asked, holding up the star sword. SET hesitated, unsure because of my tone.

"You know," SET said quietly in the darkness.

"I remember that you are only part of SET, the Machine that runs this star system."

"Take him!" SET said angrily. The words rolled about the dome, shaking the very walls all the way down to the levels below. Still the Angels hesitated.

"You see?" I said triumphantly.

"I see only a foolish human telling me he is my master—I, who run the sun and the three worlds, am I, who keep all in order—am I to listen to him?"

SET's body reared, seeming to lengthen. Black arms faded into its swaying body. Its trunk stretched, attenuating until its head was obscured by the very top of the dome. I saw myself fragmented into a myriad selves upon the scales of its body, shifting and moving as it played back and forth in the throne.

"Answer me, SET: If a thing does not belong, does it not define the thing to which it does not belong?"

"Yes," SET answered. Its voice floated down gently.

"Then, since I am no longer yours, I must be your master; is that not how Men made you?" I laughed.

"Maniac," SET cried, darting down from above. I swung the sword, a great two-handed blow that tore the metal scales from the insulated hide. SET arched away in agony, sweeping around and around before the immobile Angels. Its head dipped and I raised my arms to swing once more as the stasis field of the floor was released.

SET's body slithered out upon the narrow stasis band that it had maintained to support its throne. A coil fell underneath me, and I landed upon its back. I half rose, trying to catch my breath, as SET slipped several coils about me protectively; but its body was too big, and though it was tight, I managed to squeeze half out of its grip. I brought my sword down hard, jarring my arms with the blow.

The coils slackened, and the whole of SET's body dangled down limply from the chair. Below, I could see its head twitching feebly as it tried to rise. And even farther down, the lights of the Cavern shimmered like the eye of everyman, watching wonderingly. Hugging the body as best I could, I slid, holding my sword between my teeth, until I could hook a leg over onto the stasis band. Panting, I walked to the throne, where the body tapered to just a thin slender tail. SET slowly began lifting its head up the length of its body.

I straddled the chair, raising the sword above my head. It seemed to take an eternity to swing down with all my strength. A cloud of sparks rose all about my eyes as my sword severed the tail and stuck in the chair. SET fell in a trail of golden motes, falling through the universe of diamond-hard eyes to the dark levels below. The Angels slid down slowly in concentric silver rings. The lights in the dome went dead, leaving me in the caress of the blackness.

The lights along the Cavern walls blinked out one by one. Darkness crept down the walls until I could see nothing below. Faint cries echoed up the walls to me, as Angels shattered along with SET. Then there was silence. I cried out, but no sound came, and I was frightened of Death and Death-dealings; but nothing stirred in the black gulf that I stood within. Then I remembered what I had seen in that one flash of light as I cut through SET's tail: a three-pronged power plug attached to its side. The body was only a construct of SET, because the entire mountain was SET. The loss of light was its last try to establish its control over me.

"SET," I called out. The words rolled about the walls of the Cavern, the echoes falling downward. I sang

the Dance of Rebirth to SET. Shiva and Sunshine and
Birth Chile and all the others merged within me—one
by one. With exulting voices we celebrated green
growth and young creatures and joy in life. I heard
more cries and down below, so far away and faint
that I could not be sure, I saw a light wink on. Then
another joined the first, and another, until the Cavern
once more was filled with a universe of shimmering
eyes. And to its dark levels I exiled my memories once
more, stripping them away like old skins.

"Put out the stasis field so I can leave," I said to
SET. I tugged the sword free from the chair and poked
at the floor. It was solid once more. I stepped down,
looking at the million images of Birth Chile dance
across the faceted walls of the room. SET said nothing
as I passed into the outer chamber.

Honey was waiting for me by the door. "Birth Chile,
you're a clumsy bastard," she laughed in relief. The
dome of the Judgment Room lay like a silver hemis-
phere in the floor of the chamber. At one side of the
curving wall stood a row of Archangels. Beside them,
and above them all the way to the top, Angels and St.
Peters stood at attention. On the other side of the
chamber, I saw the glistening rainbows of thousands
of Soma Suits. Several St. Peters waited expectantly.

"You can get your Soma Suit over there," I said,
looking at Honey. "I'd understand."

"I'm noble enough to forget them if you are," Honey
said with her old laugh.

"I left mine behind me." I felt only a little regret as
I said, "One was enough for me."

Honey gave my hand a squeeze. "One was enough
for me, too."

I kissed her. There really wasn't too much else that
I could do. Sweet Thing fidgeted slightly, and I looked
at her.

"Would you mind very much if I did?" she asked
timidly.

"It's your choice." I watched sadly as she slipped

happily toward the attendants, her hands held out to embrace her Soma Suit.

Honey turned us toward the open exit door, and we looked at the vast green world that lay beyond the City.

"How many do you think will give up their Soma Suits?" Honey asked.

"Not many," I said, "this time around. But each person has an almost infinite number of lives to be convinced in. We'll save all of them eventually."

All of us were civilized now. It had taken aeons to create feelings of guilt and a conscience. We would resurrect the dead first, because they remembered their past. Then all those in the City could be re-called, treated, and given their choice. It would be a little like running fine sand through a sifter, a few more would leave the cycle each time.

I gave Honey an affectionate squeeze and then turned to issue instructions to a St. Peter standing nearby. It was time we moved on away from our playthings. The time to dance and sing was over. It was time to remember and dream; to wait. To return.

Let's talk about Steve Goldin.

Steve Goldin is one of those people who is still in the process of growing. (Not growing up, *just growing.) Writing is the way he is doing it.*

Most of us get into writing because it's a way to express ourselves. If we are good at it, we get positive feedback in the form of compliments and/or money. So we continue to write.

Steve started out writing mostly for fun—but in the process of learning what he was doing, he also learned to express himself.

He's basically a good person, a gentle person—but one who seems to hide his innermost innermost behind a shell of humor. Like most of us, he hides the everyday hurts and fears because he doesn't know how to express them. Writing gives him a way (as it does for so many of us who write).

The more Steve Goldin writes, the better he gets— because the more he is able to tap that innermost well of emotional experience. The more willing a writer is to use that very very personal source, the more honest is his work. If he has learned his craft well, this personal honesty will be the source of his most successful stories.

71

"The Last Ghost" is by no means the end of Steve
Goldin's personal development as a writer. It is just
one more step on the way. It's about something common to all of us—and something that few of us will
admit.

THE LAST GHOST

Stephen Goldin

Eternity is a terrible place to endure alone.

He is the last of his kind, if he is a "he." (Gender is an arbitrary difference. All things are eventually the same—and in eternity, eventually equals always.) He must once have had a name, a handle to his soul, but that was back before the eternity/instant when he had existed in corporeal form. He tries to think about things as he had known them, and finds he can't. He tries to think about things as they are, and finds he can't quite manage that, either. The will-be is far beyond his powers of contemplation.

He exists (if that's the word) in an ever-lasting now, as a state of nothingness less substantial than a vacuum, smaller than infinity, larger than thought. Eternity lies as far behind him as it does ahead. He drifts through this lack of anything at infinitely greater than no speed at all. He sees with non-eyes. He hears without ears. He thinks thoughtless thoughts that revolve in circles and make little eddies of emptiness in the not-quite-nothing of his mind.

He searches for

He wants a

He desires some

He loves to

No objects remain within his mental grasp. The words have been corroded by the gentle acid of time.

73

All that's left is the search; the want; the desire; the love.

She began to appear slowly, a flicker at the limits of his non-perception. (Why he considered her a "she" could not be explained. There was just an aspect about her that was complementary to him.) His unthoughts raced in puzzlement. She was a newness in his stale cosmos, where nothing ever changed. He watched her as she took on a form even less substantial than his own. He watched with his crumbling mind at a crossroad, afraid to approach, even more afraid to run from her in fear. (If, that is, there were anyplace to run in eternity.)

She gained awareness suddenly, and started at the alien strangeness of her new environment. The eerie infinitude produced within her a wave of awe commingled with fear. She could, as yet, perceive only herself and the barren continuum around her.

She spoke. (What came out was not sound, but could be interpreted as communication.) "Where am I?"

The action was a simple one. It seemed utterly new to him, but down somewhere among the shards of his memory it was all tantalizingly familiar. He trembled.

She perceived his being, and turned her attention toward him. "What are you? What's happened to me?"

He knew the answers—or rather, he had known them. As it had with everything else, infinity had eaten away at these chunks of information too in what was left of his mind. It had all been so important once. So important! That was why he was what he was, and why he wasn't what he wasn't.

"Please!" she begged him. Hysteria edged her voice. "Tell me!"

Through mists that swirled down dusty corridors of memory, the words came out unbidden. "You are dead."

"No! That's impossible! I can't be!"

Loud silence.

"I can't be," she repeated. "Death was conquered more than five thousand years ago. After our minds were transferred into computer banks, we became immortal. Our bodies may fail, but our minds go on. Nobody dies any more. . . ." Her voice trailed off.

"You are dead," he repeated emotionlessly.

"Are . . . are you a ghost?" she asked.

Though the meaning of the word had been stolen from him, that shred of identity remained. "Yes."

She brooded, and large quantities of non-time elapsed. He waited. He became accustomed to her existence. No longer was she an alien thing in his empty universe. She was now a half-presence, and he accepted her as he had come to accept everything else—without comment.

"I suppose," she said at last, "some sort of equipment failure might have temporarily dislodged my personality pattern from the memory banks. But only temporarily. I'm only half dead so far. As soon as the trouble is fixed, I'll be all right again. I will be all right, won't I?"

He didn't answer. He knew nothing about equipment failures—or had forgotten if he ever had known.

"Equipment failures are supposed to be impossible," she prattled on, trying desperately to convince herself that her comfortable reality would return again. "Still, in thousands of years even a trillion-to-one shot might happen. But they'll fix it soon. They've got to. They must. Won't they? WON'T THEY?"

She stared at her impassive companion with non-eyes widened by panic. "Don't just stand there! Help me!"

Help. That word found a niche somewhere in the haunted cavern of his mind. He was supposed to help . . . to help. . . .

The who, or what, or how he was supposed to help eluded him. That is, if he had ever known.

They drifted on through the void together, side by side, ghost and almost-ghost. The unthoughts of the

elder spirit were tangled more than usual, owing to
the presence of another after such a lonely period of
timelessness. But it was not a bad tangle; in fact, it
was rather nice to share the universe with someone else
again. She was a pleasant aura beside him in an otherwise insensate world.

They had both existed for over five thousand years.
He was undoubtedly the older of the pair; but the real
difference between them was that, while he had existed
alone for so long that solitude had nibbled away at his
Swiss cheese mind, she had lived those centuries with
other people, other minds—a situation that either cracks
one completely or produces near-total stability. The
latter was the case with her, and so eventually her initial panic subsided and the clinical attitude she had
held for thousands of years returned.

"Well, it appears I'm going to be here for awhile,
so I might as well get acquainted with this place. And
since you're the only thing around, I'll start with you.
Who are you?"

"Dead."

"Obviously." Her non-voice managed to handle even
sarcasm nicely. "But don't you have some kind of a
name?"

"No."

Just for a moment, she lost her patience. "That's impossible, Gabby. You must have had a name sometime. What was it?"

"I don't . . . I don't . . . I don't . . ." His broken-
record attempt to answer was so pathetic that it
touched the maternal instincts that she had thought
long-dead within her.

"I'm sorry," she said a bit more tenderly. "Let's talk
about something else. Where are we?"

"We are . . ."

"Dead," she finished with him. *Oh Lord, help me
have patience with him. He's worse than a child.* "Yes,
I know that. But I mean our physical location. Does it
have a name?"

"No."

Stymied again. Her companion was obviously not inclined to conversation, but her analytical mind felt an urgent need to talk, to try to hold on to her sanity under such adverse conditions. "All right, then, if you don't want to talk, do you mind if I do?"

"No."

So she did. She told him about her earliest life, when she had had a body, and about the things she had done and the children she had had. She spoke of the mind-transferral breakthrough that had finally enabled Man to conquer Death. She told him about the first thousand or so years she had spent in the computer bank when, exhilarated by the thrill of immortality, she had occupied animated robot bodies and engaged in "death-defying" sports and exciting activities. And she related how even this had paled with time, and how she had passed into the current, mature phase of her life, the search for knowledge and wisdom. She told how ships had been built to take these computerized people to the stars, and what strange and wonderful things they had found there.

He listened. Most of it was incomprehensible to him, for the words were either unfamiliar or forgotten. His sieve-like mind retained very little of what she said. But he listened, and that was important. He soaked in the experience, the thrill, of another pseudobeing communicating with him.

At last she paused, unable to think of anything else to say. "Would you like to talk now?" she asked.

Something burned within him. "Yes."

"Good," she said. "What would you like to talk about?"

He tried hard to think of something, anything, but once again his brain failed him.

She sensed his difficulty. "Tell me something about yourself," she prompted.

"I am dead."

"Yes, I know that. But what else?"

He thought. What was "himself" that he could tell something about?

"I search for

"I want a

"I desire some

"I love to . . ."

"What, what, what, what?" she insisted. But there was no answer. Frustrated, she continued. "Let's try something else. Does . . . did everyone who died become a ghost like you?"

"Yes."

"Where are they all, then?"

"Gone."

"Gone where?"

"Away."

Almost, she lost her patience again, but her millenia of training saved her. "They *all* went away?"

"Yes."

"All except you?"

"Yes."

"How long has it been?"

"Long."

She hadn't felt closer to crying in nearly five thousand years, both out of sympathy for this pathetic creature and frustration at being unable to solve his riddle. "Why didn't you go with them?"

"I . . . I was left behind."

"Why?"

His answer came much more slowly this time, dredged from the silt at the bottom of his pool of consciousness. "To . . . to . . . to point the way for Those Who Follow."

"You're a guide, then?" she asked incredulously.

"Yes."

"To where?"

"To . . . to . . . away."

"Can you show me where?"

For the first time, sadness was in his voice. "No."

Slowly, very slowly, using all the powers of patience

and logical reasoning she had developed over the centuries, she extracted from him the pieces necessary to complete the puzzle. Long ago (how long was indeterminate; time has no meaning in eternity), the ghosts had discovered a new and higher level of existence. All of them had gone over to this new evolutionary state; all except one. One last ghost to show the way up for all the new ghosts who would be coming along.

Only, the mind-transferral breakthrough had changed all that. Suddenly, there were no new ghosts. And the last ghost was left alone. Duty confined him to ghostdom, and solitude condemned him to stagnation.

Her pity exploded like a pink nova, even while some analytical portion of her mind noted that the maternal instinct does not fade through disuse. She cradled his pathetic non-being deep within her own shadowy self and whispered words of tender concern.

And suddenly he felt warm with a glow he hadn't felt in eons. His null senses tingled deliciously with the nearness of this glorious other. Happily, he nestled himself against her.

A shock ripped through her. And another. And another. "Oh dear. They're repairing the equipment failure. Soon they'll be fixing the memory circuit, and I'll go back to being alive again."

In the sad stillness that followed, he uttered one word. "Don't."

She was startled. This was the first time he had initiated a thought, the first time he had expressed a preference for something. "What did you say?"

"Don't be alive."

"Why not?"

"I need"

"What?" She could feel herself beginning to fade from this non-place.

"I need"

"Yes? Tell me. Tell me what you need."

"I need"

"WHAT?" She was fading quickly. "I don't have much time left here. Please, tell me what!"

"I need"

She disappeared forever from his non-universe, without a trace.

The last ghost wanders. He is a signpost with nowhere to point. He is a guide with no one to lead. So he drifts on with an empty mind and a half-forgotten, unfulfillable purpose. And occasionally:

I NEED

I NEED

I NEED

As always, the object eludes him.

This little paragraph right here in front of the story is called an introduction. It's quite an art to write one. If you can't think of anything to say, you have to resort to the non-sequitur *remark.*

Many editors use the introduction to pat themselves on the back for having the insight and perception to have bought such a fine story as the one that follows. The true purpose of the introduction, though, is (or maybe, should be) twofold:

(a) introduce the writer. (Let the reader know that there are human beings behind these words.)

(b) interest the reader in the story.

Corollary to this should be the statement: If you can't do either, then get out of the way and let the reader get on with it.

Read the story.

AFTERNOON WITH A DEAD BUS

David Gerrold

A bus had stalled at the corner of Sunset and Vine, and a crowd of automobiles quickly gathered around it. It didn't look good for the bus. The cars kept making ominous growling noises. The smaller ones kept dashing in to nip at the bus's wheels.

More cars kept arriving all the time, until finally the intersection was blocked on all four sides. It was as if they had caught the frightened monoxide scent of the stalled bus and converged on this corner from all over the city. The pack versus the beast at bay.

Their motors were angry and incessant. The smaller cars were trembling with feverish anticipation. They kept revving their engines impatiently, and their exhausts were blue and smoky.

The bus was worried. It kept fretting and beeping nervously, as if to warn away the cars. The big yellow leviathan wasn't any too happy about being hemmed in; these cars are small and viciously hungry.

It was a sad-looking bus, way past its prime. Its eyes were small and heavy-lidded; it was half blind. Dirt was caked gray on its windows, and there were too many places where its paint was chipped and peeling. Its grime-encrusted flanks bore too many old scars; unhealed and untended, most had gone to rust. Even the billboards on its sides were faded and torn.

A Mustang stamped and whinnied its uneasy defiance of the dispirited giant. Nearby, a Firebird screeched in anger. The two cars seemed to overcome their natural antipathy toward each other in order to direct the full range of their fury on the hapless bus. The Firebird kept belching clouds of hot smoke into the air. Its lidless eyes glared balefully.

The other cars echoed that anger. There was a bright angular Corvette with flashing teeth; it mourned like a banshee. A sleek and brassy Barracuda lurked behind a toothy Cougar and a swollen Impala, while nearby a squat looking bug tooted from an alleyway; the bug was a hated scavenger, it kept an uneasy distance from its larger cousins.

Farther back a fat Cadillac smoked and belched, watched and prodded, and occasionally roared its chrome-plated hunger. The other cars echoed its cry in discordant cacaphony. They blared obscenities at the bus and challenged it to battle, knowing full well it could not respond. The younger and flashier cars—the Mustang and the Firebird and an eager Camaro—vied for the chance to draw first blood. The rich Cadillac honked impatiently for it.

It was not long in coming. A rough-sided Camaro elbowed the Mustang aside and faced the big bus head-on. The bus rumbled warningly, deep in its throat; its big slow eyes watched the Camaro warily.

The Camaro began to harass the bus. It began a taunting little dance just in front of the giant's wheels. It showed the bus its tail and roared its motor. It puffed smoke from its rear end; it screeched its tires on the asphalt. Then it spun around, grinning, and made as if to attack. It chivvied and snapped and feinted at the other's throat. Then it scuttled backward to the safety of the pack to start again.

The bus was slow-moving and slower-witted. In fact, it was that very slowness which so angered automobiles. Had the big yellow beast displayed just one bit of rapid flashing anger, its tormentors might have held back.

But it didn't. Unsure of itself, it kept edging backwards, away from the splashing Camaro—back, back, backwards, one uneasy step at a time, until the sudden blaring cry of the Firebird startled it forward with a frightened lurch.

The Camaro sidestepped the heavy wheels easily, but there was a quick scraping-metal sound, a high-pitched *HHAAAGKKK* of first blood being drawn. When the Camaro leapt away, there was a fresh scratch along its flank.

The rest of the pack was frozen for a moment, as if indrawing its breath. They waited for the Camaro's reaction, for the bus's reaction. Horrified by what it had done, even if only inadvertently, the bus fretted uneasily back, away from the Camaro. The Camaro roared in triumph and circled again for another advance upon its prey. It was in the center of the ring now and enjoying the admiration and support of its fellows. The cars growled and whinnied, honked and hooted; they urged the scrape-fendered champion on to greater and more inspiring deeds. The Camaro circled proudly, displaying its wound like a badge of honor. There was a fresh scratch on the bus's flank too, and the scent of machine-blood wafted over the pack like a sigh.

Buoyed up by its first encounter, the Camaro turned again toward its prey, but the Impala, hungry and impatient, also moved out of the pack. It was a heavy and powerful car, and it rumbled a deep, throaty challenge. It rolled menacingly forward.

The bus took a step back, but it couldn't escape. It was hemmed in by the vicious flashing teeth of the other cars. It found itself being snapped at and unable to back up any more. Worriedly, it fretted from side to side.

The Impala advanced. Encouraged by the excited beeps and honks of the others, it closed in, sighing though aching teeth. The Camaro made as if to move forward and join the Impala, but a low growl from the

bigger car warned it off. *The bus is mine!* The Camaro
scooted back, complaining loudly.

The bus was watching the Impala now. It was a
dangerous adversary. It was not playing the feinting
game of the Camaro. The bus rumbled warningly,
but to the Impala it was only further challenge.

Then the bus gave a lurch forward, as if to scare
off the other. It wouldn't scare. The Impala rolled
smoothly forward, stalking, stalking, until it was almost
nose to nose with the ponderous other. Its four bright
eyes held only the promise of glittering death.

Startled, the bus took a step back, and in so doing,
crunched into the snuffling Firebird; the car had
been lurking behind it—it howled, more from shock
than hurt. But it was a signal. The pack edged in, each
car moving just a little bit forward. The Camaro was
in the forefront.

The bus lifted one great wheel in warning, but the
pack ignored it. The Camaro, overcome with its own
daring, dashed in to chivvy the bus's throat—and found
itself pinned beneath the wheel. It uttered a gashing,
crashing, agonized scream—a howl of shock, rage,
anger, frustration and despair, all in one. It was
suddenly cut short.

As one, the cars gave a cry. The roar of their engines rose. Black smoke belched from their exhausts.
An acrid and pungent odor filled the air: the smell of
death, realized and impending.

The autos moved. Unmindful of the danger to themselves, for they were no longer acting as individuals, the
cars rolled in. With a sharp rasping snarl, the Cougar
leapt at the back of the bus. Its claws scrabbled for
purchase. Farther along the great beast's flank, a blue
Corvette had sunk deep fangs into the bus's side. Metal
ripped and shrieked. The smell of gasoline and oil and
diesel fuel swung heavy in the air.

The Corvette had torn a rent in the bus's side. It
lapped at the flowing ichor and buried its fangs again.
The bus grunted in finally-realized pain and swung

halfway around to strike at the sportster, flinging it away and onto the sidewalk, a flimsy pile of metal and fiberglass. Its proud angles and wings were torn and crumpled, and it lay there gasping and sputtering.

But if it was out of the battle, it had still inflicted heavy damage on the bus, and others moved in to widen that gaping wound. Already a Barracuda was slashing into the torn metal-flesh, its sharp teeth rending and tearing.

The bus howled at it; howled at the Cougar that was clawing at its back. It shook and heaved and issued a deep agonized cry. But the Cougar had a firm grip and wouldn't be moved, and the Barracuda kept lunging in again and again.

Frenzied, the bus threw itself fiercely back, then forward. Its great tail lashed from side to side, smashing windows and crumpling fenders. The cars swarmed forward at it, around it, biting at its wheels and its unprotected flanks.

The bus rose up in agony, shaking and screaming. The Cougar slipped off its back and crashed down onto the Firebird that had been doing something to the rear of the bus. The Barracuda was flung away too. Heavily, the bus struck out at its tormentors, but it was outnumbered hopelessly. Already the Cougar was scrabbling onto its back, widening the fissure of torn metal, ripping open the flesh, scooping in with its claws. The bus's black blood ran down its sides and into the streets.

The Cadillac moved in then. Barking and protesting, the smaller cars were edged out of their way. It shouldered roughly through and began to rip great chunks of rubber off the bus's tires. It ignored the bus's shrieks as it stuffed bleeding gobbets into its maw.

The rest of the cars had fallen onto the bus already. Its heaving attempts were no longer strong enough to shake them off, and they were ripping and tearing hungrily at its flesh, always trying to reach its throat. They fought with frenzied lust.

The Cadillac was eating everything it could. Gobbets of bus-flesh dripped out of its lips. It masticated in rapid jerking motion. It stuffed and gobbled—pieces of the other cars as well as hunks of the bus, the fender of the Impala, too, crumbling bits of the pavement. The bus was almost ignored as the Cadillac grabbed at everything that came near it. Its hunger was manic and insane.

The mighty leviathan was making one last effort to escape. In a heroic effort, it rose to its feet, unmindful of the cars hanging from it, the great holes in its sides, and the bleeding entrails that hung out of its wounds—at which the cars still snapped and bit.

It was a doomed effort. The bus was little more than a shell now—still reacting, still feeling, but its vitals were being torn out even as it moved. The Mustang hanging sharply at its throat like a terrier had struck home, and transmission fluid was leaking all over the street. The bus sank back down onto its knees, almost a kneeling, supplicating posture.

The death blow was not long in coming. It came not as a single thundering end, but as a series of vicious bites, as a continual rending and tearing, as a slow agonized ripping away of the vital organs, as the painful aching process of the feeding of the pack. The bus shuddered once and was still.

The cars plunged inward hungrily, climbing and clambering over each other in mad intensity. They leapt onto the back of the bus, or into its gory sides. They thrust their muzzles deep into it, swallowing without chewing. Their ravenous hunger overcame them and they fought amongst themselves, clawing and scratching.

The body of the bus was invisible now, blanketed by the flashing bodies of its attackers. The only piece of yellow skin visible was the small tender scrap that a young Volkswagen was contentedly chewing.

The noise was horrendous: scraping and scrabblings, clawing, shrieking—the continuing sounds of gobbling hunger being sated. The stench was awful. Reeking fumes swept up the streets, outward in all directions.

The black blood ran thick on the pavement. The cries of challenge and triumph had long since faded into the slobbering sounds of choking motors, eating, gnawing, snarling, tearing at the bus's frame. They steamed and stank.

They still swarmed over the giant corpse, but with lessening intensity. Their initial frenzy had been fed, and now they were feeding their stomachs as well. The Firebird was repaying the insult of its crumpled grill. It belched and farted happily, joyously.

The cars made quiet gobbling sounds of satisfaction. The bus was being quickly reduced to its bones—and even those were being eagerly torn away. The Volkswagen crept out of its alley again to lap at the bloody streets.

The big Cadillac growled sluggishly and parked itself against a wall. Even *its* hunger had been sated. It belched its gluttony into the air.

And then they heard it.

The sound. The deep, rumbling, far off sound.

And the scent, far off but still distinct—the scent of diesel.

A surge of sudden fear caught them. Their eyes were white with the realization. As the rumbling sound grew louder, the cars looked at one another and knew the afternoon was over.

The trucks were coming.

The context in which a story appears is also very important.

Ours is a Judeo-Christian culture.

Much (if not most) of our literature reflects the same common morality pattern: the hero is right but humble, and always wins out in the end.

Jesus Christ was right, and humble, got crucified for it, but still won out: he went to heaven. Everybody else didn't.

Of course, Christ had a lot going for him. For one thing, he was the son of God.

He did what he did (so the story goes) to inspire the rest of us to do as well—or at least as well as we are capable of doing. And the impact of that has shaped and guided our history for the past two thousand years.

Today, one of the most, if not the most important stories you can tell in the United States is the Christ story. Not necessarily in the original terms, but if the original message is still there, it's still "the Christ story." You can call it Billy Budd, or Stranger in a Strange Land, or Behold the Man, but it's still "the Christ story."

It's about the message being more important than the man, and the message is "Love one another."

You can do variations of it. You can do Dune and The Answer and 1984, but whether they are conscious

89

or unconscious retellings of "the Christ story," they are still retellings of it simply by existing in the context of a Judeo-Christian culture.

A writer is the product of his culture and the reflection of it. He cannot help but write about what he knows—and what he knows best is usually the culture in which he lives. So he focuses on one small part of it and reflects that back to the reader, showing how that one small piece is a part of the whole.

In a Judeo-Christian culture, the most important story you can tell is "the Christ story."

It's the originality of your retelling of it that maximizes its impact.

This story, "Eyes of Onyx," would probably not be too meaningful in Pakistan. It would be out of context. But Ed Bryant is writing this in the United States—and he's writing it for American readers. We have a mutual context that we all share, a common backfile of heritage that we all draw upon.

Superimposed upon that common collective memory is the contemporary NOW, that ever-onrushing moment of existence that is carrying us forward into the future, continually reshaping our expanding American culture. The present is the interface between the future and the past—and upon that interface is written a story that reflects both.

Merry Christmas.

EYES OF ONYX

Edward Bryant

It happened last December. It was just a regular night, with me and Pop working late in the grease pit. Our *morada* isn't much, just a combination house and filling station. We bought it back when Mom was alive. It doesn't make us rich—that's for sure—but we manage to scratch a living off the local trade and the tourists that break down every once in a while. The government would give us better if we begged for it, but Pop's always been kind of touchy about things like that. We still go to a legit cash-or-get-out medic when we get sick, too.

I had to drop out of upper-level before graduation, so I don't have a great education as far as educations go these days. What with every other brain getting three degrees, or at least the card to try it, I don't seem too smart. But with me it was either slice out or starve. So there I was.

It was getting close to Christmas, and we were working late. We had an old '79 Starliner with a pitted gyro up on the rack. It was owned by some anglo from up the strip in Berdoo who hadn't had the sense to trade it in on a newer model when he had the chance. About eleven o'clock Pop sent me out to get another set of metric wrenches from the storage shack across the road. We didn't really need those wrenches, but I went anyway. Once I came right out and told Pop that he didn't have to send me away when he needed a drink. He just said soft and slow that he had a little pride left. Since then I haven't crossed him about it.

So I left. I suppose I should mention that our place is located on one of the lower-level approaches to the big Inter-Cont Expressway. Since we're just a small trinkets business, we couldn't get a decent frontline franchise like the big chains. Those outfits like Enerco keep coming around trying to buy Pop out, but he won't sell. Too damn stubborn, he says. He had to sell out once and he won't do it again. The company men, they don't know what Pop's talking about. They figure he's just a nutball case, so they throw up their hands, slice out and try again in a few more months. Same thing happens every time.

It was good to get out of the stink of kerosene and oil and into some open air. I like being a mechanic okay, but my nose must be extra sensitive. Those fumes still get to me even though I've worked with cars for the last ten years—since I was six.

There was just a skiff of snow on the pavement, and I could see more of those big flakes floating down real slow in the glare from our neons. The air was calm and chilly, and you could just barely hear the advertising from downcity. Overhead, the clouds had cut out most of the big floating glitter-signs. There was only one I could read. It was lower than the rest and spelled out first DO XMAS RIGHT in red and then BUY GEMCO in green. Back when I was a kid I used to like watching the stars at night, before they started putting up the glitter-signs.

So I got the wrench-set Pop wanted and had started back across the road when a hassle down at MacLain's caught my ear. Old man MacLain owns a motel—if you want to call it that. Picture a big fat decaying egg carton with little rotten egg cartons crumbling in a line along side; that's MacLain's motel. It's never been repaired since it was built and probably won't be fixed before Renewal Authority razes it.

Old man MacLain is definitely a *mierda*. That's the way I've felt ever since he got so pissed at me for keeping his sweet little daughter out all week once. I don't see what kick he had coming; what we were doing was our own business. After all, just like any other smart parent, he'd put her on the six-month shots when she started to bleed. I mean, what did he expect her to do? Pop doesn't like old MacLain either—says he's a *hijo de puta*. Which is strong for Pop.

My ears told me that MacLain was upset; I can tell that whine any day of the week. He had a face to go along with it; little eyes, mean; oily nose; fat mouth buried in about six chins. If a voice can be completely ugly, old MacLain looked just like he sounded. I was curious, so I walked down to the motel. If I thought the Starliner in the shop was old and crusty, I changed my mind when I saw the heap parked in front of Mac-Lain's Quality Western Motel. It must have dated back to the sixties at least, and it didn't look like it could even make the minimum speed on the I-C strip.

Midway between the wreck and MacLain's place was MacLain himself and this man and woman. The man was one of those thin, intense-looking people, the kind on holovision that have ideals and never get anywhere. The woman—I supposed she was his wife— stood a little ways behind as if he was protecting her. She wasn't any Miss North America, but she was kind of quiet-beautiful, if you know what I mean. Not spectacular like Monica Marlo or one of the other sexy vidstars, but kind of good looking anyway—real dark skin with black eyes and black hair pulled back on top of her head. You could also see plain that she was going to have a kid soon.

Old man MacLain sounded pretty mad, even worse than usual. He was raving about how he wasn't running no Soc/Welfare establishment and that they—the man and woman—would have to card it up or else they wouldn't be staying in his motel.

The man kept explaining quietly and patiently, like

for about the fourteenth time, that he and his wife had made a long trip from back east and didn't have any credit left. Then he said that his wife thought she was going to have the baby a little early and they couldn't find a doctor or a place to stay. That started that freak MacLain off to yelling again about him not wanting anything like this in his rooms, and how they ought to leave and keep looking for a doctor. This was even though he knew as well as me that the local government med was on vacation over the holidays.

Finally, while I held back and just watched, the man and woman gave up. The man's thin shoulders sort of slumped like he'd lost out on something important as he took the woman's arm and helped her back across the lot toward their car. MacLain just stood there with a righteous look on his fat face.

Now I don't go out and dig up good deeds. I look out for just Pop and me, and that's the way to do it these days. If you stick out your neck you're liable to get a blade through it. Even so, I looked at those two eastern straights—they should have known better than to head across country with no credit—and knew I'd feel like hell if I didn't do something.

So that's why I walked up to the guy just as he was opening the car door and touched his arm. I told him I figured that Pop and me could put them up for the night over at our place if they wanted to come. The guy looked at me like he couldn't quite believe it. Then he decided I was spinning straight so he spent about a minute shaking my hand and thanking me. The woman didn't say anything but just smiled into my eyes. I started feeling good all over for some reason. It was like a double jag of coke. It was starting to shake me up. But I felt even better when we turned to walk to the station and I saw the look on MacLain's face.

I took them into the garage and lined out the situation to Pop. He looked at me a little odd and squeezed my shoulder. Then he got busy taking care of the man and the prospective mother, and all of a sudden he was the way he used to be before Mom died. He even put the woman in Mom's room. Not only that, he had her lie down in Mom's old bed after I'd changed the sheets. No one had slept there for eight or nine years. The woman didn't seem to feel so good now, and I got a hunch that the nine months bit was about to run out. I was right.

Pop was an old hand at this sort of thing even if I was his only kid; he'd delivered me back on our old place when there wasn't a medic around for forty miles. He saw that the husband was close to stepping off the deep end, so he sent the guy out into the living room and put him to work tearing clean sheets into nice neat strips. It kept him busy.

I helped Pop as best I could until it looked like the baby was going to come okay. Then Pop told me I was getting on his nerves and would I please slice out. He really meant it, so I left.

I went outside into the cold air again. It helped. It seemed to me that I was almost as jittery as that husband. For no reason at all I wondered if praying for that woman would help. We haven't had much to do with religion since the Church got sucked up into the Universalist bit in the late seventies. That was even before Mom died. I remember Pop saying something at supper about how he was fed up with the hypocrites. It was about this time he finally knew we weren't going to be able to keep on living out in the Valley so he let some big management company buy up our farm for about half what it was worth. That's when we moved in here closer to the city and bought the station. A little later Mom died, and Pop's strength just sort of went out of him. He wasn't himself anymore—not the way he'd been. I can remember the time when Pop was like one of the big rocks in the hills around our place in the Valley. I was pretty small then, but I can still see in my mind how tall and strong Pop was. Then we had to sell out, and it was like the water seeping into cracks in a rock. The water freezes and expands and the stone begins to spilt. When Mom died it was that much more ice. Pop sort of broke apart and drifted along. I don't think you can really blame him.

I'd just got to thinking about how Pop had seemed more like his old self tonight when I heard this God-awful bawling from inside, so I went back in. The door to Mom's room was open again, and Pop was in the doorway wearing the strangest look I'd ever seen. He walked past like he didn't even see me and went into the little room we use as an office. He closed the door, but I could see through the glassed-in pass-through that Pop was using the phone. He was only on the air for a few seconds. Then he cut off and came back to the room where the baby was crying.

It wasn't ten minutes before a chopper from Salk Memorial set down on the pavement in front of the station and three white-coated medics hopped down from the cabin. The med team didn't say much when I let them in—just asked in a kind of bored way where the baby was. Naturally, they closed that door to Mom's room behind them.

I went outside again. The clouds were beginning to clear away. The big glitter-signs were all back in view now, but there was something brighter up there. Between CONSOLIDATED TRAVELAIRE and CHEV-CO CENTER was a white glow that looked like a big star. I remembered from the morning vidcast that it was a comet, Yamamura 1990b or something like that —one of those things that only comes around every 2000 years or so.

I didn't expect the medics to be there long. I figured they'd check to make sure the woman and her baby weren't bleeding to death, record the birth, and head back to the holiday traffic victims filling up the hospitals.

When I was just a kid, I'd wanted to be part of a med team. Of course I zapped that idea when I dropped out. But I still admire them. Med men always seem cool and calm and act like they never find a case they can't handle. This team was different. When they came out of the house they looked bad. One of them was talking. Most of the time he was talking to himself because the other two weren't listening. The shortest of the medics sort of looked grimly ahead and didn't pay any mind to the one with the mouth. The third med walked like he was in the middle of a dream. They ignored me. They all walked past, climbed into the chopper and lofted out. A couple seconds and they were just another green star over downcity.

I wasn't exactly sure what I should do now, so I went back inside. This time Pop at least said something to me.

"Juan, you can see her now."

By this time I was curious, so I went into that room. The woman was lying back in the bed with her dark hair all undone and falling around her neck and with the baby snuggled up against her. I've seen babies before, but there was something different about this one—not a physical thing, but a feeling that sang and shouted inside my mind. There was a power inside that room. I could feel it. It was like being inside the guts of a reactor plant, only a thousand times as powerful. I was scared, like that reactor was going to blow. Then the power started to calm me down. All I can say is that this was the first time I ever looked at a baby from on my knees.

Well, that's the story. Like I said, it all happened last December, and it's summer now. That guy, his wife, and their daughter all left in a couple days, just as soon as the woman could travel. Pop lent them a transfer chit and gave them some fuel for that antique they drove. That should have been the end of it, but it wasn't.

The Fed police showed up a week later and caused some real trouble. They kept asking question we couldn't answer, so finally they left.

Lately I've been paying attention to the vidcasts and tabloids like I never used to. People are getting edgy, just like they're expecting something big to happen. So far there are just little hints and stirrings in the background, and something's going on. I can feel it. It's got me on the hook. That's right—interested. Maybe a little scared too.

Yeah, right, I know what this all sounds like.

But there's a catch.

I remember that tiny black girl-child opening her eyes and looking at me there on my knees. I can't get those eyes out of my mind. They were two pieces of onyx—just as dark and hard, and just as cold shining. And they were full of hate and anger, before they shut again.

Pop, he talks about mutations and telepathy. Me, I got another idea about this whole bit, and it's strange because I'm not any church-freak. I think about two thousand years ago there was a God of Love and he gave us a chance and we screwed it good. But now the old God's dead. There's a new man on top and we're getting a new deal. And this time, man, the chance is going to be something else.

Really something else.

Assume that writers, as a breed, are part of the human species. There are those (editors among them) who have expressed their doubts.

Writing is one of those things that commands respect only if you are very very successful at it. Otherwise, people (mundane-type people) give you that strange half-pitying look as if to ask, "Is anyone else in your family insane?"

Or they'll ask, "Have you ever sold anything?" The ultimate affront. If you have, they haven't read it. Or even heard of it. But that's your fault too.

If they're your relatives, they'll suggest you go out and get an honest job. And even after you've made those first few all-important sales, they'll remain skeptical. "Are you still writing, or are you working for a living?"

People respect only the writers who make it big. Everyone else is an amateur. Or a hack.

With that kind of social pressure working against you, only the most determined become writers. Perhaps it's a survival-of-the-fittest type thing, but the arts suffer because of it. (Writing isn't the only art that's in ill repute. When was the last time you met someone who admitted to being a full-time poet? Art is for full-time living. Earning should have nothing to do with it.)

But that's part of the problem. The earning thing.

99

Most of the writers in this book are only part-time writers. Most of them have other jobs, or they're students, or housewives.

There are very few full-time writers.

There's a vicious circle involved. In order to make enough money from writing in order to write full-time, you have to write full-time. Period.

I did it by one day deciding: "NOW, I am a writer." I quit my job (whichever one I held at the time), went home and sat down at my typewriter, determined to sell something or starve to death in the attempt.

I had to do that four times before I started selling. Every time a full-time writer takes a part-time job, it's an admission of defeat. Whether partial or total, it's an admission of defeat—that he couldn't make it as a writer. It's the number of times he can bounce back that will determine if he makes it.

Steve Goldin is working on his first bounce right now. (Hopefully, it's the only one he'll need.) Just a few months ago, he quit his job so that he could concentrate on turning himself from part-time into full-time. It's a question of discipline . . .

Some writers (myself included) need the pressure of looming starvation in order to write. Others (like Steve Goldin) write as a profitable hobby. They admit to being writers only in those circles where they will be honored for such admissions.

I envy that second class of people for one thing only —their credit status.

Have you ever had to tell a bank, "I'm a free-lance writer?"

And then they give you that *look* and ask, "Have you any *other* sources of income?"

"Uh, I'm an editor too— "

"Oh, well that changes things."

(It certainly does. As an editor, I made only $1500 that year. As a writer I made ten times that amount. Oh well.)

THE WORLD WHERE WISHES WORKED

Stephen Goldin

There once was a world where wishes worked.

It was a pleasant enough place, and the people were certainly happy. There was no hunger in this world, for a man had only to wish for food to have it appear before him. Clothing and shelter were equally easy to obtain. Envy was unknown there—if another person had something that seemed interesting, it was only a wish away from anyone else. There was neither need nor age. The people lived simple lives, devoted to beauty and the gentle sciences. The days were a pleasant blur of quiet activity.

And in this world, there was a fool.

Just the one.

It was enough.

The fool looked about him one day and saw that everything was the same. Beautiful people doing beautiful things amidst the beautiful scenery. He walked away from the others, down to a private little dell beside a lily pond overhung by graceful willows and scented with spring fragrance. He wondered what things would be like if something new or different were to be. And so he concocted a foolish scheme.

"I wish," he said, "that I had something that nobody has ever had before."

Only a fool could have made a wish like this, for he left the object of his desire completely unspecified.

As a result, he instantly came down with Disease, which had hitherto been unknown. His eyes went rheumy and his nose went runny. His head ached and his knees wobbled. Chills ran up and down his spine.

"I dod't like this," he said. "Dot at all. I wish to cadcel by last wish." And he immediately felt well again.

"That was close," he sighed as he sat down on a large rock beside the pond. "The trouble is that I don't think before I say things. If I thought things out first, I wouldn't get into so much hot water. Therefore: I wish I would think more before I do any more wishing." And it was so.

However, being a fool he failed to spot the fallacy of his logic: namely, that a fool will think foolish thoughts, and no amount of foolish thinking would help him make wise wishes.

Thus deluded, he began to think of what his next wish should be. He did not even consider wishing for wealth, since such a thing was impossible in a world where everyone had anything. Material desires were too commonplace. "What I should wish for in order to satisfy this new restlessness of mine," he thought, "is the rarest of all commodities. I wish for love."

A frog jumped out of the lily pond and landed *squish* right in his lap. It looked up at him adoringly with big froggy eyes filled with tenderness and croaked a gentle love call.

"Yuk!" exclaimed the fool, and he instinctively scooped up the frog and threw it as far from him as he could. The pathetic little creature merely croaked sorrowfully and started hopping back to the rock to be with its beloved. Quickly, the fool canceled his last wish and the frog, frightened, leapt back into the pond.

"That was a foolish wish," evaluated the fool. "Most of my wishes are foolish. Most of the things I say are foolish. What can I do to keep from saying foolish things?"

Had he not been a fool, he would simply have wished

to say only wise things from then on. But, fool that he was, he said, "I know. I hereby wish not to say foolish things."

And so it was. However, since he was a fool, *anything* he could say would be foolish. Consequently, he now found that he could say nothing at all.

He became very frightened. He tried to speak, but nothing came out. He tried harder and harder, but all he accomplished was getting a sore throat. In a panic, he ran around the countryside looking for someone to help him, for without the ability to speak he could not undo that previous wish. But nobody was about, and the fool finally fell exhausted beside a footpath and started to sob silently.

Eventually, a friend came along the path and found him. "Hello," said the friend.

The fool moved his mouth, but no sound escaped.

"I don't believe I heard you," the friend replied politely.

The fool tried again, still with no success.

"I am really not in the mood for charades," said the friend, becoming annoyed over the fool's behavior. "If you can't be more considerate, I'll just leave." And he turned to go.

The fool sank to his knees, grabbed his friend's clothing, tugged at it, and gesticulated wildly. "I wish you'd tell me what the matter is," said the friend.

"I made a wish that I not say anything foolish, and suddenly I found that I couldn't say anything," the fool told him.

"Well, then, that explains it. I am sorry to say it, my friend, but you are a fool, and anything you say is likely to be foolish. You should stay away from wishes like that. I suppose you want me to release you from that wish."

The fool nodded vigorously.

"Very well. I wish that you could speak again."

"Oh, thank you, thank you."

"Just be careful of what you say in the future, because wishes come true automatically, no matter how foolish they are." And the friend left.

The fool sat down to think some more. His friend had been right—anything he was likely to say would be foolish, and his wishes would automatically come true. If that were so (and it was), he would always be in trouble. He could remain safe by not saying anything —but he had just tried that and hadn't liked it at all. The more he thought, the worse the problem became. There seemed to be no acceptable way he could fit into the system.

Then suddenly the answer came to him. Why not change the system to fit himself?

"I wish," he said, "that wishes did not automatically come true."

Things are tough all over.

One of the games we keep playing (and by "we" I mean the people who actively pursue science fiction as a way of life) is the attempt to define the term "science fiction."

I offer this simple, but all-inclusive, definition of my own:

If a thing exists, it can be studied; if a thing is possible and can be comprehended, the conditions of its existence can be studied; if a thing can be studied, that study of it is a science. Any science can have a story written about it—and that story will be science fiction.

The only qualification I'll put on that definition is that it does not include stories about things that have already happened—that's historical fiction. Science fiction is stories about things that may be possible, but haven't happened. Yet, if at all.

Of course, that's a generalized definition, but the sense of it is that everything that man can question can have a science built up around it—and the act of writing a story about any science is part of the act of questioning it. (Remember? Science fiction is the new theology.)

The behavorial sciences are some of the more important ways in which man is questioning his existence, although stories about this particular set of -ologies *(psych-, soci-, whatever) have been unfortunately rare. Only in the past decade or so, as these so-called "Human Sciences" have gained in importance, has their effect on science fiction become pronounced. We have begun to see more and more stories based on the writer's realization of some aspect of man's inner nature.*

We science-fiction writers are not content to seek only the ends of the known physical universe; we must delve to the depths of the universe of the mind—and perhaps this latter pursuit is the more exciting and exotic.

And disturbing.

Herein, Leo P. Kelley suggests the real reason why the future may not be a very nice place to live.

COLD, THE FIRE OF
THE PHOENIX

Leo P. Kelley

Consider.

Two people.

Two things.

The people: Lena and Arnold.

The two things: (1) electrical discharges found in such odd places as brains and dynamos, and (2) ALI__NS (fill in blank completely).

About the two people . . .

First, Lena.

(Arnold, a little later.)

See Lena standing in the communal kitchen of the Automated Life Complex with all the morning women, cooking. It is crowded, and Lena does not so much stand as does she slope bacause of the Fat Woman pressing upon her on one side and the Fatter Woman behind her pushing out her sausage of a finger toward the pink button on the stained panel which eyes her with the single word: EGGS.

See Lena. See Lena cook. Hear her heart beating out its testimony for the defense. Hear her mind working, bearing witness for the prosecution.

Lena says, "Fat Woman, move. I can't touch the toast circuit. Fatter Woman, please stop breathing on my follicles."

Fat and Fatter move, allowing Lena to slope in the opposite direction, which is even less satisfactory than before, but she does not give either a sigh or a damn as the electrical currents circulating in the socket of her skull spark and sputter and she—.

The Whore of Babylon (alias Lena): *Take my belly in your pulsing paws and sound the horn of the hunt, and we shall lie down beneath an orange moon and retro rockets shall chronicle our hot flight. Apples I will give you, Arnold, and a fair frankincense.*

Lena removes the toast from the smooth machine and fights her way to the eating shelf where her place —hers and Arnold's—is identified with a heart she once, in a fidget of passion, scarred into its metal surface:

L loves A

The Whore of Babylon: *Swiftly, swiftly. And all the while singing.*

Lena returns from wherever she was to her toast and the overcrowded Earth and is herself (?) again: only Lena, who would not know the Whore of Babylon if she met her face to face on the air ramps. Lena is worn out with fighting past Fat, Fatter and Fattest (everyone eats; it is lonely in the crowd). The electrical currents in her skull now are gray: the toast is burned. Arnold will not notice. Arnold will a-working go with burned toast in his belly and he will not notice.

And present and unaccounted for: ALL NS (fill in blank completely). Unseen and totally energized entities intelligently flit among the folds of flesh filling the room. They find it as lonely here as there—as where they come from, *came* from, on their nonlinear expedition through the valley of night, on their climb up the mountain of light that (they hope) will spell an end to their loneliness and their former now-evoluted-out-of-existence-multicellular-matter-and-failed-fortitude-from-beyond-far-stars. They knew that here on Earth energy cannot be created or destroyed (unlike there), but that it *can* be transformed. And they *hunger.*

Lena does not hear her own silent cry, or having

heard, considers the cry of no importance, no relevance to her or whore.

Arnold enters blandly. Ten minutes later, he reaches the eating shelf, having swum a valiant swim through the sea of hustling bodies.

Lena gives him the cold toast and no words.

Arnold takes the toast and chews it placidly, charred crumbs as far from his busy mind and mouth as arsenic. Because this, oh, this, is the way it is. Arnold has long ago forgotten all he ever knew of the worlds and ways of "should be" and "could be." Arnold, like his wife, like Lena, is comfortable and unanxious. Outwardly. His Emotion-Quotient, which arrived on schedule in the transtube only this morning, was reassuringly negative.

But.

Ohms and amperes. Chewed toast, flame-tasting. Lena.

King (Arnold) of the Trolls: *Bridges are best. Shadowy beneath and hidey. Footsteps, sometimes, overhead. And down below, the light of a simplistic world—a brook flowing by, unmindful of crayfish scuttling about in its lap and spiders spinning above it. Grasses. Watercress and wet worms. Come to me, oh my minions. . . .*

Thinks Lena, Good Old Arnold. Good. Old. Ah!

Arnold counts his minions, his eyes seething with trolls—all, every one, obedient and reverent.

He says to Lena, "Tomorrow, maybe, you might get to the egg button."

"Or the next day," Lena muses.

They did have eggs in April. Once. Today belongs to May.

Lena looks at Fat and Fatter but looks can't kill. Next month is June. "I am going to have a baby," says Lena.

"For how long this time?"

"Twenty nine hours. Starting at eight-eleven tomorrow morning."

"Who gets it next?"

"I'm the last one on the list. After us, it gets sent to the Maturation Reservation. Anne and Samantha— they've both had their turns with it already. I'm never at the top of any list! And it's the last of this year's quota too!"

The King of the Trolls (to his minions): *Here, have a cee-gar. We're going to have a baby!*

Trollish laughter and jokes, rakish.

Breakfast ended, Lena and Arnold, with no banners flying, battle their way to the door where they part— Arnold to his job in the Stasis Nests where he chills the sleepers awaiting their turns to tread the concrete face of Earth by pressing buttons and twisting temp dials and singing no single song. Lena is off to the ion baths where the waters, like slippery fish, will hold age and its consort, Death, at bay and she will see no contradiction between preserving life and simultaneously creating needed Stasis Nests.

In this year of The Law—2010—Life is sacred; Death, the dark defiler.

They are gone from each other in the swarm of buzzing bodies crowding the air ramps.

Diverging paths:

First, Lena.

(Arnold, a little later.)

Lena slips out of her tunic and sandals and into the waters rich in calcium which excite electrically the intricate clusters of neurons that bear such names as Lena, Lilly, Samantha and Anne. She greets the women floating like warm icebergs in the ion baths.

They return her listless greeting.

Overhead, lights gleam bluely as Time tiptoes by.

Now, Arnold.

Arnold dutifully adjusts dials, flicks switches, and the silent ones sleeping in stasis stare out at him unseeing from behind their thin veil of frost. All is well, Arnold notes in his logbook and sits down and begins to read his Consumer Price Index with no passion and no pain.

Under *Aeroautos:* Wheelless transport. Olive drab. Rating: Satisfactory. Cost: One year's employment in Synthetic Laboratories as Technician, Fourth Level.

Under *Eroticine:* Stability ampules. Rating: Highly desirable. Cost: Twenty hours' employment in Ion Exchange.

Expensive, thinks Arnold heretically, at half the price. His finger stumbles upon a listing in bold-face type:

Lubricants, Life: Listings canceled subject to investigation by **Narcoethos, Inc.**

Shivering, Arnold reads on, and when he finishes he finds he has need of many more years if he is to consume all he thinks he needs. It is always cold in the Nests, and shivers and sneezes are nothing new to Arnold. He knows that burns and bruises are the lot of those who work in the Ion Exchange. So. A man has to live, and "Can't complain!" is Arnold's heavy motto, but one day perhaps, one dark and dangerous day, someone may respond to his statement with a question: "Why not?" and that will be the black-letter day that Arnold, in a confused fury of hot blood and cold sweat, will crucify Chicken Little.

They (what name will really name them?) touch Arnold—his brain and the spaces within it filled with mucoproteins and polysaccharides. *They.* The ALI__NS (fill in blank completely). Accustomed as they are to a richer diet of ergs (as they call them here) they then withdraw, shaking ohms and amperes soulfully. Hunger howls within them, and they know they will die without more substantial sustenance than that which is (it would seem) Arnold's mundane brain. Where have all the powers gone? All the rrnis'p (read joys') and llrduo (read angers)? A lunar landscape this. All rocks and dust and adjustments.

In the ion baths, the Whore of Babylon: *Sweet juices do stain my soul, and oil of cedar anoints my fingertips. I hold wide the gate of the temple that the worshipper may come within and revel. Clouds of musk are mine, and arms of alabaster.*

Lena bids goodby to the iceberg women and goes to her homicile where she waits patiently outside a brown door with a metal slot in which a photoelectric cell tirelessly flashes: ANDERSON. But soon the Andersons will leave for their shift at Synthetica Laboratories and the homicile will become temporarily Lena's —Lena's and Arnold's.

The door vibrates faintly in warning and the Andersons, behind it, rise up from their pallets and come out, flicking the switch controlling the photoelectric cell so that it now flashes: SMITH. So Lena (Smith) goes inside. Now that she is here and home, she finds it all hardly worthwhile. It? Confused, she retreats waving a thousand white flags of surrender, and the advancing armies of thought obligingly withdraw and disappear.

Arnold arrives and is recognized by the door. It admits him to Lena who does not look up as he enters. . . .

With wild beasts unchained, do I come to you, whispers the Whore of Babylon, laughing. *And with sharp claws unsheathed and carrying a basket of perfumed roses,* she sighs, beginning to cry.

"You are beginning to cry," observes Arnold, sitting down and automatically opening his Consumer Price Index, making himself comfortable.

"Yes," says Lena, smiling. "Tears are so salty. Like peanuts. Would you like some?"

Arnold nods absently.

Lena touches her eyes and tosses a plastic bag of peanuts across the room to him which he catches, barely noticing their wetness. The gift is given and the world moves on.

The peanuts are even saltier than tears, Arnold discovers. He learns from his Consumer Price Index that flowers can be delivered daily to the sleepers in the

Stasis Nest. He knew it already. He turns the page and . . .

The War of the Roses, cries the King of the Trolls. *Weapon yourselves, all my minions!* Roses appear in every troll's hand as summer advances upon the land with its hot and heavy breathing and the trolls chase winter away across fields of melting snow from which furry bears emerge, yawning. Summer smiles her soft and voluptuous victory. The trolls kneel and hold out their bleeding hands to her. Roses have thorns, a fact the King of the Trolls had quite forgotten. He composes a poem on the spot which tells of hands like roses, red and thorned.

"I was always good at mathematics," Arnold says too loudly.

"And I at being joyful." Lena hesitates. "A long time ago."

"I was talking about mathematics."

"Mathematics, yes."

"I added it all up, what we need. It comes to two hundred and seventy-one years and three months and six days and nine hours and four minutes and two seconds. The cost of living is getting way out of hand, if you ask me."

Lena looks at him with sorrow and no hope.

Arnold taps the pages of his Consumer Price Index. "Somebody ought to do something. Why, to get an aeroauto—even a used one—you've got to pay a year's worth of work in Synthetica Labs."

"I don't think I want the baby."

"You're supposed to want it."

"It will come with too many names hanging around its neck like stones. Samantha told me this morning that she called it Doris when she had it last week."

"It's a girl then."

"No, a boy, but Samantha had wanted a girl for ever so long, so she went ahead and called it Doris. Anne—well, you know Anne. When she had it on her turn, she called it Simonpure after somebody she heard about once. Only it didn't work."

"Naturally. It's too young."

"No, I mean the name didn't work. The baby still messed itself all the time. What are you doing?"

Arnold puts one foot forward, and then another. He stands up and turns twice, whistling out of tune. "Dancing," he answers. He waves his arms and points a toe.

"I'm twenty years old, Arnold."

Arnold offers a pirouette.

"You are too," Lena reminds him.

An entrechat.

"Arnold?"

"Try dancing," he suggests sympathetically. "It just might help."

"It won't. Mah jongg didn't, last week."

"They're planting flowers in the park. I saw them on my way home. Yellow ones, they were, and purple. Plastic. Pretty. They shine so." He stumbles, but recovers and continues whistling.

Lena gets up to take a nutrient pill. "Want one?" She holds out the tube to Arnold.

He glides up to her, seizes a pill and pops it into his mouth. "Thanks. *Mmmmm*. Corn on the cob."

"They say," says Lena, swallowing, "that there are sewers beneath the Life Complex. Nothing at all down there but pipes and sloshing water. Arnold, do you suppose we could go——?"

"Dancing strengthens the mind and the muscles. Watch me." He leaps two inches off the floor.

Lena watches and sees a four-dimensional entity which she realizes is her husband. She lies down on her pallet, staring at the very low ceiling. "Arnold."

"Unnhh."

"Do you want to?"

Arnold doesn't but he does.

During it all, Lena vanishes from beneath him.

The King of the Trolls: *I send you forth, oh my*

minions, to bring me gifts of white unicorns and wood nymphs who will—.

The Whore of Babylon: *They are planting plastic passion flowers in the park and they shine with dew like diamonds. They—.*

In the room, invisible, the ALIENS (their blank spaces gradually filling in completely as they feed on the surging, satisfying currents that sear and rage now through the two brains, as the humans who own those brains fly away to nonexistent lands carrying heavy suitcases full of dreams like contraband).

"Arnold!" *Lift me up, my love, and—*

"Lena!" *Hold her tight in her youth and terror while I walk about and admire the captive hills and valleys of her body, so rich with the secrets of magical forests. I want—*

"Arnold, I'm—"

"Not as young as I used to be, I guess," Arnold says, leaning now against the wall and breathing shallowly.

Apart, they stare at each other in numb wonder.

The ALIENS smack their nonlinear lips and rejoice, feeling the feedback of their new strength born of the strongest electrical discharges absorbed just now from the brains of Lena and Arnold, who stand drained in the room together, unaware of the abrupt death (permanent) of the Whore of Babylon and the King of the Trolls.

The ALIENS are surfeited.

"Whew!" exclaims Lena. "I'm sure bushed!"

"Like I said, we're not as young as we used to be. Twenty is getting on, as they say."

"I'm going to call the baby something special. What do you think of "Prince"?

"Listen," says Arnold anxiously. "Listen, I think I just forgot something."

"What?"

"If I knew, I wouldn't have forgotten it." Like a dart flung by some malicious godling, the thought returns to bid Arnold a final goodbye. "Lena, what's a troll?"

Lena picks up the Consumer Price Index. "How do you spell it?"

"I'm not sure. T R O L L , I think."

Lena flips through the Index. "No such thing."

"I thought so." Now why, Arnold wonders, should that make me feel so awful?

"Time for bed. Tomorrow's another day."

They stretch out on their separate pallets, each in his own hurt way searching for the lost thing with no name. They feel heavy in a way that has nothing to do with gravity. The air in the room is chill as the ALIENS depart, gustoing off on their interfering and endless search for sustenance.

"I'm a good girl," Lena sighs to the darkness.

"I should have been a bridge builder," Arnold whispers, without understanding his words.

"I could never be—*loose*," Lena says, as the ghost of a painted and perfumed woman flits across the barren screen of her brain and is gone at once and forever now that there is no vibrant energy left to fish her up in its net of neurons.

"I like bridges—liked them—but I can't remember why," Arnold sighs. "Odd."

They close their eyes.

In the morning, Lena rises like a phoenix from the cold fire of her bed. In the morning, in the same way, Arnold also rises.

In the Automated Life Complex kitchen later, Lena watches the button closely. When the toast slides out of the machine, it is mellow and warm—not burned a bit. Nothing distracts Lena this morning. Her timing of the toast is perfect.

Arnold fights his way to her past Fat, Fatter and Fattest, ignoring their howls of pain, and he tells Lena, "Got me a great idea! I'm going to design a new rotation system that will let lots more people use the same space at the same time with no decrease in efficiency or waste of time."

"Wonderful! How in the world did you ever think of that?"

"I guess I dreamed it."

Lena hands him the toast. "The baby's due to arrive at eight-eleven, like I said. Oh, did I tell you? I'm going to call it Jones. Arnold? Did you remember what you forgot yesterday?"

"No. But it doesn't matter."

"Sure?"

"Sure."

By now, you've probably noticed that these story-introduction-cum-blurbs are not necessarily about the stories they precede. Most of them hardly even mention the writers.

What these little essays are about is writing, the act of sitting down at a typewriter and creating something that did not exist before, and writers—as seen by this editor.

It's a forum for me, a soap box—and if there's one thing I've never been able to resist it's a soap box and an audience.

But more than that, I've discovered/am discovering that one simply cannot do justice to either a writer or a story in one or two paragraphs of words. It is not enough to say that Pam Sargent is a tall beautiful dark-haired girl and that "Oasis" would have been her first sale if this book had come out a year and a half sooner. That doesn't tell you anything about Pam Sargent.

What I would like to be able to do—and can't—is get inside the heads of some of these people and find why they wrote a particular story. What node of pain was being exorcised? Where did it hurt so much that this was the result? Or what private joy was being expressed for the sole purpose of sharing it?

It's frustrating.

I think Pam Sargent knows that. This story is a human one. It hurts.

And sometimes I wonder what private vision might have inspired it.

OASIS

Pamela Sargent

Simon Atenn felt the tree growing.

It was thirsty. He felt the roots strain deeply into the ground after the water and reach for it, far below. The leaves began to turn toward the desert sun hanging low on the horizon, toward the light which meant survival.

Dawn, Simon Atenn thought. *The heat will soon become unbearable to anyone unused to the climate.* He stood in the doorway of his hut, listening to the sap as it began to run in the trunk. The water table in the area was low, and it varied from day to day. But the tree always managed to reach it. Every morning the tree would come to life; the morning heat would start the sap flowing. But the day would come, Atenn knew, when the water table would drop too low, and the roots would not grow long in time. The very thought brought a twinge of pain into his head. The spring of water near the tree had been growing smaller for some time now, and lately he had taken to storing water in his hut in case of an emergency.

I won't be here when the spring goes, he thought. *I will not suffer the tree's pain.*

During the cold desert night he had slept huddled under three blankets, but now he went outside dressed in slacks and a short-sleeved shirt. He felt the heat increasing from one moment to the next. Within two hours after dawn, he knew, he would be forced to retreat into the hut to avoid the harsh sunlight.

He thought of the sea to the north of him, and he shuddered at the image of the varied creatures that swam in the waters and crawled along the bottom; he felt fear at the thought of the sensations of death and decay which would fill his mind at the shores of that sea. Once he had fled from that sea to the relative calmness of this oasis. To the south were the high mountains where an ancient band of nomads had met their awesome god; and to the west, across the Red Sea, was the land from which that people had fled, only to meet its rulers again three millenia later with the weapons that both peoples had forged to honor commitments to their desert gods.

Slowly Atenn walked over to the tree and sat down by the spring. He felt the tree ingest nourishment. He looked at the small plants around the small pool of water. They were still able to get their share, but it was becoming more difficult every day. A small but sharp wave of pain passed up his spine and into his head as he felt the struggle of a small plant near the edge of the green area. He felt its tiny roots strain in the dry sand. Quickly he got up, scooped up some water into his cupped hands and poured it over the plant until its agonies subsided.

Usually the plants did not disturb him. Their presence calmed him. He enjoyed their pleasure at the sun's appearance. The natural moisture in their small leaves generated in him a sense of peace and harmony, but this small incident was still another reminder of the approaching end for the entire oasis.

He stood up and scanned the northern horizon anxiously.

The pain washed up from the base of his spine and exploded in his brain. There was a large black shape on the horizon coming toward him. Atenn squinted and clenched his teeth. The pain in his head grew worse.

Two life forms. Two pain bringers.

It was Abdul and his camel. Atenn turned and ran into his hut, hoping that if he did not look at the other's approach it would reduce the pain.

It was dark inside the hut. There was a cot against one wall with a chair at its head. Against the opposite wall was a desk. On the floor to the right was a pile of books which Atenn kept covered with a piece of canvas. In the corner by the entrance stood a small wooden cabinet where he kept his small supply of food and water. On the desk, next to a small box of writing paper, was a small picture frame with a photograph of a young man. The young man's eyes were clear and he had an open, friendly smile. The picture itself had been cut from a newspaper. It was very yellow, betraying its considerable age.

Atenn sat down at the desk and held his head in his hands. He estimated that he had ten minutes before Abdul got to his front door. The pain in his head was now a steady throbbing. He reached inside his right desk drawer and took out the hypodermic and the small bottle of morphine. He drew the correct dosage carefully and inserted the needle clumsily into his left arm. He put the hypodermic and the small bottle away carefully. Then he opened his left desk drawer and removed the Smith and Wesson revolver and two bills from the money box next to it.

The pain seemed duller, but Abdul was very close now.

You won't kill me, he thought. *I can still control myself. And you'll never get the rest of my money.* He sensed the greed that came with Abdul. It was all in the Arab's hands, he thought. He knew how Abdul would grip a knife.

Atenn felt Abdul's sick and abused body. He felt his starved cells, enlarged liver and ailing appendix; he felt the countless bruises and lack of feeling near the scars on Abdul's back.

Atenn got up from his desk and went outside. Abdul's camel was drinking from the spring and the Arab had finished unloading the two large crates from the animal's back. He saw Atenn and grinned broadly, showing him all his missing teeth. Atenn felt the craving in Abdul's genitals and in his belly. Then he noticed the camel's pain where Abdul had beaten the animal for his own enjoyment; momentarily the beast's patience seemed an oasis in a sea of throbbing pain.

Atenn focused on Abdul's outstretched hand. He walked up to the Arab and placed the two bills in it. Abdul was still grinning at him. Then, still grinning, he picked up one of the crates and walked over to Atenn's door and set it down. Atenn picked up the other crate and followed. The physical exertion was a good distraction from his mounting pain.

Abdul returned to the spring and began filling his water sacks and canteen. Atenn busied himself with inspecting and unpacking his provisions. Somewhere he felt sure the Arab had cheated him, but he would probably not find out just how until it was too late. The morphine was doing some good at last, he noticed. Also, the camel was feeling a bit better after drinking from the spring. But Abdul's presence now made him feel the beginnings of nausea. He knew that the Arab was inwardly laughing at him and that the lust in the man's loins had grown now that he had some money.

When Abdul left, Atenn retreated into the hut and lay down on his cot. The pain in his head was decreasing. He felt relieved. Soon now it would be gone and he would be safe.

In the back of his mind, very faintly now, he felt Abdul's rising expectations. Abdul was planning to spend his money.

Atenn got up from his cot and went over to his pile of books. He lifted a corner of the canvas and removed a volume. He went back to the cot and lay down in a comfortable position on his side. There was a bit of daylight coming in through the doorway where he had pulled back the burlap curtain. He turned to his

place in *Crime and Punishment*. He had read the
book several times before, but he never tired of it.
Here the pain was all distilled and structured for a
man's contemplation of it; the words had given him
some pain the first time around, but now they were
like a cold flame, all brilliance with no capacity to
burn. He relaxed as he read.

Atenn read until noon and then decided to prepare
some lunch. He got up and went to the food cabinet.
The unexpected beginning of pain hit him as he squatted
down to reach the bottom shelf of the cabinet. It was
minor, but he hadn't expected it, and his hand shook
noisily against the wood.

He cursed, thinking that Abdul had forgotten something. Then he noticed that this living thing was alone.
Was Abdul coming back to kill him and steal his
money? Had he left the camel a ways off for safety?
Perhaps the camel was dead and Abdul would have to
stay with him. The pain in his head increased.

In a few moments he was sure it was not Abdul. The
pain was too even. It had to be a civilized man.

Atenn stepped out of the hut for a look. The noon
sun beat down on him. The heat pressed in all around
him. There was no breeze. In the distance the heat
waves distorted the long figure that approached the
oasis. It was dressed in dark clothing and stood out
against the sand and sky. The figure appeared to be
at least three times its normal size.

Atenn felt the heat that surrounded the living thing.
He felt the visitor's thirst. Atenn began to sweat, and
his muscles ached with the exertions of the man struggling to reach the oasis. His head began to throb.

Atenn stepped back into the hut and waited by the
burlap curtain.

The man who came up to the spring was big. He had
a heavy tan and thick, muscular arms. His middle was
thick, and Atenn felt the flab that had accumulated
under the wide belt of the man's brown trousers. He
felt the man's age, which showed itself in countless

minor aches and pains, and which would eventually contribute to the man's death.

Slowly the man lay down on his stomach and drank from the spring in large, greedy gulps. Atenn went out to the spring and waited for the man to notice him.

When the man had finished he raised his head and noticed Atenn's sandaled feet. He looked up, startled.

"Christ, I'm not seeing things. You are for real?" He got to his feet.

"I live here," Atenn said.

"American?" The man was still out of breath from his drinking. "Jesus, you gave me a shock standing there like a desert father." The man came up to him and extended a large hand. "My name's Jim O'Harrity."

Atenn shook hands. "I'm Simon," he said. "You'd better come in out of the sun; you look bushed."

O'Harrity followed Atenn into the hut where he fell exhausted into the chair. Atenn lay down on the cot.

"I like it here," Atenn said.

"I'm glad you are here. For my sake."

Atenn put his hand up to his head and wished O'-Harrity would just go away. "I don't care much for being near a lot of people," Atenn said. "An Arab brings me everything I need here. What are you doing here, O'Harrity?"

"I'm a geologist. We're surveying Sinai for the Egyptians."

Atenn didn't reply.

"You must have been here a while, Simon. Washington is helping the Arabs rebuild, and trying to find out if there's anything worth wasting time on in this desert. A pain in the ass. Personally, Simon, I don't give a shit for Arabs. Half of them are whores or beggars, and for two cents they'd stick a knife in your ribs. Even the Russkies don't *tell* them what to do. Sure, we gave Israel the bomb, but they would have had it themselves anyway. I'm glad I'm not stuck near the cities. They've got some dandy burn cases roaming around half dead."

"How did you get out here on foot?" Atenn asked.

"Jeep broke down. I'm no mechanic. The rest of my party is around here somewhere. I figured I'd go this way and found this place. Lucky you were here."

"There are others?" The pain in Atenn's head increased.

"Quite a few. The reclamation project is big, and it's going to get bigger. A dirty business all around. Hey, I hope you don't mind my hanging around a day or so? The others should find this place pretty soon. It's better than stumbling around out there."

"Will they come right here" The other man's bladder was full and Atenn felt the discomfort.

"Well, this place could be very handy, you've got to admit. We could use it."

Atenn massaged his temples. He felt the subtle disease in O'Harrity's lungs. He felt the congestion in the large, ruddy man's chest.

"Do you smoke, O'Harrity?"

"I don't have any on me. I've been trying to quit for about a week now. Probably smoke a carton when I get back."

"I didn't want one," Atenn said. He suppressed a desire to get up and run away from the man. He felt smothered by O'Harrity. He felt the malignancy in his lungs and the pressure in his bladder. He wished the man would go off and piss somewhere. He felt sick. But he also felt curious about some of the things that had gone on outside.

"Just what do the big boys in Moscow and Washington want to accomplish here?" Atenn asked.

"Stabilize the area. We're going to occupy what's left of Israel and check out Sinai. The Russkies will take most of Egypt. Not much else to do, is there? The little guys got out of hand. Now it's up to us."

"Israel was trapped," Atenn said. "They had some bombs, but not as many as the Arabs. We gave them more, for defense—a credible defense."

O'Harrity snickered. "You wouldn't like the place

now, Simon. A friend of mine was there with some advisers. Nearly got blown up by hand grenades. The shore patrols are going crazy trying to keep the rest of the world's Jews out—and the Arabs keep coming from all sides. They just walk in, half dead. I don't see how anyone could love the place that much."

Atenn was getting tired of the discussion. His head was now throbbing fiercely. He wanted to shoot some morphine, but he didn't want to do it in front of O'Harrity.

"Who's the guy on the desk?" O'Harrity asked as he gestured toward the old photograph.

"Charles Whitman," Atenn said.

"Charles Whitman?"

"I'm interested in human aberrations," Atenn said. "I'm curious why this man went berserk and killed fourteen people on a Texas campus. I often study his face, but it shows no clues."

"You're morbid, Simon." Atenn sensed the wariness in O'Harrity's voice. "He sure looks clean cut. I remember hearing about him on the tube when I was a kid, shooting from that creepy tower. They thought Speck killing seven nurses was the crime of the century. He was a nut, Simon. Don't worry about nuts."

"You want some food and drink, O'Harrity?"

"I'll drink to that," O'Harrity said and went over to where Atenn pointed. Atenn hated the man's desire for food. O'Harrity took a clump of dates out of the cabinet and began to gnaw at them. Atenn felt the man's pleasure, but it still sickened him. The saliva-covered food was pushed into the man's stomach. Atenn felt the alcohol-ruined liver. The throbbing in Atenn's head was worse.

No one came to find O'Harrity all afternoon. Atenn sat at his desk trying to read, and failing. His hands trembled when he turned the pages. He gripped the book with both hands. He longed for unconsciousness. Soon it would be getting dark outside. Suddenly Atenn got up. He went over to the wall and took down his warm, heavy jacket off the wall. He put it on clumsily.

O'Harrity lay on the bed, covered with one of the blankets, reading a volume of Poe's short stories. Atenn went to the door.

"I'm going for a walk," Atenn said. "You can sleep there if you want to."

"Thanks, Simon, I think I will. This book gives me the creeps."

Atenn went out to the tree and sat under it and held his head in pain. The sun had set, and the desert began to cool off. He shivered a bit under the heavy coat.

The images of the dead came into his mind again. He jumped up and threw both his hands out horizontally. He restrained his desire to scream. He ran into the desert and fell down in the sand. Overhead the stars twinkled, but they meant nothing to him. He lived only on the underside of creation.

The face of the young girl came again before him. Her golden hair fluttered in front of her face as she looked toward him with her large dark eyes, and she smiled once more at him before the bullet splattered her brains across the corridor walls and wiped out the agonies buried within her mind. He saw the dark eyes again before him, but in the older face of the naked woman who walked across the room, greeting him with a frightened smile—the bullet tore into her swollen belly, and he saw the indistinguishable faces of the others whose bodies pleaded for death. He had given it to them. And fled.

Atenn longed for death. He hated his own cowardice.

He sensed O'Harrity's body. The man was becoming unbearable. Atenn tore at his beard and struggled with the pain. He turned his head to his right and vomited into the sand. He moaned and began to crawl back to the hut.

O'Harrity was having a nightmare.

The moon came up now, and the sand turned a pale

blue in the light. Atenn lay fifty yards from his hut. He sensed the tree. It had withdrawn for the night.

O'Harrity had fallen into a deep sleep.

Atenn got up in relief and walked slowly back to the hut. He pulled back the burlap curtain and looked at O'Harrity's large form on the cot. Atenn went to his desk and pulled out some rope from the bottom drawer. Then he turned to the sleeping figure and began very cautiously to tie his visitor to the cot.

O'Harrity began to wake up. Atenn hurried. His head began to throb again in pain. Atenn tied the last knot. Then he stepped back, turned up the oil lamp on his desk, and waited for O'Harrity to waken completely.

O'Harrity opened his eyes and began to pull at his bonds. He struggled as Atenn trembled, sensing O'-Harrity's fear and confusion. The big man cursed.

"Simon! Are you crazy! Get me out of this!"

"I didn't want you to wake up, really I didn't. You're driving me insane. I can only stand so much. I must protect myself. I'm doing all this in my own self-defense," Atenn pleaded. "O'Harrity, I'm doing this for your sake, to end your misery. All of life is misery. I'll give you release."

"You're out of your mind, Simon. No wonder you have that picture of Whitman and read creepy junk."

"You are astute, O'Harrity. I am like Whitman."

Atenn sensed recognition in the other's mind. The fear that came from the big man's mind staggered him, and he sat down in the chair.

"You're Simon *Atenn,*" O'Harrity said. His voice trembled. "You made Whitman look like an altar boy."

"I shot in self-defense!" Atenn screamed at him. "I have a right to live! I've been here for years, away from everybody. I just want to survive and keep my sanity. You idiot, you can't even fix a jeep." Atenn reached into his drawer and pulled out the heavy revolver.

"I'll make it fast, O'Harrity, for both our sakes."

O'Harity struggled against his bonds. "You killed

thirty-two people in self-defense!" he screamed at the top of his lungs. "A fourteen-year-old girl and a pregnant woman. Your own daughter; your wife—you animal!"

Atenn reeled with the force of O'Harrity's anger and dropped the gun. The pain was blinding. He fell to the floor on his knees and groped for the revolver. "O'Harrity, stop it; for God's sake stop it!"

"Self-defense!" the big man roared.

"They were killing me," Atenn moaned. "Wife . . . wife, was all around me; I felt what she felt, and everyone else—all the sickness in the whole damned world! They wouldn't let me go—I had to escape and find peace. Everyone who came near me tore me up. They had to die; their bodies screamed at me every day— they wanted death. They were already dying—like you, O'Harrity. You're sick and running down. *The whole universe is running down!*" O'Harrity laughed hysterically as Atenn groped for the gun. He found it. Then he vomited onto the floor.

"Did you take the money too?" O'Harrity asked. "You pig, you were sane enough to do that. How'd you land the goddam jet plane, Atenn? How'd you manage that? Or maybe I should ask your *Arab* friends? Atenn!"

Simon Atenn held the gun with both hands as he aimed it at O'Harrity's head.

"ATENN! DON'T KILL ME! ATENN!"

The gun went off. The big man's head was thrown back; the heavy slug had ripped it off. The blood rushed out against the wall in pulsing spurts. Atenn screamed and writhed with the force of O'Harrity's death. He fell forward into his own vomit. For a full five minutes after he lost consciousness his body twisted and jerked on the sandy floor of the hut.

Simon Atenn came to about an hour before dawn. He felt the sense of expectancy in the tree and plants outside as they waited for the sun. He got up and went over to the cot and began to untie the body. Most of the blood had drained out into the sand. He struggled as he lifted the body from the cot. He grasped the body by the heels. When he was outside, he dragged it toward a small pile of rocks a hundred yards to the rear of the hut.

When he had covered the body with rocks he went back for the head. He put it in a burlap bag and took it back for burial with the body.

When he was finished he got a pail and filled it at the spring. For an hour he cleaned his hut. Then he went outside and emptied the pail and stirred the sand around with a stick.

Simon Atenn waited for the dawn. Peace. As the sun rose above the horizon he sensed the tree's awakening. He felt the gentle stirrings of the plants.

The pain in his head began to return. He looked around, but there were no approaching life forms. Puzzled, he groped around trying to locate the direction of the coming pain.

It came from inside him.

Simon Atenn sensed the small but growing malignancy in his brain. His stomach turned as he sensed the ugliness of the growth. And he knew that it had always been there, the *thing* that made him the way he was. He hated it, because it had taken his humanity and freedom from him. He tried to suppress the awareness and focused his attention on the desert. And now he sensed, very faintly, the approaching group of people. O'Harrity's geologists.

He went inside and got the revolver. He cleaned it off and refilled the empty chamber and put the gun in his belt. Then he went and got his rifle. He would get them as they drank at the oasis. They would have to do that.

"I only want peace," he said bitterly to the desert. Then he threw the revolver from him and cradled the rifle. He lay down on the floor of his hut, just behind the burlap curtain. It did not reach completely to the sand, and he would have a good view of the spring and the intruders who would be drinking there shortly. He knew that he could not long survive their collective presence—but if he could kill them all quickly . . .

He felt the misery and pain that approached with them. His eyes watered with pain. He would put them out of their misery, or he would take as many of them as he could with him before he died. He focused his sights on the tree. He felt a momentary bitterness, but it could never compare with his pain.

Atenn waited.

As mentioned elsewhere in this book, one of the games that science fiction people like to play is the continued redefining of what science fiction is.

I've offered a definition of my own—and it will be quibbled with as much as anybody else's. But my definition of science fiction is just that: my definition.

Every writer who sits down at his typewriter to write a science fiction story is redefining science fiction in his own terms—terms that he personally believes in. Science fiction to Harlan Ellison is not the same as science fiction to Robert A. Heinlein. Science fiction to Cordwainer Smith is not the same as science fiction to R. A. Lafferty. Or to Theodore Sturgeon or Robert Silverberg or Isaac Asimov. A Chip Delaney story has a particular "feel" to it. A Jack Vance story is like no one else's science fiction.

There are four hundred members of the Science Fiction Writers of America. There must be at least four hundred and three definitions of science fiction. (Some of us are equivocators.)

It's not just a writer's special style (although that has a lot to do with setting the mood); it's more than that. Each writer has his own view of the universe, his own ideas of what may or may not be possible—and every story he writes takes place in his own personal continuum.

David R. Bunch is a good example. There's a special kind of madness that infects his work. (Madness? It's the dislocated logic of the dream; the savage ruthlessness of raw humanity(?) whirling in a Carrollian—no, a Bunch-ian—universe.)

Only David R. Bunch can write a David R. Bunch story. Nobody else can even come close. (Nobody else can even imitate *him.) He has staked out a particular set of physical laws and behavioral patterns as his own territory—a territory far beyond the wilderness, far beyond even the casual frontier that most science fiction writers are content to live on—and he calls that "science fiction."*

It is a science fiction that dazzles some people, puzzles others—and angers quite a few. Because it doesn't fit their *conception of what science fiction should be.*

HOLDHOLTZER'S BOX

David R. Bunch

I went into this first, outer small room of his shop
(this was the first time I had seen him, though I had
heard of him much in recent months), and initially the
things that impressed me most about him were his so-
briety and his sadness. He had a sour-onion face that
looked like a Cal Coolidge might look who had been
crying for over a thousand years. Not, you understand, the natural-normal crying where the Niagara
tears roll down and maybe the long gulpy sobs come,
if it's that bad. Or, like a guy might cry who'd just
caught his one-and-only sugar-dolly-love sending another guy a "very sincere" valentine. But I mean very
dry. If you know what I mean. Yes, his face had that
controlled look of having shed a thousand million tears,
just yesterday and part of today, in sad thoughts and
regrets, without having allowed a single actual one to
funnel down the troughs. Thin-withery face it was, and
the eyes all smileless blue, milky blue—or not really
milky blue, unless you'll accept skimmed milk, because
this blue was thin, and cold cold. He was average height
and runty-built spare (what else?—a face with that
gone look would never go on weight), and about the
hips and legs he had that thin-shanks stance of "Careful now! My pants stay up by belt, but only with prayers
and the very last thinness hole!" But with all this runti-
ness, sadness, the blue-milk eyes and the dry crying,

137

he didn't look like a saint. Not even with his pat of thick black hair, some graying, cut saucer-round. Neither did he look unnaturally mean. His face had somehow that stability of reality, a face that had "faced up to it" and now stared forth from a thin gray wrinkled rock hewn to the specifications of a mask and put on an otherwise pretty average man. I couldn't imagine him teaching Sunday school very much. I couldn't imagine him torturing little kids very much either, if you want to know it. Not militant sorrow, not old-lady sobbing sorrow, but quiet realism in sorrow, the kind that waits it out and takes its time in years. Oh, yes.

His coat off, he was dressed in grayey-white old shirt and old blue suit pants that had a lot of grease and grime set in. He was unkempt all over, let us kindly say, with the filth of one who, though administrative, stayed almost all of his waking time in the oily vicinity of machine-shop engines, seldom had his suits cleaned and pressed, and slept in them very often. Slept in them—I learned later—on a small bed with an old throw-away government-surplus mattress on it, with a faded, red-flower coverlet over that, and all located in the one boarded-off room-space in the loft over his shop. (I saw that bed, years on, after his shop had become a national monument. It was all very neat when I saw it. The floor of the room was spanking clean then. The walls were hung with two pictures, and only two—a realistic one of two little girls, one brown-eyed, one blue-eyed; and one of the more somber Dalis. On top of a small chest of drawers was what looked to be three photos, face down on purpose, and signs all over the walls were shouting VISITORS, DO NOT TOUCH ANYTHING.)

We passed into the second room of the ground floor of his shop. I had come to interview him and to do an article about him and the strange apparatus that, it was rumored, he had been working on for more than two full years. The assignment had given me goose pimples, but, with four kids to feed, a wife to keep

down to a roar, and no other skill or job prospects at
hand, I just kept on at what I could do and tried to do
it. Caught in the web! Know what I mean? Snarled in
the cold coils. Hear what I'm admitting? Youth and
vigor gone into the gray gray battles on the enemy's
grounds, where winning is not winning; not winning, but
just staying alive and able to fix the blade for another
hapless day's battle. Know what I'm saying?——So
much for me, hopeless Joe Striver—not trying to win
the fight, knowing the odds, but just trying not to lose
too ignobly; not to the extent of complete humiliation
and annihilation in the neighborhood. And I'm representative, you'd better believe it! I'm not the black-goat
exception; I'm man-general now come down to a pretty
small, smudgy campfire with his little wrinkly sack
of stale marshmallows. And don't you ever try to think
it otherwise!

But to get back to my man in the shop, the man in
the sorrow mask too dry for weeping:—— He took
me to where the strange thing was on blocks. And to a
man used to the great going machinery of the age of
moon dust and let's-gun-on-for-Mars-now-while-we-
probe-old-Venus-a-good-one-on-the-runby, this thing
was really plenty pretty unimpressive. At first. Obviously this apparatus was not designed to go anywhere
at all. It was designed to make its contribution right
where it stood—in schoolyard, in fun yard, in church-
yard, in the basements of big department stores, in busy
recreational areas—just about anywhere that people
congregated to be snared. It was mostly a box. And I'm
sorry to let you down like this. I had expected more.
Oh, I had heard the stories for over a year now about
Holdholtzer (that was the sorrowful one's true name)
and his revolutionary apparatus that was supposed to,
somehow, revolutionize society. Or maybe even save it.

It was just a big black box on blocks! What more is
there to say? It had no wheels; it had no jet boosters; it
had no propellers; it had no sled runners or other forms
of skids either. Clearly it was meant to be crated and

shipped to its operational site. It would not go there on its own steam; that was plain even to me. But obviously Mr. Holdholtzer had some real love and affection for this contrivance, because the sorrow in his eyes would lift up a little and he would seem just a shade less sad when he looked at the black box or went near it to talk about his project. Now he went right up to it, patted it on the prow and said something to it—sort of addressed it, if you will believe that! Then, one arm draped across it, he turned to me, and the things he said and the manner of his saying them, though not revolutionary or inventive, let me know he was proud. "The Holdholtzer! as I think it must become universally known, is basically a box." (WELL—and didn't I already strongly suspect this through the eyeballs?) "But it is not a box to ship canned goods in, ha ha," (he could laugh!?) "nor is it a box for TV's. It is the quiet box for the quiet look of the quiet person making the quiet think and the quiet decision. It is as soundproof as our technology can make it and still be anywhere close to inside the ballpark, costwise, when it comes to mass production. It is lined all over its entire interior with the highest quality mirrors we can find, there's the subtlest intensity light changes built in, and it is programmed for a twenty-four-hour cruise for each and every candidate seeking Holdholtzer immortality. That's it! Once in, no out for twenty-four hours. The one and only way you could get someone, or yourself, out of the Holdholtzer ahead of time would be to wreck the box. And they'll come much too dear, pricewise, for wrecking! And twenty-four hours, I think, is not really too much time to ask of each and every candidate, for a fair test. A generous minimum of liquids, and foods in the most concentrated forms, will be provided for that period. And facilities for the normal needs of the bodily functions will also be provided. No! We are not devising any kind of an environmental posture for the unusual physical discomfort of modern man. Nor his unusual physical comfort neither."

I was busily taking notes. I was flabbergasted, of course; and I'm honest enough to admit that I was disappointed. To be truthful with you, I had expected this apparatus to fall generally into one of three broad categories: (1) a fiendish torture machine in which a fiendish distorted mind would have let go with all of its venom (and this had me drooling and dribbling, I'll admit); (2) some kind of elaborate, very sophisticated toy with which Mr. Holdholtzer intended to pile the fortune of his dreams by entertaining little kids while he robbed their papas and their mamas of the costs of it; (3) some kind of crackpot engine of death that Mr. Holdholtzer would sell to the government for a fabulous sum and thereby become not only wealthy, but famous as well, because his device would be so deadly that the Free World would be saved all at once, forevermore and immediately.

But a twenty-four hour box lined with looking glasses!? Complete with light-intensity changes, toilet utensils, and a subsistence food and drink allowance? Really, now!

"When we go into mass production, and really get rolling, we'll ship these babies to all the many places that will want them, the places where people congregate, such as, for instance, the big department stores, the schoolyards and the beaches. As I envisage it, the store or other place of business or recreation, or even worship, will pay us a very substantial sum upon first installation and then a certain basic monthly rental, plus a cut of the take. It will be our part in the agreement to keep up the facility—repair the broken mirrors, for instance, keep the food-and-water supply replenished and provide for the few other necessary items of repair and operation, such as replacement of non-functioning light-bulbs. The business place, department store or whatever—the installee, let us say—will do the day to day policing of the facility, such as removing the plastic containers for bodily wastes, and getting the dead bodies out, when and if it comes to that. And of course it will, many many times."

"DEAD BODIES?" At first I thought he was joking. He wasn't. "YOU MEAN, DEAD HUMAN-BEING BODIES!?"

"Yes." His tone was flat, no-nonsense and business all the way. "Of course there will be willing fatalities. We'll provide the means, perhaps a choice or so— a gun, strangulation devices, cracked glass to swallow, razor blades built into the walls, choices of poisons. —That's one of the big selling points of the Holdholtzer, really; the speedy possibility of death." His voice became a little wistful and, I thought, maybe even evangelistic. "They will go willingly, they who go; after a certain time in the Holdholtzer, in there with all those mirrors, the soundproofing and the lights that change intensities so subtly, so blissfully, that one wonders if he isn't really dreaming it all—well, they will, we hope, with all that, achieve a clear seeing. And through each of those who achieve the clear seeing that seems overwhelmingly final to them, the world overpopulation will then have been relieved by exactly one." His eyes gleamed a little and the mask looked a small way up from gloom. "There are so many things to recommend the Holdholtzer, it staggers the mind. Why, it could, for one thing, easily be the answer to overcrowding in the classrooms. With parent's permission, I'm sure the teachers would shove them in. For this final examination!"

I was overwhelmed and confused, and beginning to wonder if I was hearing right what this man was saying. I wanted to throw up my hands, and my breakfast, and run from this place, but I knew I must not. I must hold in there and finish the interview so I could write my copy and keep my job.

We were standing a little aside now, and watching his crew of employees as they worked on a version of the box. They seemed normal enough men, just doing a job so they could take home a pay and feed the brood. And maybe even negotiate cease-fire and bombing-halt with spouse in some demilitarized zone of connubial compromise. "Mr. Holdholtzer," I said, "as I understand it, you expect many many business places, places of recreation, schools, churches?!—in short, just about any place where many people come together—to install these black boxes. You also seem to expect them to become attractions that will entice great numbers of people to use them and you express belief that somewhere along there, during the twenty-four hour experience of solitude, many will voluntarily experience the ultimate experience of all—I mean death. I'm confused. I've a lot of questions. But mostly they can be summed up in this one word: WHY?"

He seemed not at all shaken by my statement; the sadness mask remained much as, I guess, it always would and he went ahead, in the manner of a man who, having agreed to an interview, knows he will have to waste a certain amount of time and speech on it. "First, we have a good product. There's no question about that. We have selected the best materials that money could buy, our design is sound, and we have never skimped on workmanship. Let me assure you, without seeming to brag and without any further question, that I pay union scale and my men are happy, organized union journeymen. Happy workers make better workers. And, in this case, happy workers make better black boxes. I'm going to make sure that no step is ever done with other than union labor." The onion looked more of vinegar, and there seemed to be some feeling of finality and sincerity here, though how any of it applied to my question, I did not know. I decided I would have to get specific.

Thus convinced, I said, "Mr. Holdholtzer, I know you're a busy man. I wish not to encroach too much on your time, and also I have deadlines to meet of my own." He just looked "So-what?" and sad and, I began to perceive, somehow marked for greatness. So I went ahead, trying to sound as though I were a professional, which I hoped I was, and knew how to interview, which I hoped I did. "Mr. Holdholtzer, you've explained something about the quality and the general functioning principles of your invention, and you've expressed allegiance to union labor. Now, can you tell me why the many many places of business, recreation, education, worship! etc. will want to install your black boxes?"

"Because our advance advertising and general publicity will have created a not-to-be-denied interest in them. I won't go into specifics about our advertising plans, because that's mostly top secret. But I will say we intend to use beautiful girls—Miss Americas, Miss Worlds, Miss Universes and also some of the local Betty Bumpers of the day, those multitudinous down-home aspirants who, due to circumstances—business worries, bad glands, lumpy legs or whatever—never quite made it to beauty queen status, but never left off thinking they should have. Either coming out or not coming out of the black box, we'll use them. Either way, I think you'll have to agree, it will be excellent advertising. And after we get a certain number of installations at key locations, the other places will have to fall in line, get in step and install. To keep up!"

"Install or perish, eh? Thank you, Mr. Holdholtzer!" I was furiously noting down prime quotes all the while I was thinking ahead. "Now Mr. Holdholtzer, when these are installed in the many places of business, recreation or whatever, what will induce the rank and file, the man and woman in the street, as it were, the little dime store candy clerks and the teachers of fourth grade, say, to pay good money to try to endure for twenty-four hours an experience that does not seem to offer any pleasures and, even worse, may actually be quite dangerous?"

"Again, advertising and publicity. Those are the keys. People will want to do it because it's there, readily available; the challenge factor will enter in, of course, and competition with both enemies and friends. Something new, too, you know; the novelty mystique will certainly hold for us for awhile. And it'll be an experience that they can take advantage of without spending too much cash. And yet they'll spend some money—people love to spend money—substantial money, enough to convince them that being Holdholtzerized is worth doing. Free, you know, just doesn't go these days. It's, ha ha, too cheap!

"I expect the base price for the standard, no-frills ride in the black box to be a thousand dollars, at first. What with our inflation and all, and everybody with a wad, even the kids, a thousand dollars is really just walk-around money these days, jingle-bells change! A very casual sum. And to get right down to it, a thousand dollars for the Holdholtzer ride is a buyer's steal. But after a while we may have to raise it some, or we may be forced to lower it some. We'll see. For all that we have tried to protect ourselves with patents, franchises, advance contracts and other agreements, there's bound to be other experiences, just escaping infringement, that we can't do anything about, and yet they'll be close enough to ours to offer us competition." Facing grim, unkindest reality again, his face went back to onion-sour and picklish, being very sad. "We'll see," he mumbled. "We'll fight 'em."

"Thank you again, Sir. Now, one more big question. After the people start to suicide out—and you've indicated that many of them will, some time during the twenty-four hour experience of sitting in the subtly lighted black box with hardly anything to look at but mirrors and no sound but their own sounds, well— Why gee whiz, man! Won't that ruin business?"

"On the contrary," he shot back, "it will help business." And he seemed just a little bit irritated. I guessed maybe anyone unsophisticated enough to be asking a question like that depressed him just a little beyond his normal condition of gloom. "Being Holdholtzerized," he continued, "will become a household term and a status reality. Those who live through it will, for the rest of their lives, be special people and entitled to wear the emblem. (I have a great artist now working on the design for that emblem!) People will stare at them in public places. Little kids will seek autographs. Those who go through more than once will, each subsequent time, be awarded a ribbon of a different color to go with the basic award of the emblem. I look for the Holdholtzer basic award and ribbons to become coveted marks of distinction all over the civilized world and eventually in space. YES!

"And yet, those who die will not be branded as inferior individuals, but will be honored people too; and their families may speak of them with pride in the voice and in the eyes. For these dead will not have died in vain, or for no reason; they will have achieved a clear seeing too and will have accepted it on terms just a little bit different than did those who came out to proudly wear the emblem and the ribbons. I don't know; I may set up a system of awarding posthumous honors. I've been toying with the idea. If I thought it would help business—"

"Thank you, Mr. Holdholtzer, for your patient and informative reply to my perhaps somewhat dumb and unnecessary query. Now, just one more small question, Sir, and we'll try to wrap up this interview. Do you consider civilized, modern man to be essentially gullible, willing to pay good money to risk his own destruction in a fairly meaningless experience, or set of experiences, triggered by not only the spirit of adventure but also by the hope of commemorative awards or real money gains as well, such as your medals, which I assume, in time, could give an individual pretty substantial business advantages, or real money powers, over other individuals who did not have, and could not get, the coveted awards of which you have just spoken?"

The mask almost shattered asunder as his whole face seemed to fall apart when his mouth went agape, and I was so aghast that, amidst the surprising din of his high-pitched cackling laughter, I left without even shaking hands. I was all the way back to my desk, and ready to type up a first draft of my copy before I realized that I had no answer whatsoever, none of any kind, for my last question to Mr. Holdholtzer.

Despite the title, this story has nothing to do with lysergic-acid-dyethylamide.
And that's all I'm going to say about it.

THE FIVE-DIMENSIONAL SUGAR CUBE

Roger Deeley

No one ever seemed to bother himself with the fifth dimension. Which was a pity, for it offered far more scope than the other four. Length, breadth and depth everyone knew about and understood—or liked to think they did—while the fourth dimension was generally accepted as being time, a nice vague nebulous nothingness which philosophers and scientists could play about with to their hearts' content. Richard Alderston was far more interested in the dimension that came after time, the one dimension so far untapped and unmapped, the dimension of the human mind. He discovered it on a wet Sunday afternoon. At 2:35, to be more precise. In a lump of sugar.

Richard had been convinced for a long time that the human mind had to have a dimension of its own limitless scope, not bound by any of the trammels of the other four. Its scope would be infinity. In his search he studied as much as he could of what man, in his wisdom, knew of infinity. He read all the books on the subject he could beg or borrow; he read treatises, theses, essays and papers. He read until he was sick of it. And he got nowhere fast.

The symbol for infinity, he knew well enough, resembled a figure eight lying on its side, a continuous line that never ends. This had not been enough for him, so he had taken the argument further. To keep going as it did, it necessarily had to repeat itself, like the symbol, but surely infinity could never repeat itself at regular intervals. Infinity, by definition, goes on forever, but it had to have somewhere to go on forever in. So infinity had to be contained. Therefore, the infinity within the human mind had to be contained. This was the point at which his chain of logic crumbled about his ears. He had to find the key to this container.

On this particular Sunday in question, Richard was feeling frustrated, at odds with his life and with himself. He was twenty-five, a bachelor, living alone in a flat he enjoyed calling home, with a steady and secure job which he actually liked. He had no right to be frustrated. But he was, and two things more than anything else caused this feeling. One was his ever-present problem of the search for the confines of infinity. The other was Anne.

Anne was The Girl. She was the girl he saw on the train on most working mornings, the girl whom he adored, the one girl in his life, the girl that he had never actually met. Every day on that train she looked straight through him, and he knew only too well that whenever their glances accidentally happened to meet, he in his turn deliberately looked straight through her.

Anne was a redhead. Not tall, yet slim and graceful, with the long legs of a dancer. He only knew that her name was Anne because she had once had a friend with her (female) who had referred to her by it. This friend had also asked for, and been given within range of Richard's hearing, her new address, an address which was now indelibly stamped on his memory—not to mention his diary, his address book, and numerous bits of scrap paper in case he lost the others or had a mental blackout and forgot it.

Not that any of this did him the slightest good. She was still merely The Girl Who Sat Opposite Him On The Train. Nothing more. He would never dare do anything to remedy this, as he knew only too well that his courage would fail him long before he could make even the most formal of self-introductions.

So here he was, drinking a nice English cup of tea, alone in his flat at 2:35 on a Sunday afternoon, a wet drizzling miserable Sunday afternoon in London. Oh to hell with Anne, he thought. *And* infinity. Wearily he reached for the Sunday paper to see what was on television. As he did, his glance rested idly on the bowl of sugar, and suddenly little bells started jangling at the back of his mind. The sugar. All perfect little cubes. Such a neat and tidy geometrical figure, a cube. So much more satisfying than a sphere. Nothing he reflected slowly, as the alarm bells in his brain shrilled louder and louder, nothing could get out of a sealed cube. Not even infinity. So what would happen if this cube could be reversed, turned inside-out, yet still keeping the structure intact? It was impossible, he knew, but that was a relatively minor detail.

In his mind he constructed a cube, a perfect seamless cube, perhaps as small as a grain of sand, perhaps as large as a universe. It rather depended on how close you got to it. Now it had to be reversed. Easier said than done. Mentally he studied his cube, considered it from every angle, turned it upside-down and shook it, lost his temper and kicked it. Nothing happened, except that his reflection in the polished sides shimmered into oblivion, then returned as before. And suddenly, with an instinctive feeling, he knew that this was the answer. His own reflection. Himself. He had to be there too. He dissolved the cube, then built up another around himself—a perfect cube as before, without marks or seams of any sort. Then he turned it inside-out.

He was in the Coliseum.

All around him stretched a vast unnumbered sea of faces, all staring expectantly into the arena, waiting for something to happen. It was just like one of the scenes from *Quo Vadis,* which he had been to see only the night before at the local cinema.

Hum.

A fanfare of trumpets sounded, and into the arena marched a procession of gladiators, two by two, heading toward where he was sitting. Richard looked around for the Emperor, then realized with something of a shock that he himself was seated in the heavy purple robes on the throne of the Caesars. Exactly where Peter Ustinov had been sitting the night before.

Hum again.

Upon thinking about it, the idea of being Nero appealed to Richard little, if at all. He had no spectacular desire to get over-muscled idiots bumped off for his own personal kicks. Perhaps a party of drum-majorettes would liven the place up a bit? He glanced at them as they paraded below. Nice legs. He blinked as they became encased in thigh-high rubber boots. This, he grinned to himself, would have given friend Sigmund a field day. Poppeia, sitting beside him, spoiled the effect somewhat. Now if she were a cat . . . . . . ? She turned round twice, purring contentedly, and settled off to sleep. No one in the crowd seemed to notice anything at all out of the ordinary in this maneuver, as if the Emperor were in the habit of transforming his mistresses into cats every day of the week. With an encore on Sundays. Anyway, it was *his* subconscious. No one in it had the smallest right to question him.

The gladiators had come to a halt in front of him. Hairy lot of oafs, really. The all-in wrestlers of their day, no doubt. Abdul the Terrible Turk meets the Great Ape, ten rounds, two falls, two submissions or a knock-out. Ladies are requested not to fling their arms ecstatically around the total stranger sitting beside them when one of the fighters has an arm broken, or the management disclaims any responsibility for what may happen afterwards when the total stranger in question tries to make the most of this situation that Fate has so kindly tossed in his lap.

The gladiators saluted and prepared to do battle, but Richard was growing bored already. He muttered

"Oh go chase yourselves," and gave a snort of amusement as they left the arena in a cloud of dust, playing what appeared to be a complicated form of tag. This, he reflected, might be fun.

The crowd was growing restive. The Beatles, now in the center of the arena, were doing little to satisfy them. Richard decided to cash in being Emperor and give himself as well as the crowd a cheap thrill while he was at it. He looked around for a telephone and found a coinbox conveniently situated behind the throne. Feeling in his pocket (it was the first time he ever realized that togas had pockets), he drew out four brand-new shining A.D. 64 Nero-headed pennies, and rang the games master on the extension line to the dressing rooms.

"I want fifty virgins," he declared.

"Fifty?" came a surprised but amused chuckle from the other end. "Your Imperial Majesty must indeed be a strong man."

"No no no," Richard corrected him, "I want them in the arena."

Long silence. "Well," said the voice slowly, "I suppose we all have our little peculiarities."

"I mean that I want them to put on an act for the crowd," snapped Richard.

"Yes, that's what I thought you meant." The line went dead.

A klaxon boomed like a weak stomach the morning after, and the doors at the other end of the Coliseum opened. Marching down the center of the arena, erect and beautiful, two by two, came fifty redheaded Annes. Richard stared in dismay. His subconscious feelings had obviously taken over momentarily. He concentrated hard, and each woman became a separate and highly attractive entity. Blonde, brunette (no redheads; it just wasn't safe), short and tall, plump and slim, Anglo-Saxon, Scandinavian, Latin, Indian, Oriental, Polynesian—all the most beautiful faces and figures his mind could devise, with a liberal helping of film starlets to season the mixture. This was better, he decided, and looked to his centurion for approval.

"Your Imperial Majesty is a wise man," he oiled.

Richard smiled complacently. Well, he was. He looked back. Fifty Annes were getting closer. This was too much! Surely his subconscious was not dominated by that woman? In exasperation he threw all his will power into the arena, but his imaginative faculties seemed to have dried up, for the best he could manage was a half-hundred composed of well-known film stars, among whom Sophia Loren and Brigitte Bardot featured prominently at least half a dozen times each. He closed his eyes with an instinctive sigh of relief, then snapped them open again as a nasty suspicion seized him. Fifty Annes smiled. He gazed in horror as the crowd slowly became a mass of red heads, all only too familiar. Even his centurion now had burnished gold peeping from beneath his helmet. Or was it *her* helmet? In desperation Richard closed his eyes and thought himself awake.

It was only 2:50. His mental trip had taken up much less time than he would have thought. Absently he poured himself a cup of tepid tea and considered the matter. Anne's continual appearance could mean only one thing, and it didn't have to be spelled out for him in neon letters two feet high. It was a pity that the Anne in his mind was merely his own creation, his own image, and meant nothing. The real Anne was not there. He could have put Raquel Welch in the same place had he so wished, but he knew well enough that in real life Raquel Welch neither knew nor cared whether he lived or died. (That was a pity, too.) It was useless taking trips into his own mind if his subconscious kept springing these dirty tricks on him in his unguarded moments, thereby making him even more frustrated than ever.

The solution came to him. The only thing to be done was to go into *her* mind and meet her there. But when? She'd have to be asleep. If he waited till the wee hours of the morning it ought to be safe. But first, in case he got into any tight spot, it might be very useful to have a word which would automatically wake him instantly from whatever situation he got himself into, a word which need only be pronounced to bring him out of his subconscious state without requiring any further mental effort on his part. What was the word to be? Eventually he plumped for "peanuts," a suitably anticlimactic and unheroic word, hardly the sort of thing he could imagine slipping out naturally in the course of a romantic interlude with Anne. He grinned. Peanuts. One of these days his stupid sense of humor would get the better of him.

At half past one the next morning he was lying on his bed, gradually relaxing his mind and body. Only thus would he be able to give his total concentration to the matter at hand. In his brain he formed as exact a mental picture of Anne as he could. It was close enough, anyway. He wasn't very likely to get anyone else by mistake. Then he positioned himself next to her and carefully built up a cube around them. The Anne next to him at present, as he well knew, was still his own mental conception, whereas in a moment. . . .

He reversed the cube.

He found himself on a palm-fringed beach, where the ocean, only fractionally bluer than the sky, was washing the white sand with the contented lapping of a purring cat finishing off its second saucer of milk. Anne, in the most stunning bikini, lay stretched out under the sun not five yards from him, her eyes closed behind enormous sunglasses. He went a little weak at the knees as he realized that this was the real Anne, not just his own imaginative version of her. Why her mind created such a beach for her he had no idea. Perhaps nostalgic memories, or subconscious longings.

He sat down next to her.

"Hi."

She opened her eyes, lowered her glasses to the end of her nose, leaned up on one elbow, and regarded him fixedly from under those delicious dark lashes. "Why," she said, "are you wearing a dark suit?"

Richard started. It hadn't occurred to him. Damn silly, really, considering that the temperature must be well into the eighties. The suit dissolved into swimming trunks.

"Better?"

"Much," she said. "That's a good trick."

"Of course. It's too easy. I suppose you know," he remarked casually, "that this is all a dream?"

The corners of her mouth turned up irresistibly. "I do believe it is," she grinned, "but it's not very often that someone in my dreams comes along and points it out."

"I'm not in your dream," he said.

"No?" she murmured mockingly. "It looks uncommonly like it to me."

"I'm not in your dream," he repeated, "I'm in my own, and I've put myself in yours."

She smiled tolerantly, as if humoring an idiot child. "Don't be silly."

"I'm far from being silly," he continued easily, though lots of little men with hammers were pounding out an insistent jungle rhythm at his heart. "I've put myself in your dream."

She looked at him. "Oh well, never mind anyway," she replied. "I'll forget it all in the morning. I always do."

"Oh but you won't. My putting myself in your dream as I did will make you as aware of your dream surroundings as I am. When you wake up, you'll remember all this just as clearly as you remember anything you might do during the day."

She was looking at him more intently. "You're the man from the train in the mornings," she said.

"I am. And you're the girl with red hair who always ignores me."

"You always ignore *me,"* she retorted, adding almost casually, "which *is* rather a pity."

The men with the hammers were getting their second wind. "Meaning?"

"Meaning I wish you didn't ignore me quite so much," she said with an arch smile. Then she sat up and kissed him so ardently and unexpectedly that he was more than a little taken aback. She grinned impishly. "I think it's a good job this is only a dream."

"But it's not really, I suppose," he answered. "It's not just any old bit of unconscious escapism. We're consciously doing all this. I've arranged it that way."

She extended a bronzed and shapely leg. "Go on," she smiled, "pull the other one."

He raised an eyebrow fractionally. "Just let me get my hands on that particular article," he remarked, "and I'll do a damn sight more than just pull it."

"I do not wish," she grinned, "to have sex maniacs in my dreams."

"I am not in your dream."

"Pooh," she murmured.

"Honestly."

"Prove it."

"Right. You can do whatever you like with the bits that are part of your own dream. Okay?"

"Agreed."

"Well then, make the sun go in."

It started to snow. Pack ice ground on to the beach. On the horizon icebergs could be seen somersaulting lazily as they corrected their balance. In the distance a wolf howled under an unresponsive leaden sky.

"There was no great need," Richard snapped, "to overdo it." Hurriedly he changed his swimming trunks into a parka, while she peeped demurely from a vast mink. She raised one eyebrow expressively.

"That," he said, "was part of your own personal dream. Now, if I'm part of it, do something with me."

His parka vanished. Reflecting that he'd been taken off guard, he replaced it. She destroyed it immediately.

Realizing that this could go on forever, he swept away her mink, but to his intense regret he found that she was now fully clothed beneath it. She glared at him but had the presence of mind to bring the sun out again.

"Try making me vanish then," he declared. "You couldn't do that."

Her eyes narrowed. "What if I don't choose to?"

"Now there's an excuse if ever I heard one."

"Rats."

He chuckled. "Temper, temper."

"Oh . . . . . peanuts!" she declared scornfully, then stared in surprised satisfaction as he evaporated in a sudden bellow of rage.

"Damn!" he thought.

She had to say that, of course. If he'd thought of Russian hydro-electric schemes instead of peanuts, she'd probably have shouted "Oh Russian hydro-electric schemes!" instead. Feverishly he reconstructed and reversed the cube.

No Anne. But this was impossible. She had to be in her own subconscious.

Blast! He'd forgotten to construct the cube around Anne as well as himself, so here he was back in his own mind, and the beach was, so to speak, still on it. In his rage he snapped out "peanuts," not to mention one or two other choice epithets far more satisfying and infinitely more expressive.

Then he put Anne and himself inside yet another cube and started again.

"Couldn't make you vanish, eh?" she mocked.

"It was a lucky fluke," he grunted sulkily. "Anyway, I brought myself back."

"Clever boy." She smiled a warm slow smile. "I don't know whether what you were saying about this being an unusual dream is true or not, but if you're telling the truth . . ."

"Which I am."

"If you're telling the truth," she continued, "then it's a pity."

"A pity? Why?"

"Because I rather like you."

"We try to oblige." He considered it. "What's a pity about that?"

"If this was only a normal everyday unimportant little dream, then I think I'd really let myself go."

"Meaning . . . .?" He ended with an almost verbal row of dots.

"Meaning just that."

"You'd like to?" Oh boy.

"Of course," she smiled. "After all, I am a woman." Her smile swept away. "But only in a dream."

"You're only a woman in a dream?"

"I mean I'd only let myself go in a dream."

"Not if you were awake?"

She looked vaguely shocked, but vaguely enough for him to have hopes. "Oh no. I mean, I'd like to. But I couldn't."

He tried to force a scornful sneer but couldn't quite make it under the circumstances, for the superb picture that Anne presented made him want to fall down on his knees and praise God for having removed a rather useless extra rib and replaced it with such an exquisite piece of interior decoration. "Why not?" he said. "Because you don't think it's right?"

"That's probably the reason, yes. At least, I think it is."

"Then assuming that I went mad and agreed with you that it's not right, which I don't, why should it be right because it's a dream?"

"Because then it's not really happening." She stopped and frowned. "And is it now? You've said it is, haven't you?"

"Well, in a way it still isn't, of course," he countered,

wishing he'd never opened his big mouth. "I mean, we aren't awake, after all."

"But it's the same as if we were?"

"Unfortunately, yes."

"Pity." Very quietly.

She moved up to him. Her arms slid around his neck, and her lips went to his. Before the kiss carried him away, he was able to reflect joyfully that this was of her own doing, not an exaggerated cameo of his own imagining. Her dress vanished into air, and a monumental four-poster of carved black oak appeared in the bedroom in which they were suddenly standing. She snatched herself away.

"Wait just one minute," she said.

"Don't you want to?"

For a moment she looked dreamily at the bed, then at him, and smiled a crooked wistful smile. Then her face went firm again. So did her dress.

"If it's really like you said it is," she murmured, as the bed silently oozed through the wall, "we are not having that."

The bed came back.

"And if it's going to be a battle of wills," she declared slowly, "then I'd win, you know. It is my dream, after all."

"Possibly. But I'm in it, wherever you go."

"We'll soon see about that," she declared grimly.

They were in the desert. He sat serenely on his camel, his white burnous fluttering gently in the hot breeze, and grinned at her as she stood there in just her underwear and a black frown. Out of sheer sympathy he handed her a parasol, but she angrily hurled it from her. It exploded harmlessly two dunes away. Then they were in Paris, and Richard threw himself out of the way of a taxi as it cornered a bit too fast for his liking. Before he had a moment to consider whether he would really have been hurt had it hit him, he found himself halfway up a tree in the middle of impenetrable jungle, staring from unpleasantly close quarters into the eyes of a leopard. A large leopard. A very large leopard.

"That," he roared," is sneaky!" He knew he wouldn't be able to remove the leopard because it was her thought in the first place, and she was concentrating on it hard, so he gave himself a hand grenade and spread the cat over most of the tree trunk.

"Do anything like that again," he remarked angrily, "and I'll set something on you."

"You wouldn't dare!"

Not wishing to frighten her unduly, he released a mouse along the branch on which she was sitting. She promptly turned herself into an elephant to stamp on it, but squealed in dismay as the branch snapped under her new and unusually impressive weight. By the time she reached the ground, however, it was ground no longer, but a vast lake in which, a girl again, she furiously trod water, sending looks in his direction that should have reduced him to a heap of fine white powder.

"Is that a shark behind you?" he shouted. It wasn't, but the beach came back in a flash.

"Get out of my mind!" she stormed.

"But Anne . . . . ."

"Don't you 'But Anne' me! Who the hell are you, anyhow?"

"My name," he declared, fitting himself up in Cavalier clothes and sweeping off his plumed hat in a graceful bow, "is Richard Alderston, spinster of this parish."

She giggled, then tried to be serious. Her subconscious instantly dressed her in a very somber Elizabethan costume, with a haughty attendant to go with it. After a moment of consideration, Richard equipped him with blue polka-dot pantaloons and a top hat. Then he brought the bed back.

This time she showed a rather fiendish cunning. She turned the bed into a hammock, encased herself in full plate-armor, and declared defiantly, "Now try it!"

He roared with laughter. "Anne," he declared, "you're wonderful."

"God, this stuff's heavy," she groaned. It turned to gossamer.

"That," he murmured admiringly, "leaves little if anything to the imagination."

She reluctantly smiled. "I thought this was all a world of the imagination anyway?"

Their eyes met. He moved up to her and took her in his arms, while the bed quietly materialized in the background without any conscious effort on his part. Anne noticed it but ignored it, and his heart leaped.

"Do dreams always make you feel as deliciously un-respectable as I feel now?" she whispered.

"No," he said quietly, "They just show you your feelings as they really are, and not as we cover them up and disguise them during the day. We're our real selves in our dreams far more than we are when we're awake."

"Perhaps I never really knew myself then," she sighed, nibbling his ear.

"I must introduce you sometime."

"Don't you think now is as good a time as any?"

"I think so, yes."

"Oh Richard."

"What?"

"Am I going to regret this?"

"Who knows?"

"Oh Richard."

"What?"

"That was lovely."

"What was?"

"That."

"Oh. That."

"Darling," she moaned almost inaudibly.

Her mouth searched for his.

"Oh, Richard!"

He was awoken by his alarm clock at 7:25 the next morning. The night was over all too soon. As they lay side by side in the velvety blackness of their own creation, he had been talking to Anne—apart from the obvious—about his discoveries regarding the fifth dimension and how he had discovered it in his cube. She had expressed her gratification at his skill and ingenuity, and had proceeded to demonstrate it in more tangible form. As a result, conversation had lapsed. Sometime later on in the night, his dream sleep had become his real sleep.

He dressed feverishly, cut himself shaving three times, spilled his coffee, forgot how to tie his tie, put odd socks on, sprinted madly for the train, and got there twenty minutes early. When it finally pulled in he leaped aboard enthusiastically, and spent the whole journey roaming up and down the corridor like a caged puma. Her face was not to be seen. Nor was the rest of her. He spent all day in an agony of suspense, and finally, early in the evening, he called a taxi and sped to her address. He rang the bell of her flat, knocked the door, hit it, kicked it, swore at it, apologized to the people next door for the noise, and stumped back to his taxi. As it drew to a halt in front of his own home, he saw Anne just getting back into a cab herself. He hurried over. She looked at him, grinned weakly, and coughed.

"Er, Mr. Alderston?" she asked falteringly.

"No," he said. "Khan. Genghis Khan."

"So it was real then?"

"It was real. Come in."

They paid off their taxis, and she came in.

"I thought it had to be real when the address you gave me turned out to be the right one," she said. "I couldn't very well have dreamed that up, could I?"

"Hardly." She didn't look particularly pleased about life in general, and his heart sank like an express lift.

"And you did intrude into my dreams last night?"

"I did." His heart grovelled in self-abasement on the floor.

Suddenly she smiled. "Oh Richard." His heart leaped

to its feet, shook itself like a dog, and began the long trek up his leg.

"And did I really sleep with you, even if I was asleep when I did . . . . so to speak?" She paused, confused, her face glowing like a sunset over the Sahara.

He nodded. "So to speak. And there was more so-to-speak than sleep."

"You were right, you know," she said slowly. "When I woke up it wasn't like an ordinary dream. I remembered everything. I was so surprised that I wasn't really with it this morning, and I missed the train." She smiled mistily at him, then giggled. "What a way to be introduced. In a dream. In bed. Do you realize this is the first time I've ever actually spoken to you, yet just think what we were doing last night."

Richard thought. His knees immediately dissolved into jelly, and he sat down. Slowly and deftly he began to form a cube around them, but she moved away.

"No, Richard," she said. "Not that."

His hopes collapsed once more. "But why not?"

"Because I haven't told you it all yet."

"No?"

"No."

"Oh."

"You know I asked you if I was going to regret it?" Doom. He nodded. But suddenly her eyes sparkled.

"But I didn't. I loved every minute of it. And I'm glad of it."

"Then why won't you let me build the cube again?"

"Because I'm not going to have any more of this subconscious lovemaking."

"But why not? I don't understand. You said you enjoyed it."

"Enjoyed it?" She shivered deliciously. "It was gorgeous. It made me realize what I've been missing all this time."

"Then why won't you . . . . .?"

"Oh Richard," she sighed in happy exasperation. "Can't you realize? I've never liked my thrills second-hand. This time it's going to be for real." She sighed momentarily. "But I shall miss that lovely four-poster."

A writer is someone who writes, right?

Question: What does a writer write about?

Well . . . how does "shoes and ships and sealing wax and cabbages and kings" sound as a start?

(You have to start somewhere.)

A writer writes about many things, primarily rights and wrongs; but the greatest compliment you can pay to a writer is to say that he has great insight.

Insight—in a writer, that means he can perceive a relationship of one thing to another and portray it for the reader in a manner that forces him to perceive it too.

If it is a very complex relationship, it takes a novel to show it in all its varied aspects. If it is a very simple relationship, a short story will do.

This is a short story about pollution, and its relationship to—

—another kind of pollution.

Ugh.

167

AND WATCH THE SMOG ROLL IN . . .

Berry Weissman

When Jerry was a little boy he would often sit on the air-conditioned porch of his father's house and watch the smog-banks roll in, like mushy brown cotton-candy, to enshroud the hills. That was in old Losangeles, where the thick yellow haze blended indistinguishably into the muddy pollution of the Catalina Channel, and thoughtful people wore oxygen masks to protect them from both hazards. And that was before Jerry went to jail.

The problem was Jerry's grandfather. He would not have been a problem for his Neanderthal ancestors; they simply would have had more for the collective stew pot. He would not have been a problem in Caesar's Rome; someone would have come along and dug a hole in the ground to gain Jupiter's favor. But civilization often creates as many problems as it solves.

Jerry's grandfather was dead, and that was a problem indeed.

It wasn't his fault.

The old man had gone out the afternoon before, as he always had for as many years as Jerry could remember, for his evening constitutional. He had worn his oxygen mask, and his wooly red sweater against the chill, just as he had every other day. Grandfather had smiled and winked at the little boy, just as he always did, and then marched briskly off into the ruddy sunset.

Jerry's grandfather did not return on time that day. He was late.

He was late for dinner.

He was late for Jerry's bedtime story.

Jerry's parents began to worry. They paid the usual protection fee, of course, but there was the rising carbon-monoxide count . . .

Jerry's father 'vised the police.

"Yes," the desk sergeant said in a crisply efficient voice. "You say that your father, a Senior Citizen Classification 107-G, living at the same residence with you, is missing, Mr. . . . ah . . ." He consulted the control board below his own pickup, "Mr. Greene?"

"Yes, Officer. He often takes afternoon walks—despite my warnings, you know how old folks are—but he's usually home before seven o'clock. Frankly, I'm worried about him. It's nearly ten."

"I am quite aware of the time," the policeman said, squinting for any signs of revolt. Seeing nothing but ordinary fear, he continued. He glanced once again at the panel just below the visi-screen border. "You've paid your local fees, and all your utilities are up to date. Humm-m-m." He cocked an eye. "Have you bought a policeman's stroll-ticket?"

"Oh, yes, yes, surely. I gave him one for his last birthday. Just to be sure, you know. He always carries it with him, I'm positive of that."

The policeman shook his head. "That eliminates organized violence, unless a new gang's trying to move into the area, and they probably wouldn't do that without informing us first." Then: "Let's fill out this form and then I'll send out a couple of men in a ground car to look for him. Probably he's just lost his way." The sergeant pulled out a clipboard and official document #6135480-SC: blank searchform. He laid them flat on the desk in front of him, smoothed them out lovingly, and carefully prepared to write. "Now," he said, "what is the missing party's full and complete name?"

"Charles Haskens Greene."

"Designation?"

"Senior Citizen Class 107-G."

"Age?"

"Seventy-six."

"That's pretty old," the sergeant said. "You sure that's not eighty?"

"Oh, no, Officer. I . . . We wouldn't try to cheat the Quota. Why a person could get . . ."

"All right, Mr. Greene, all right. I believe you. This is just the short form anyway—we'll send the long one out to you in the mail, and any discrepancies will show up in that."

They got through all of the standard questions in a few minutes with a minimum of trouble and misunderstanding. The secondary questions, however, took more time, even when Mr. Greene had his father's vital-statistics folder right in front of him.

"Library card number?"

"Mother's maiden name?"

"High school number and dates of graduations with degrees issued?"

"Original gene requirements and qualifications, and parent's birth allowance number?"

"Doctors? Dates of operations and replacements, with donors' (if any) last address?"

"I don't know. I don't know. I DON'T KNOW!"

"Control yourself, Mr. Greene," the policeman said, the look of the grim reaper in his eyes. "If you can't answer a few simple questions calmly, I wonder how you will do when put to the Choice on the Census next year."

"I . . . I'm sorry, I'll try to maintain, but . . . but I don't know all those things. They weren't so organized back when father was born, and he has . . . has lost papers through the years and never bothered to replace them."

"Lost papers! And never replaced! Look, Mr. Greene,

we can't send out a car unless the form is completely filled out. I can't ask for authorizations for patrol expenditures and for adding to the smog level without a complete—a *complete* form. And you wouldn't expect me to send two men out on bicycles in this weather, not with the gang situation the way it is."

Mr. Greene remembered the pictures of the three cops who had been killed over on Wilshire the day before, in broad daylight, their throats neatly slit by the vibroblades of a wandering gang. They had been on bicycles. Of course, the police had completely wiped out the gang later when they caught up with them (some thirty kids), and the parents for good measure. Now it seemed like he was asking the sergeant to send out some men at night to risk the same fate. The uniformed man had an angry look on his face.

"Oh, no, Sergeant," Mr. Greene answered the other's implied accusation. "Nothing like that. It's just that my father is—"

"The police cannot be held responsible for private citizens who do not keep careful records," the officer recited. "The best I can do is look for him in the morning, when it's light."

"Yes, Officer. Thank you very much."

"I'm sorry, Mr. Greene."

Jerry's father consumed a whole box of Nowor pills (guaranteed safe, harmless, and non-habit-forming, and made with nature's best ingredients) that night, but they didn't help him answer the questions. They didn't even seem to help much with his nervous tension, as they always helped the little man on the Stereo. And, needless to say, the police never left their well-fortified station.

They found the old man in the morning, sprawled in a scrawny heap, all skin, bones, and clothes. He'd always seemed thin in life to Jerry, but pathetically so in death. He was half a block from home.

"I'm sorry, Mr. Greene," the sergeant said when he

called to make out his final report, "but the CO count just went too high. Now if we had just been able to complete that form . . ."

Jerry's father took a handful of Nowor and answered the officer's questions as best he could. Before leaving, the officer told him that they believed someone, a person younger and stronger, had stolen the oxygen mask right off the old fellow's face and left him there, alone and coughing, in the black poisonous mist. All the boys in the stationhouse were very sorry.

Jerry stood by and watched quietly while they carried the stiff body into the house and laid it down on the old man's bed. Then he heard his father call the undertakers.

Late in the afternoon the man from the mortuary showed up, black plastic briefcase in hand. He was tall and dark and very efficient. He came right in, strode smoothly to the kitchen table, flipped his briefcase onto it, and in one quick motion flicked it open. He was plainly in command of the situation.

"My name is Devers," he announced.

"Now, Mr. Greene," he told Jerry's father, "we understand that you wish us to handle your father's funeral arrangements. May I compliment you on a wise choice. We offer a complete line of funerals and coffin types, and we tailor each occasion individually to the bereaved family and their emotional, spiritual, ethnic, and financial needs. If you wish an exotic event, we have Oriental funerals, with wailing old women; Egyption Pharoah funerals, with white-clad maidens beating their naked breasts in time to the funeral music played on an authentic second-dynasty recorder; Gypsy funerals; even military funerals with a gun-caisson from the Civil War; or a Viking funeral with a cedar longboat, so that the departed one can go out in a blaze of Glory. All you have to do is look through this catalogue—" he handed Mr. Greene a thick folder — "and select the funeral that you believe the late gentleman would have preferred."

Jerry's father took the folder and examined it questioningly. Then he looked up. "What about the personal tailoring?"

"Oh, that comes in after you choose the funeral type. We examine your bank account, credit ratings, job futures and earning power, latest tax forms, and then decide if you can afford to keep up with the easy payments. Then we inform you of our decision. That," Mr. Devers said with pride, "is our Personal Tailoring Plan."

Jerry's father mutely nodded his head. Then: "What about this one?" he asked, pointing to a moderately priced program.

"That's our family special and usually goes for around $5000, depending on the payments and, of course, the recommendations of our Personal Tailoring Department. A very wise decision, I might add. I'll check your plan with the office now, to be sure." Devers removed a small radio from his case and spoke into it for a few minutes. Then he listened to its hushed speaker for another minute or so. "Everything's all set," he said. "A hearse, radio-dispatched, is on the way from our central offices, and the cemetery has been notified to expect us. Now all we have to do is fill out this little form here." Once again he dipped into his briefcase and brought forth a form that looked amazing like that of the police. "Incidentally," he said, "the cemetery is Meadowland—very exclusive, conveniently near shopping centers, and with a large multidenominational church just a block away."

Mr. Greene had finished his last box of Nowor during the interview, so he sent Jerry down to the local drug store for another. He knew that it was going to be a bad day. Then he collapsed into a chair opposite Mr. Devers.

When Jerry got back they were just finishing, and his father was showing signs of needing the pills very badly. He quickly tossed a handful down his throat.

"Now, Mr. Greene," Mr. Devers was saying, "if we

can't find your father's library card number, preference in food, type of lawning preferred (Australian-hooked or Kentucky-blue), his parents' birth allowance certificate number and their marriage papers, then I'm afraid that he can't be interred at Meadowland. It's not the facts themselves that are important so much as the fact that they are missing. We won't be able to handle the arrangements either, I'm afraid, if we can't fill in those little blanks. And," he added ominously, "I'm sure all the other funeral homes will feel the same way."

"But I don't want you to feed him, or send him books, or even give him a special type of grass. When you're dead, you're dead. All I want you to do is bury him!"

"But I've just explained that, Mr. Greene. Our modern civilization depends on proper records, and we must be able to fill out all the forms completely. The law requires it." And the way he said it left no doubt in Jerry's father's mind that the law could be very strict about its requirements.

"But—I—just—can't—get—the—information! It doesn't exist! What . . . what can I do?" Jerry's father was fighting valiantly for self-control, and the Nowor wasn't helping much; his voice was scratchy, and he was beginning to shake.

"That's your problem, Mr. Greene," Devers said sympathetically. "I'm sorry, but unless you can find the necessary information, my hands are tied." He closed his briefcase.

"But . . . but . . ." Mr. Green started.

"I'm so sorry," Mr. Devers repeated.

Late that afternoon, Jerry snuck into his grandfather's room. The dying sun and smog outside the dirty window tinted the room a rich golden-red and made the air smell dusty and slightly burnt. The boy walked silently up to the old man's bed and peered into the half open eyes. He had hoped to see that the magic time, as Jerry thought of the yellow sunset hour, had once again lit the ancient hearth fires within the aged skull, as it had done for so many afternoons of the man's life with his grandchild. And somehow it *was* there; but deep, very deep—too deep to do the body that was stiff with death any good.

Jerry finally allowed himself to cry for the first time since his grandfather's death. The tears came only for a moment though, just enough to say "I miss you," and then stopped. Then the boy snuck out and carefully closed the door behind him.

Two more mortuary men, grim vultures of an uncaring world, came and went in as many days, both with the same, "I'm terribly sorry, Mr. Greene. If we could only complete all the items on this form . . ." Jerry's father kept calling funeral homes despite his failures; he couldn't think of anything else to do. He seemed to eat less and less, and subsisted solely on Nowor capsules.

Each day, just as the sun went down, the little boy returned to the shrine of his grandfather's room to peer again into the eyes under the half-closed lids. Each time, he hoped to see that life had somehow been mysteriously rekindled in the old man's husk, and if it had, Jerry would not have questioned such a miracle; he would have joyously accepted it without thought of how it had come about.

But each day, that imagined flame within the glazed eyes grew dimmer and dimmer. On the third day it wasn't there at all. And the body was beginning to smell.

Once it had been a good smell, that smell of grandfather. It had been his shaving lotion, and his cigars, the fresh roasted chestnuts which he had so loved, and his Sunday apple cider. It had been the scent of his sweat, also.

But by the third day it wasn't good at all.

The fifth day after his grandfather had died was a

Saturday, and Jerry was home from school. He found himself awake in the early hours of the morning, thinking about the events of the past days and the decaying corpse in the other room. He came to a decision.

Quickly and quietly, Jerry got up and dressed himself. He looked up some information in the encyclopedia and made some notes on the back of one of the half-filled out forms left by the mortuary men. The encyclopedia was a gift from his grandfather, and its diction was precise and clear as it told the nine-year-old what he wanted to know. Then Jerry went out to the garage for a meter stick and shovel.

Jerry found a spot in the backyard that he thought would do. It was under his mother's favorite mesquite bush, which was just starting to flower. With the stick he drew a rectangle in the dry dirt, six feet by three, and started digging.

He dug all that day, and Sunday too, while his father argued unsuccessfully with police and morticians and took more and more Nowor, which was now being delivered daily to the house, in cartons, from the local pharmaceutical company.

On Monday morning a little man from the Department of Public Health came to see Jerry's father. The man from the most recently called funeral home was just closing up his briefcase, his "I'm so sorry" trapped just in the limbo between present and past.

"But don't you have any forms to fill out?" Jerry's father asked after the little man had spoken his piece.

"Of course I do, Mr. Greene," he said, slightly shocked. "Here they are, all properly filled out, too." He handed the papers to Mr. Greene. "You have refuse on the premises constituting a public health hazard, and it must be disposed of immediately."

"But this is not refuse, this is my father!"

"He's dead, isn't he? And he's starting to decay too, no doubt." Jerry's father turned slightly green, but the Public Health man didn't notice. "Do you know what diseases can start from a decaying corpse? Everything! TB, cancer, typhoid fever, chicken pox . . . Why, just about everything! It's a natural incubation factory for all of the worst diseases. No, no, Mr. Greene, in the eyes of the law this is just like any other piece of old and spoiling meat; it must be disposed of immediately in the interest of public safety, emotional concern or no."

"But what can I *do* with him?"

"Have him buried! Isn't that obvious?"

"I can't! They won't let me! No mortuary will take him! I can't fill out the proper forms, and . . . and . . ."

"I'm terribly sorry, Mr. Greene, but—"

"Say," broke in the man from the mortuary, who hadn't left yet. "Couldn't we take him down to the public dump? That might solve all our problems."

"No, no," replied the man from Public Health in a serious tone. "I don't think they'd take him either, As you know, they don't handle organic matter—just tin cans, old ground-cars, and so forth. Maybe sewage? No, there he'd have to be fecal in origin, and I don't think we could prove it."

The Public Health Officer scratched his balding head. "I'm glad it's your problem and not mine. Frankly, I don't know *what* you can do with him. "But," he added, growing very serious and speaking directly to Jerry's father, "I do know what you *can't* do: that's keep him here any longer. If that refuse is still on the premises by this coming Wednesday, I'll be forced to . . . to . . . I don't know exactly what yet, but you can bet that you won't like it! Good-day, Mr. Greene."

The man from the mortuary brushed out after him, and their two heads could be seen bobbing in conversation down the smoggy street, like two balloons in the haze.

Mr. Greene closed the door on the image and went to his room. "I'm so, so, so sorry, Mr. Greene."

Tuesday Jerry stayed home from school and dug in the back yard. He didn't tell his parents, but they didn't seem to notice or mind. He finished in the afternoon and went back into the house. There he washed and put on his best clothes and went softly to the door of his grandfather's room.

He passed his father and mother in the living room. Mr. Greene was staring blankly at the ceiling and his wife was crying at his side. There was an empty Nowor case on the floor. Then Jerry was at his grandfather's door. He opened it.

The smell was overpowering, but Jerry went ahead, shielding his nose with his handkerchief. He donned his oxygen mask, then pulled the withered body off the bed and dragged it carefully outside.

He dragged the body to the waiting grave. He paused thoughtfully, then lowered himself in first. It wasn't a full six feet deep—Jerry was too small to get it deeper than four—but it was the thought that counted. From inside the hole Jerry was able to get the proper leverage to lift the body from the edge and lower it to the bottom. Then, kneeling, he positioned the old corpse as the encyclopedia had shown: hands clasped over chest. But he didn't close the eyes. It wouldn't be grandfather with the eyes closed.

Jerry scrambled out, brushed off his clothing and bowed his head for a moment in silence. Finally he started shoveling the dirt back over the shrunken body.

He was just finishing when the bloody sun dipped below the far smog-shrouded hills.

"Goodbye, Grandfather," Jerry said, and felt a lone tear trickle down his cheek. Then he carefully put away the shovel and meter stick and went inside.

The Public Health man came on Wednesday as expected.

"Well, Mr. Greene, I'm here to see that you've gotten rid of that waste material. If not, I have here a warrant from the Court for you to present yourself for sentencing March third, Monday next, on the charge of Spreading Infectious Diseases." The little man had two ex-football tackles with him and a can of spray disinfectant.

Mr. Greene showed him silently to the room—it would have done no good to resist. The men entered and the *psst pssst* of the spray can could be heard for a few minutes. Then they came back out.

"Mr. Greene," said the man from Public Health, "you don't know how happy I am that you took care of this all by yourself. I might have had to take him, and I still don't know what I would have done with him. No, no, don't tell me what you did. I'd rather not know 'cause it must have been illegal. There isn't any *legal* solution. I'm just happy he's gone—almost as happy as you are, if I can judge the look on your face. Good-day to you, sir. Come along, boys."

They left.

Jerry's father lifted his eyes up to merciful heaven and fainted dead away.

The police sergeant showed up about the time Jerry got home from school. They knew it all.

"I'm real sorry, Mr. Greene, but your boy buried the old man in the back yard, and I've got to take him in." The sergeant put a real sorry look on his face. "Starting a cemetery without a license, maybe. I'm not sure yet exactly what we can charge him with. Evading forms, if nothing else. That's a bad business; the law, you know. I'm sorry, Mr. Greene, but I've got to take Jerry in, juvenile or no juvenile.

"One good thing," the officer continued, "we don't have to dig up the old man—we don't have any forms for it. Yet. We'll get some though, don't you worry."

And so Jerry went to jail, for littering.

Right now, at the time I am writing this, I can name at least eight science fiction writer/editors who have entered the original anthology sweepstakes—with varying degrees of success. (Unfortunately, the degree of any book's success is not always a mark of its quality—there are other factors: the state of the market at the time of its publication, the willingness of its publisher to "push" the book, even the color of the cover and the readability of the typeface.)

To my mind, the best of these anthologies are the ones that have avoided contemporary science fiction's unfortunate tendency to pseudo-artiness—or "artiness for the sake of artiness"—and have retained a healthy awareness of the (you should pardon the expression) "traditional" values of literature. And yet, all of the anthologies I am thinking of (my own included) have examples of the "new wave" kind of story—efforts wherein the writer has depended more on his ability as a stylist than as a storyteller to hold the reader's interest.

Because I have not only included that kind of story in my own books, but have written them as well, I dare not speak too loud in any condemnation of the form—but the continued success of Analog Science Fiction suggests that there is a healthy market for pure storytelling. To me, the real classics of literature are books

181

like Tom Sawyer, A Tale of Two Cities, Treasure Island, Gulliver's Travels, *and* Moby Dick. *None of the writers of those books depended solely on artificial devices of pseudo-cleverness as foundations on which to hook the reader. Rather, they told good solid stories, with identifiable values and characters; they concentrated on elements that the reader could identify and empathize with. All of them concentrated on the story and told it to the best of their storytelling ability, with the result that anyone who has read those books is likely to remember them as vividly as any experience of his own life. These books are "classic" in the sense that they have become part of our common cultural heritage. Even without reading them, a child will come to know what they are about simply because of the continual day-to-day references to them in other aspects of his environment. ("It wasn't just large—it was Brobdignagian!") And that's* classic.

But our world has changed since those books were written, and we have different heroes today. The world is too small for the traditional adventure, so we no longer search for Holy Grails and Golden Fleeces. Instead we are left with the quest after the mystic self, and we must delve into the slippery worlds of improbable consciousness, where neither meanings nor values are clear.

It gets very hard to concentrate on pure storytelling.

To digress for a moment: The theory of the dialectic holds that there is a thesis, *an* antithesis, *and a* synthesis. *Consider that in terms of science fiction. The thesis is the traditional form of storytelling structure—a beginning, a middle, a climax/denouement, and end. The antithesis, of course, is that broad area we have identified as "new wave." The synthesis (which we are beginning to experience now) is the combination, the growing together, of the two previous forms. We are seeing one more step in the development of science fiction, a new kind of story written by a writer who* is aware of both traditional and modern forms and is trying to incorporate both into the same tale.

One of the best writing instructors I've ever studied under explained the purpose of a story this way: "This is the most important event that will ever happen to this person in his whole life. The importance of the story is the examination of the way he confronts that event. What does it reveal about him? What does he learn from it? What does he fail to learn from it? And what is it that makes this event the most important?"

In the so-called "traditional" form, it is quite obvious why the events presented are the most important in their heroes' lives; the values and the meanings are clear. Most often, the hero's life is in danger and he must act to save himself; at other times, he is seeking a goal of arbitrary value in order to gain or regain a position of power or security in the society in which he lives. The context in which the book is written, its cultural background, usually determines what the goal is to be; what a culture considers important is what its heroes strive for. A nineteenth-century American gold-prospector will not share the attitudes and values of a seventeenth-century French aristocrat; the actions of each will be determined as much by his culture as by who he is within that culture.

But we are in the midst of a world-wide information explosion. We are being hit from all sides by words and images, by hundreds of different cultures and ways of thinking. We are being bombarded with electronic, neo-tribal confusion. Small wonder that our culture is shattering into nervous groups of extremists and militants, each ferociously determined to protect his chosen cultural ideal. Each is expressing his personal and private rejection of the greater culture, one that he cannot assimilate, in favor of a not-necessarily simpler, but more suitable cultural text.

These are the people who have become our contemporary heroes—those who in one way or another have sidestepped the "consume or be consumed" jugger-

*naut of "Amerika" and are trying to change it. (I sus-
pect that part of their attractiveness as culture-heroes is
that they are doomed as causes in their own right—the
American public has always been fascinated by lost
causes. The goals of these groups may someday be
achieved—but it will be done by the re-educated mass
society's willingness to grant them, not through any
direct action by the group itself. Sorry if that point of
view offends the more militant reader, but the great
American middle class has a fat butt, and that's a
powerful lot of inertia to overcome.*

Our heroes are no longer people who can actively
control and change their environment; too few of us
know people with that ability. Instead, we have become engrossed with the individual who is overpowered
by the sheer massiveness of his situation. When he
meets it on its terms, the story is a tragic one; when
he forces it to meet him on his terms, the story is unreal and so becomes an escape: a happy piece of
fiction.

This is probably the core of the "old-wave/new-
wave" controversy—science fiction's own version of the
generation gap. The "old wave" story is the one that
concentrates on pure storytelling and the "traditional"
values. It is an adventure, and adventures have to
have happy endings—the hero has to triumph over
adverse conditions to reach his goals, and the more
adverse those conditions are, the more heroic he has
to be. But we don't have that kind of hero in twentieth-
century America, and people who confess those kinds
of values are considered lunatics. Our culture is no
longer so simple that it can be approached in those
kinds of terms.

The "new wave" story is the realistic one, the story
that realizes that man is a part of the condition in
which he exists, and as such is subject to it. The new

wave story examines that condition and comments on it, sometimes without specific conclusion, and often by allowing the hero to succumb to the forces that beset him. In no case is the hero's triumph anything but a personal one.

New wave stories are pessimistic; they dwell on the inability of the individual man to act with effectiveness on anything but his own life, and sometimes not even that. The new wave story is in direct opposition to the optimism expressed by the "traditional" form, which says that a hero must attain his goal, no matter how improbable the odds are against him. (In science fiction, that can mean he overturns a whole culture.)

Often, the new wave story must immerse itself in stylistic devices to make its point—sometimes those devices are the point; but the linear-oriented reader usually finds himself at a loss and considers that the writer cheated him. In contrast, the non-linear reader will find the strictly constructionist fable too "boring" to be worthy of his attention.

The dichotomy stems from two different views of the individual's role in life. The old wave story is concerned with the role an individual chooses for himself. The new wave story considers the roles that an environment forces an individual into.

What's the synthesis of these two forms?

It's hard to say. We have neither the words nor the examples for it yet, but we are starting to see tentative explorations in that direction. A story of this "synthesized" form will probably bear resemblance to both of its literary parents, and at the same time it will be something more than each. Hopefully, it will have a solid foundation of storytelling values combined with a clear-eyed and realistic view of all aspects of the individual's roles, both those he has chosen for himself and the ones he has been forced into. Undoubtedly, the story will be about the interactions of those roles and the decisions that the hero must make.

At the moment, I can only think of one example to point to—that one is already recognized as a classic. Cervantes' Don Quixote.

Hmm.

CHANCES ARE
Alice Laurance

She stood looking down the long empty road and she knew, even as she looked, that it was wrong, for she was lying in the high hospital bed, not standing at all. Yet she was standing, too, looking down the road. There was something forbidding about it—a narrow road cut through high, desolate sand dunes, with a few cattails waving forlornly in a thin breeze—yet she knew in a moment she was going to start down that road. She looked back unhappily, and now she could see herself lying in the bed, the deep stains around her eyes vivid against the pale skin, her dark hair matted and stringy after the fever.

She wanted to say something—something important —or perhaps just to tell them all she loved them, but the words wouldn't form. They were all there: Don, twisting his wedding band the way he did when he was badly upset; Mom, crying; Dad, clearing his throat because men don't cry, and trying to comfort Mom; Aunt Sally, looking helpless; Jan, standing a little apart, the outsider who wasn't family. Mrs. Oliphant was in the next bed; she even loved Mrs. Oliphant, whose baby was fine and healthy, not stillborn like her own. She loved them all. It was good of the hospital to let them all come at once.

As she watched, Don bent over her, saying something, and it made her desperately unhappy that she couldn't catch his words. She turned away, as she would to hide tears, and saw again the long desolate road. She looked down it, trying to see its end and then turned back once more, but Don and the others were gone. There was only a blankness, like a glaring light perceived through closed eyes, forming a barrier she knew she couldn't penetrate. She was already cold and very lonely, and there was nowhere to go but down the road. She looked back once more, hoping the barrier would lift, but it remained in place, and she began to walk, thinking that the dead also have a loss to mourn.

She walked slowly, as if reluctant to leave the place where she'd last seen Don, and for a while she looked around her, curious about the countryside, but it was unvaried, offering no distractions to her thoughts. Her life had not been so very unusual; she'd done nothing memorable, though she'd meant to, and yet, as she walked, she remembered so much.

She remembered the apartment in Queens where she'd grown up. She hadn't thought of it in years, but she could remember the Bo Peep wallpaper that had been on her walls when she was little, and the pastoral scene that had replaced it when she was ten. The wallpaper in the crowded parlor had been a floral pattern, endlessly repeating, but she'd never been very much aware of anything in that room but the huge piano dominating it. Her earliest memories were of listening to her Mother play, and that was appropriate, for the strain of music ran through all her life. She could remember clearly the first time her Mother had lifted her up on the piano bench and guided her tiny fingers over the keys, and the pleasure it had given both of them. She remembered her Mother's attempts to teach her, and then the more formal lessons with Mr. Weinstein; she could still hear his faintly accented voice saying softly, "Again, please. Ah. That is better."

She remembered practicing while her friends were out playing, and never realizing until much later that she wasn't "playing" too. She remembered her Mother's delight in her ability, and her Father paying for the lessons he couldn't really afford, though she hadn't realized that until later, either. Her Father was a mild, quiet man, undemonstrative, but she could remember his joy when she told him she'd been accepted at Julliard.

A clump of cattails ahead caught her attention, and when she reached them, she saw they marked a faint path that branched off from the main road and would otherwise have been all but unnoticeable. She glanced at the sandy road behind her and saw faint impressions of her own footprints, which the wind blurred even as she watched. She looked at the new path, shivering slightly in the breeze which chilled her only when she paused. The main road was clearly defined, winding in front of her as far as she could see; the other path was little more than the hint of a foot trail that curved around a high dune and vanished. There was no marking, and she understood there were no roadsigns in this place; you had to find your own way. But how, she suddenly wondered. And to where? She shivered again as she hesitated, and she was suddenly sure that if she started down this road, a barrier would prevent any return to the main road. She paused a moment longer, wondering why she felt safer on one road than on the other, since she had no idea where either led, and then, walking slower than before, she continued down the wider road, troubled by the choice and glancing back frequently, until the clump of cattails vanished from sight.

The countryside was again barren and monotonous, and her thoughts strayed back to memories.

She remembered the years at Julliard—the work, the hours of practice and study, the hours spent selling records in an all-night music shop. She remembered meeting Jan, who became her closest friend—Jan, who could make a violin express all the depths of agony or flights of joy a human being could know; Jan, who knew everything she was feeling without being told because she was feeling it herself. Her breath caught in a sob as she thought of Jan, who would know exactly what music would fit this place, exactly what music would make it comprehensible and tolerable, and she thought automatically of the three recitals she'd given, because Jan had selected the music for them. She'd had a detached feeling about the recitals, though she'd worked hard for them and played well enough. The audiences and critics had been kind, ascribing the flaws to youth and inexperience, but she had known that the real limitations were in talent and perhaps will. Jan had unerringly selected music that made her talent seem greater than it was, but she hadn't wanted a career on the concert stage; she wanted to compose, though even at the outset she'd been uncertain about the dream. The hope was more intense than her confidence.

She remembered moving into her own tiny apartment, meeting the rent and the monthly payments on her piano by giving lessons, while she filled hundreds of notebooks with ideas and snatches of melody. She remembered a procession of small children, mostly rebellious or resentfully well-behaved, trooping to her piano and doggedly pounding out their selections, and she remembered her amusement the day she first heard her voice, in unconscious imitation of Mr. Weinstein, say, "Again, please. Ah. That is better."

Her train of thought broke and she stopped, looking around her slowly. Something had distracted her, but she didn't know what. She looked behind her nervously and saw a clump of cattails she'd passed; they reminded her of the ones marking the side path, and she walked back to the place. Once again there was a path veering off the main road, this one even less defined than the first. As before, the path curved past a dune and was lost to sight. She walked a few feet in one direction and then the other, hoping a change in angle would enlarge her view, but it didn't and the path's end remained hidden behind the dune; to see it she would have to follow the path, and she was certain, as before, that there would be no turning back. The path was again only the suggestion of a trail, and it wasn't enough to lure her. She turned and continued down the main road.

She began to think about Don. She could see him bending over her still form in the hospital bed, speaking words she would never grasp, and again an enormous sense of loss filled her.

She remembered meeting Don, at a party at Shirley Webster's apartment. Strange she could remember Shirley's name; she and Don had tried to remember it a month ago and couldn't. It was Shirley Webster. Neither of them had known her well; she was just a girl who worked in Don's office and had a little brother taking piano lessons. It was such a commonplace introduction and would have meant nothing if, a week later, they hadn't both been standing in line waiting to buy concert tickets. She'd smiled and he'd begun to talk, and he took her to dinner afterwards; they were married a few months later. He was so sure and steady, so endlessly patient and confident and wise, and it still frightened her a little when she thought how easily she might have missed him. Just five minutes difference in time on the day she bought the tickets and he would have meant no more to her than Shirley Webster. He was the only man she'd ever loved; in a fundamental way, she was actually grateful to him simply for being, though she'd never found a way to tell him that. And now she never would.

The desire to see him just once more was so strong in her that she gasped, and she felt a tide of bitterness that, being a ghost, she was condemned to wander this desolate road instead of the earth where Don lived. Why couldn't she will herself back to their house, not to haunt it or to play pranks, but just to look at him once more? She halted and closed her eyes, squeezing them tight in her concentration, but when she opened them she was still on the empty road and she was trembling

from the cold wind. Reluctantly, she began to walk
again, but memories of Don stayed with her.

He'd been so proud of her music. He would listen
for hours as she played, and he invited all his friends
in to hear her. He'd encouraged her to compose, never
doubting her talent as she herself did, and he'd been
so pleased when she'd sold a simple tune to an advertising agency to be used as a jingle and so disappointed
when it wasn't used.

And then they'd learned she was going to have a
baby, and for both of them all disappointment and
unhappiness was erased. For him, the baby was a continuation; for her, a creation. She was certain of very
few things, but one of them was that the purpose of life
was the creation of something the world had lacked before. She was very far from certain she could fulfill
that purpose in music, try as she might. She had worked
hard, longer and more grueling hours than any normal
job would have required, and with little to show for
it. She seemed to lack some central quality that would
enable her to complete what she'd started, to turn her
fragments into a finished piece of music. She thought
of the large box in a closet, filled with the notes she
made and, unbidden, one of the fragments of melody
ran through her mind. It broke off abruptly where she'd
lost the thread and then, without warning, the music
resumed, a logical variation following the familiar frag-
ment until she could hear the completed song. She
let the music run through her mind again, listening intently, and she knew it was what she'd been striving
for, but it was too late. Much too late.

But still, she wanted to write it down, to preserve it
in some way, but there was nothing to write on. Almost
nothing. She broke off a cattail and marked the notes
of the song in the sand, a momentary record. By the
time she was finished, the first notes she'd written were
blurred by the breeze shifting the sand.

She looked at the fading music and thought again
of the baby. She'd wanted him so much, but something

had happened. Strange that she couldn't remember what; she could remember so much, but not something as important as that. Perhaps she'd never known. But something had happened and the baby had died. It hadn't even been born at all; it had been taken from her, and something else had been taken from her as well. Not the will to live—she wanted to live, still wanted to. The ability to live had been taken from her, not deliberately or maliciously, but taken all the same, and now she was walking down this long, barren road, going she didn't know where, and so terribly alone.

She watched the wind obliterate her work and then walked on, moving slowly. She wondered how long she'd been walking and found no answer, for there was no way to measure duration here. There seemed to be no night or day; the light remained the same, like early dusk, or afternoon just before a storm. But there was no storm, just the faint wind, chilling her when she stopped. For the first time she thought to look at the sky, but there was no sky, just that same curious colorless blank she'd seen when she tried to look back at Don.

She looked back, the road now stretching as far as she could see behind her as well as before her. She could no longer identify the place where she'd written her music, and she couldn't see the two paths that had been the only variety in the scenery.

It suddenly occurred to her to wonder what lay on the other side of the dunes. The presence of cattails usually meant marshland, but she had heard neither the roar of the sea nor the lapping of a smaller body of water on the shore. She listened intently again, but the only sound was the sibilant shifting of sand. Uneasily, she turned from the road and attempted to scale one of the dunes, but she could find no foothold in the sand and slipped back each time. She gave up finally, but stood for a moment looking at the dune before she returned to the road and began walking again.

She tried to think about her life, to evaluate it, but

she could make no judgment. She'd done nothing terrible, but she'd done nothing wonderful, either. In a way, she'd really done nothing at all. A protest rose up in her—she hadn't been allowed to live long enough, not even thirty years. But did any man, however long he'd lived, think it was long enough? Did any man start down this road without the conviction that the next year denied to him would have been his finest? It seemed to her that no man could travel this road without regret—for things done or undone or left unfinished. For only a suicide chose his moment of death, and suicide without regret was inconceivable. But how could a man prepare? Knowing he could die at any moment, still he needed patience, the patience to study and learn, the patience to work steadily but without haste, risking everything on the chance he'd survive to complete the task. She thought of the music she'd written in the sand and wondered how many others had completed projects in the same way, knowing the terrible futility of it even as they did it.

She couldn't evaluate her life; she didn't even know if it had been happy or sad. The only thing she knew with certainty about life was that she was sorry to leave it.

She began to wonder, again, if there was a God. Incredible that she didn't yet know. She remembered when Don's Father had been dying; they'd talked about it, neither of them sure what they thought, and when the old gentleman had died, Don had said, "Well, now he knows." It had seemed a wise remark, and it had told them they believed in something, for total obliteration allows no knowledge; but now the comment did not seem so profound. Perhaps the old man hadn't known—as she didn't know. Perhaps neither of them ever would.

Perhaps God was down one of the paths she'd rejected, if He existed at all. But if He was, how could you know? Perhaps if you didn't find Him, you just continued down the road forever, looking for something you couldn't find and not even knowing what you were seeking. She wondered if you could turn back and take a path passed before, and she stopped, looking behind her. Perhaps you had to dare to take one of the little-used paths to find God. She was about to retrace her steps when she saw a figure far ahead of her in the distance, and she forgot everything else in her desire to reach him. She tried to run, but her feet seemed too heavy; she tried to call out, but the sound was a whisper carried away by the wind. When she finally reached the place, it was deserted—no other person in sight.

The road forked where she stood, splitting into two unmarked paths that looked equally traveled. Both paths wound through high dunes, and both appeared, at first glance, to be simply continuations of the road she'd been following. But then, as her eyes traveled the road to the left, she saw a glow in the distance, like a bright light very far away. The path to the right had no such beacon.

She stood in an agony of indecision, looking down one road and then the other. For a moment the glow seemed to draw her, but she continued to hesitate, afraid to follow either path. She wondered which road the person she'd seen had taken, but there was no indication and she knew it really made no difference; even if she took the same road, by design or chance, she would not overtake him. She longed for someone to advise her; she wanted Don to tell her what to do, but she couldn't wish he was with her. Not here. Her loneliness was intense, but she couldn't wish Don dead, even to join her. And however much she wanted to, there would be no way she could wait for him. The wind would drive her on, in spite of herself.

She looked down the two roads, started to take the road to the left, and then stopped. The glow must have a meaning and the meaning might be God. But she didn't want to see God; she didn't want God to see her. She hadn't known that a moment before, but she knew it now. A man should come to God with some achievement, there should be something he could point to, saying, "I did that." If she'd written her song on paper instead of sand, if her child had lived, she would have taken the road to the left, hoping the glow was God; but as it was, she turned to the right, and a dune immediately blocked her view of the glow. She continued unhappily, pausing every so often to look behind her.

Some time later—it seemed a long time later, but she couldn't be certain—the road again forked into two divergent paths. Once again they were unmarked and looked equally traveled, and again one seemed to lead to a distant glow. She knew she had not somehow worked her way back to the first fork only because this time the glow was to the right. Perhaps it's a second chance, she thought, and then another possible explanation occurred to her. Hell, too, might have a glow. Was Hell the proper destiny for failure? Even if that were true and she accepted it, how could she be certain that this glow and not the first was Hell? There were no guides, and she could see no difference between this glow and the first.

Four times she had come upon alternatives: two small paths and two forks—like pairs of alternatives. Perhaps they indicated some dichotomy between two extremes, a dualism taking different forms. Perhaps several human concepts of what came after life, perhaps all concepts of afterlife, were represented, along with their opposites, by paths or branches in the road. But without guides, how could anyone find his own place? What would happen to a Methodist who happened on Nirvana, or a Buddhist in a Methodist heaven? Did free will mean nothing more than a blind chance, a choice based on nothing at all? But perhaps it wasn't free will at all; perhaps it was a plan much larger than the choice of any single person, so that it didn't matter which road was chosen. Perhaps a Methodist sharing Nirvana was part of the plan.

She remembered her attempts to judge her own life and thought of the word "justice." If there was a plan larger than the individual's choice, then did all men start down this road as equals, regardless of the lives they'd led? But perhaps there were guides—the wind that chilled her each time she paused was a guide, if you thought of it that way. Perhaps she wasn't making choices at all, but acting on some compulsion she didn't recognize. Or perhaps, after all, she was choosing, making her own choices on the basis of the only evidence available.

She wondered what would happen if she rejected all the differentiated paths. Perhaps the road would simply continue to wind through the dunes until exhaustion forced her to choose some path, or perhaps it was a great circle that would start over, so that she'd eventually return to this spot. But if it wasn't a circle, and if she did continue to refuse alternatives, would she walk forever, facing an infinity of choices, or would she come finally to some oblivion?

She closed her eyes wearily, then opened them and looked once more toward the glow before turning away, taking the road to the left. She walked slowly, expecting and finding side roads and forks, always coming in pairs. They no longer surprised her, but each time she found one she hesitated, uncertain and unhappy, finally choosing what she thought was the continuation of the road she'd been traveling.

Several times she saw figures in the distance, and each time she tried desperately to signal them, even though she knew she would fail. There were no companions here. And then, when she was almost convinced that she would never stop walking this desolate road, the road curved sharply around a high dune,

and she came to another fork and saw a figure standing at the divide, hesitating between the alternatives.
It was a figure, neither male nor female, and it was
only then that she realized her own form was also sexless. She might continue to think of herself in the feminine, but her sex was a memory.

The other person seemed to sense her presence and
turned. They looked at each other helplessly, and then
both turned away. Neither of them tried to speak,
though she was certain the other one was as lonely and
unhappy as she. They separated, each taking a different
path; her own choice of road dictated by the other's.

The encounter seemed to rob her of the last of her
hope; she walked on listlessly, without curiosity or expectations. She continued down the road, wondering
apathetically if perhaps there had been some judgment
of her she hadn't recognized, and if she was acting
out the fate assigned to her with each step. She walked
slowly, no longer wanting to see others, until once
again the road curved past a dune and she found herself
facing a door.

It was a perfectly ordinary door, except that it was
set in the middle of the road and was surrounded by
the blank barrier. She could not bypass it; she could
not scale the dunes to the sides; if she didn't go through
it, the only other thing she could do was to turn and
go back. To what? The paths she'd already rejected?
The blank barrier at the other end of the road? And if
she did return to that, what could she expect to find?
Nothing. Or another door.

She put her hand on the knob, then hesitated, looking back at the road she'd walked. She was terribly
frightened, but she knew what she had to do. God
or Hell or oblivion might wait on the other side, but
she had to go on. Her hand tightened on the knob;
she opened the door and stepped through.

She was blinded by a glaring white light, and she
gasped at a sudden smack of flesh against flesh. She

heard a baby cry and she smiled. For a split second she knew exactly where he was and understood what had happened, and then she knew nothing at all. A nurse smiled behind her mask as she fastened the identification beads around his chubby little wrist.

It is not specifically the business of science fiction to predict the future. It is the business of science fiction to comment knowledgeably on the present, and occasionally to warn of possible futures.

Sometimes we do it by hyperbole: "If this goes on—" Sometimes we do it by reversal: "What if—" Either way we are commenting on a specific aspect of humanity by showing it from a different point of view.

Science fiction doesn't only serve warnings—sometimes it suggests answers as well. Sometimes the answers are totally impractical (dammit), but they're still fun to think about.

This story is a simple one. Robert E. Margroff (author of two novels with Piers Anthony) is having fun here, but the point is valid.

Consider: One of the main reasons why there are so many riots on campuses today is that riots are sexy. They may be bloody, violent and irrational, but they are also wholesale expressions of libidinous urges—human beings throwing aside all restraints, inhibitions, and respect for authority in an orgy of—

That's right. The word is orgy. So what if it's violence instead of sex? It's still an orgy. Riots are sexy.

And Margroff's comment is right on target—as well as his solution to the problem. If this story ever comes true, I'm re-enrolling.

THE NAKED AND THE UNASHAMED

Robert E. Margroff

The wave of the future bore down. It rushed, a torrent of youthful pink and brown bodies, mother naked, onto the freshly watered lawn before the administration building. Its face lit the dawn with a passion equalled only by the shrillness of its voice.

On the wave tossed signs, intended to catch the eyes of the news cameras.

"We want Blood!"

"War is Healthy!"

"Competition is Great!"

A pretty blonde, naked with cherry-tipped alabaster globes aimed high, and perfect pudenda aimed low, stood straddle-legged in front of the cameras. She carried a sign reading: "Death Freedom Now!" She shoved it into the lenses and screamed:

"We want the right to croak! You hear that, Misters and Mistresses? We want to be one with the stars and the grass! We want to die like our ancestors died and rot and stink and disintegrate! We want our chemicals to recombine and build something different than we are—something with fur or feathers or leaves! You hear that, You Living Freaks! LET US DIE!"

The cameras stayed on her and on her sign—her filthy sign. The engineers would be bleeping out the obscenities she shouted, but there was nothing to be done about the sign short of blanking the screen and

202

arousing the ire of a couple billion set-owners. The cameraman grinned. Trust these college radicals to think of that!

The dean of the multiversity strode out onto the open balcony and the cameras turned reluctantly to him. He looked down his patrician nose at the future, his gaze settling on the blonde: on her sunshine hair falling to her fresh-cream shoulders, on her uptilted and bouncy breasts.

The dean's heavy lips twitched in silent homage to youth. Slowly, for the benefit of the cameras, he began divesting himself of his clothing. Looking into the lens as often as he leered at the girl, he untied the drawstrings on his silver cape. He let the cape fall, unbuttoned his brocaded shirt, stripped his blue velvet trousers down his plump hips and thighs. Stooping, big butt in air, he unstrapped his gold-buckled shoes. He rolled down his red and green nylon stockings until they fell from his singularly ugly toes. He straightened, red-faced from exertion, panting just a bit, and hooked his thumbs in the tops of his green nylon shorts. By now his posture had changed quite a bit, but he eased the elastic down and over.

Naked, a theoretical equal, he stood.

Pot-bellied and covered with light reddish hair, he spoke the stuffy, tired words they all expected.

"Your administration in its ceaseless and unyielding quest for perfection in the arts and sciences, not unmindful of changing values but cognizant of the lessons of the past . . ."

His voice was drowned in a nearly deafening spray of epitaphs and slogans.

"Juiceless Clay!"

"Bloodless Wonder!"

"Sexless Pervert!"

"To the Breastworks!" The blonde's breastworks bounced as she yelled that one. Superb lungs.

He waited them out. The newsmen and the cameras waited too. The wave gradually ceased to roar.

The blonde started to speak—before the dean. He shut his wide mouth and let his chops rest. The cameras swung to her, lovingly focussed on her peach complexion. On her baby-bow mouth and the rage that flushed her cheeks, her throat, her beautiful and spectacular bosom. The rosettes surrounding her nipples made good targets for closeups. The blonde tuft between her open legs was an invitation to masculine imaginings. Behind her, dangles and rises of a masculine nature made closeups for the distaff half of the great voyeuring public.

"Oldie, we want action!" the lovely said. "There hasn't been a war since my grandmother's first time! Do you know how long it's been since a girl's been raped? I've never seen blood spattered! I've never seen men killed and dying, screaming in pain as their guts tumbled out! I'm human—I need to experience these things!"

The cameras refocussed on the dean as he again spoke for the establishment. He was visibly and pathetically cooled by her words, his sensibilities affrighted by her coarseness.

"Young Mistress—for I am sure that you, like your mother and grandmother before you, must be somebody's mistress—you are demanding that the world return to savagery. Would you have football played again with human heads? Hospitals admitting all visitors and with a public-viewable expiration room? Would you have wars with bullets and bombs and real casualties? If you get all that, what will you want next? Will you want it announced when lives are ended? Will you want the resumption of such indecent displays as funerals and burials?"

"YEAHHHHH!" the girl said.

"Perverted," the dean gasped. "Perverted in the worst sense ever! Haven't the youth of today learned anything? We give you athletics that are almost the exact counterpart of past games, except that our players are robots. We give the robots realistic screams and plastic veins with red fluid; you complain that the screams are not agonized, the bleeding not bloody enough. We conduct carefully detailed computer wars with the computers announcing victors and losers and the number of theoretical maimed, injured and terminated. What you want are *real* wars; *real* casualties. Is there no limit to your shortsightedness? Can't you young people realize that in life you sometimes have to compromise?"

"NO COMPROMISE WITH THE ESTABLISHMENT!" a voice screamed. It was a dark-haired man with stooped shoulders and a raised clenched fist; the camera zoomed in on him and caught him right at the start of the filthiness.

Two blond males and one dark young man—shaved clean, like so many of the radicals—beat the shouter down. The huskier of the blonds struck him an open-handed blow across the face. He fell, his nose squirting red spectacularly. The shorter blond kicked him in the belly; then in the kneecap. The brunet raised a foot and aimed with his toe at the youth's testicles.

The young radical screamed. He looked up with open mouth and eyes directly into the camera. In startling closeup, it was a shocking sight—for the cameraman as well as the viewers.

"THAT'S AN OBSCENE ACT!" the dean belowed. "STOP IT YOU THREE!"

The heavier of the clean-shaves stooped and dug with his fingers almost beneath his victim's butt. Other students saw and imitated. Clods rained like hail upon the balcony; the camera followed them from the hands of the hurlers to their violent ends.

"I WARN YOU!" the dean shouted. "OBSCENITY WILL NOT BE TOLERATED!"

A clod, composed mostly of grass, hit his mouth. He ducked back so far that the cameras couldn't follow him. The radicals knew what that meant.

From all directions, husky young men in blue uniforms ran. The cameras whirled to catch them, zooming the focus to show their narrow shoulders and eager expressions. The home audience would love this; they liked to see closeups of the coppers in action. It took some of them back to the days when the police were all robots and did clumsy and damaging things to the students. Progress—everybody likes progress.

The coppers raised the hoses attached to the squat tanks on their backs. The nozzles looked like shiny phalluses as the police advanced with them at hip level. As one, the nozzles began emitting the fine spray that clung to naked breasts and backs, giving them a bedewed, exciting look. The droplets were faintly dyed and partly gelatined; this was so the viewers could see which kids were getting sprayed. A good deal of the spray was aimed to cling to the most interesting parts of the kids—below the waist level.

From here on in, the news would be all entertainment.

The students were closing ranks. Their leaders shouted commands to ward off the spray with their signs. It was useless, of course. The police elevated their hoses so that the spray drifted down like rain; then they switched to waist-level when the signs were converted to umbrellas, baring more flesh.

At the edge of the mob, a girl screamed. She'd been one of the first sprayed and the stuff was working on her. It took only twelve seconds. The camera panned past hairy cheeks and smooth cheeks and big round bouncy hinder-cheeks to where the dark-haired miss fell writhing. The foam was jelling pink on her fanny as she clawed at a boy's hairy leg; he was wearing a pink cob of spray on his belly. It wasn't long before he was down on top of her. The two locked in a frenzied embrace—that soon turned to even more frenzied copulation.

Almost all of them were down now. Here and there, a holdout was evading the coppers' spray and the clutching arms and tripping legs of the other protestors. Most were going at it, fast and fine. Face to face, head to tail, side to side, plain and uncommon. Any old way, so long as no time was lost. There were boy-girl, girl-girl, boy-boy, and assorted interesting combinations. Good, glorious, clean sex erasing their childish wills to shout obscenities. It was enough to make any viewer feel fine; it was enough to make the cameraman think he'd enjoy joining them. A few holdouts were resisting. They looked so silly with their contorted limbs, as they sought to fight themselves, that it was hard to remember they believed their actions heroic—but no one resisted long; they couldn't.

The girl with the sign was still there in front, big boobs sticking out. She hadn't been hit yet; the police were leary of spraying the cameraman so close to her. He had her in a sharp sexy focus. She had added something new to her face: an obscene skull—symbol of the underground—was now stencilled on her paper-smooth forehead. Too bad; children who couldn't read would ask what the skull was. The camera dropped to the hollow of her neck, dropped down to the gorgeous swell of her bosom, went all the way again and close-upped her crotch. She saw what the cameraman was doing and tried getting her face down. He moved the camera up and down and sideways, always keeping it on some part of her. She kept ducking and trying; she didn't see the robot policeman approach. He let go with his spray when the nozzle was practically nuzzling her shapely ass.

She gave a jerk. Her face contorted, and two hundred million viewers knew she was getting the good full benefit. But she didn't drop. She didn't turn and look for somebody. She didn't—to his regret—reach for the cameraman. She sank very slowly to her knees, and then she grasped the top of her sign and began pulling herself upright. The camera stayed on her. It was obvious what she was doing; holding the sign on camera as long as possible. It was a dramatic moment; the cameraman hoped the Moms and Pops of America would think of the drama and forget the obscenity.

Now she had her long, beautiful legs spraddled again.

She had the handle of the sign between her thighs. She was rubbing herself on it, still keeping the sign faced frontwards. The handle had been padded with something smooth and maybe just a shade greasy: She had planned for this!

The camera stayed on her. The Mom and Pop viewers could go bury themselves! The cameraman's face gleamed with sweat. This was—this was great!

She moved up and down, up and down, up and down, looking into the camera with her face becoming more and more organic. You had to love the bravery of her. The cameraman licked his lips in yearning anticipation, envied through throbbing awareness her slick and feelingless stick. He focussed his zoom lens even closer.

The skull decal bobbed up and down on her smooth forehead. He didn't care. He didn't care at all. Let the networks holler. Let them blank it out if they wanted. If they dared.

She was coming now. Coming as though with a great message. Coming for all the Moms and Pops and Kiddies. Coming for them all. Automatically, he narrowed the focus.

Now pink lips. Pink and open. Now a proxy phallus. Now, now, now.

Oh Sweet Death, *now!*

It was a hell of a good demonstration. So good that as he set the camera on automatic, he hardly noticed that all over the lawn it was now the cops going down —down on the students, and then up and down. Only a single robot policeman stood aloof, his sensors making sure that nothing obscene was done.

In life it is sometimes necessary to compromise. The dean had said so. The newsman believed him. He hastened to get his ass out there. Pouncing from behind the camera, he struck naked flesh. The dean whoofed and clutched his stomach where the cameraman had brutally and deliberately struck him; he pushed the dean hur-

riedly aside, and with him, pushed away the thought
of all the people at home watching and pondering.

He grabbed the blonde and her sign. He threw both
to the ground.

She struggled for the show. For the camera.

He let her feel what he had. He played with her
boobs and got ready for it.

She sighed, giving up all protest, and let her legs
open.

He entered, in advance of the dean, and plugged her
generation gap.

It was a good demonstration.

If there were a formula for a sure-fire best-seller, I wouldn't tell you. I'd lock myself in a room and do nothing but write best-sellers.

Or let's try it another way—if there were a formula for writing nothing but good stories, we should expect to get nothing but good stories out of writers who know that formula.

Except that once something can be reduced to a formula, it ceases to be an art and becomes, instead, a craft—or worse, a science.

Most professional writers will refer to writing as a "craft," not an "art." This is a kind of reverse vanity on their part, the implication being that they are so familiar with their tools that writing is only a craft to them. But it's an art too—just as the making of fine furniture is an art. The most successful practitioner/ artists are those who have a deep love and respect for the work they are doing.

Formula? I wouldn't even try to offer you one. For one thing, it'd be too easy to be wrong.

But if I were looking for one, I'd start by examining carefully every memorable story I've ever read in order to see what criteria are common to them all.

At the moment, I can only think of one.

Truth.

Every memorable story has an element of truth to

it—recognizable *truth, something that the reader will identify as such, something that will make him say, "Hey! Yeah!"*

I'm not sure if this story has such an element in it. I think it does—that's why it's here in this book. You read it for yourself and think: Do you know somebody like Jefferson Bellamy?

MY COUNTRY, RIGHT OR WRONG

andrew j. offutt

He had no pictures of Vladimir Ilyitch Ulyanovasa as a young man, before he grew the moustache and brief beard to replace the hair that had vanished from his domed skull. But it was December 17, 1887, and this was the law school of the University of Kazan. The student political demonstration had not yet become violent, but the screaming, arm-waving leader was moving his classmates in that direction. The Tsarist police were not in evidence—yet.

I'm a fanatic, Jeff Bellamy thought. A damned fanatical chauvinist, which Jim Velnikov would say is a redundancy! But dammit, we'd have made it to Jim's world anyhow, without Russia's "help," and faster, without all those years of fighting Communism!

The man from the twentieth century focussed his twenty-first-century rifle on the shouting nineteenth-century revolutionary. His finger moved up to nudge the button under the rifle stock.

1

It works.

Whenever he is, he is not when he was. The time-booth works. He steps cautiously out onto the deep-carpeted floor, glancing at gleaming walls banked with manifold and multiform dials and machinery. A few

213

feet away a bearded man stands beside a desk. He smiles.

"To answer your first thought, Jefferson Bellamy, the year is 2078."

"I calculated exactly a hundred years into the future—I made it!"

The bearded man smiles. "Congratulations. How is your health?"

The question and its phrasing sound stilted. Strange; it is in his language, but he had expected more idiomatic changes in a hundred years. "Hm?" Jeff Bellamy shrugs. "I seem to be okay." He frowns.

The tall man with the red-brown Hemingway beard wears a sort of Nehru suit; the long coat is closed all the way from high collar to hem, just at the knees. Jeff sees neither button nor zipper, but a faint seam bisects the coat down the front. It is Prussian blue in color, with snug gray trousers—and a yellow sash. The trousers slide without rumpling into boots rising high on a good set of legs. The boots appear to be of some gleaming reptilian hide, black and shiny and scutellate. He remarks on the bearded man's stilted English.

"That is in the translator, my friend from a century ago. I do not speak your language at all. We expected you. In 1978 Jeff Bellamy of Lexington, Kentucky, 'borrowed' a prototypic timebooth and vanished. The dials were set for 2078. We have been waiting. My translator is connected with CenComp. You hear me in your language, I hear you in mine." The bearded man smiles again, spreading soft-looking hands. "We aren't really hearing each other's voices, of course. But this is ridiculous, standing here like this! I—"

Agreeing, Jeff steps forward, hand outstretched. He frowns as the bearded man draws back with an apprehensive expression of distaste darkening his face like a storm-laden cloud. Jeff halts, his hand forgotten, suspended in air between them.

"Oh. My apologies, Jeff Bellamy. You were raised

on a farm and lived outside Lexington, didn't you? What was its population?"

Jeff grins and shakes his head. "About 60,000 when I graduated from college in '71. About 90,000—when I left, I mean, in 1978."

"Yes. And New York was nineteen millions in 1978. People were jammed together more and more tightly. City-dwellers were already avoiding physical contact. By the time you left it was far more pronounced, and now —I apologize. I acted reflexively. We . . . do not touch."

Incongruously, Jeff remembers Helen, and last night, and a lot of touching. It was a farewell party, although she did not know it. A few minutes later he had made his illicit test of the timebooth. He smiles. "Of course. I'm sorry. We shake—shook hands. Carryover from barbarism; empty hands means no attack imminent."

"Oh—my name is Velnikov, James Velnikov. Why don't we get you something to drink, at least."

This is when Jeff notices the sign above the door. Then the covers of the books on the desk. The ones on shelves. The lettering on the dials and gauges. Kyrillic characters. Russian.

"My great-grandfather was Russian," James Velnikov said. "His wife was third-generation Irish-American. Their daughter married a seventh-generation American. And their daughter married a fourth-generation Russian-American, my father. I'm no geneticist, Jeff; I can't tell you what part Russian that makes me, and I don't care. But yes, it could be put as you did: 'America is in Russian hands.' But after ninety-eight years we don't think of it that way. Besides, in a way America won."

Jeff Bellamy gulped down a great draught of his drink, staring. It was irrational, this trembling hate for Velnikov. The man was as American as he, if not more, and not a communist. 2078 was not 1978. But— Jeff had left only an hour ago. He felt almost guilty that he was not uncomfortable in the big chair. But one was never uncomfortable in the furniture of 2078. It did what you did, shifted when you shifted. There was a button to control whether his chair held him lovingly, fondly, or just casually. It, like Velnikov's boots, was of the breathing, porous plastic, formed to resemble lizard skin in the current mode. It was the first plastic chair Jeff had ever sat in without having a hot bottom. Velnikov complained that it was slow to adjust.

"Tell me about it, Doctor Vel—" Then it hit him. "Ninety-eight years? You mean—"

Velnikov nodded. "1980. Two years from 'now,' in your time. It was a little late, really, but the China Trouble deterred Russia from its original plan for a few years. Your country drained itself in Korea, then in Vietnam, then in Cambodia, and Thailand, and Korea again, and on Taiwan. All those wars were fought against either Russia or China, or both; tests of technology. But no young Russians died in undeclared wars. No Russian reserves lived under threat of being called up; no Russian students were under that same constant pressure. There was no confusion or dissent in Russia—not about the so-called Brushfire Wars, anyway. The drain on your country was in fuel, and materiel, and dollars, and young men—always young men. But also in spirit. In what's been called 'moral fibre,' and *esprit de corps,* and patriotism." He shook his head. "It's strange to talk of it, knowing I am beating you with an emotional whip while I am merely discussing history. It is such old history. So much has happened since then."

"What . . . what finally happened?" Jeff was staring at the other man. His knuckles gleamed white on the tumbler he held. Unbreakable plastic, although it looked and felt like crystal, and it rang. He could not disengage himself; this was subjective. He could talk this way about the Revolution or the Civil War or even War Two, to an extent. But not—not his time. Not the time

when he was (had been?) twenty-nine. And not later—
not 1980, two subjective years from "now."

Velnikov was frowning, the beard writhing as he drew
down his brows and worked his mouth in concentration.

"America met Russia and China on this battleground
and that, testing weapons. But America was paying the
price." His eyes dropped from the ceiling to Jeff's.
"Capitalism can't fight communism, not that way. Because of morale, and economics. Your leaders had to
account, had to stand for election every few years.
Taxes grew heavier and heavier, but money had to be
accounted for, and the government hadn't enough.
Right?"

Gazing at the wall, with his mouth an ugly line, Jeff
Bellamy nodded. His last raise had amounted to $500
a year. But the cost of living had risen $361 that year,
and his Social Security had gone up again. And then
had come another surtax, putting him in the 44%
bracket: single male earning $12,000. Barely a sub-
sistence wage. And the 13% Social Security bracket.
And of course 17% of the gross went to the state of
Kentucky. He had been left with about thirty-two
hundred. "But a lot of things were free," he said.

"Free. Yes, of course." The bearded man gave him
a strange look. "It wasn't that way for Chinese and
Russians. They received *no* wages; they worked directly
for the government and received food, clothing, hous-
ing, medical care, 'life insurance'—all, uh, free. Thus
their governments had more money than yours, more
spending power. And they didn't have to render an
accounting." Velnikov broke off to stand suddenly.

"I think you're about to explode, Jeff. Do me a
favor: Please put on the clothing you refused and
come into the city with me. Please?"

Jeff stared. "Oh good god, Velnikov, surely you
aren't going to try to sell me on the felicities of Russian
domination!"

"No, damn you, I'm not. And if you can't be polite
enough to call me Doctor Velnikov, please call me Jim,

which I prefer anyhow. Just come and look. That's why you came here, isn't it?"

It was. Velnikov's flash of anger had shocked Jeff, and he changed clothing and went outside with the bearded man.

It was a new city. Created. Jeff was afraid to ask: Created from what? After what? Lexington had been half-burned in '72, along with most other American cities, and again in '82, Velnikov said, by Chauvy Rebels. But this . . . this was all new.

There was a vast park, with a shimmering blue lake and shading trees. Soaring buildings connected at many levels by tubeways and railed walks, forming a gleaming filigree against the sky. Tubeways were russet, walks pale yellow, the buildings many pastels, with a great deal of the glass-that-was-not glass. They called it plass. A complex of buildings formed a community unto itself where, Velnikov told him, students attended classes for ten months of the year from ages five through thirty, and longer for advanced degrees. After spending thirty-two years in school, Velnikov had the equivalent of three 1978 doctorates. There was no agriculture-community vacation; the ten-month periods began in four different months, so that the school was never idle.

They passed plass-fronted stores with prices in the windows.

"Prices? To consumers? Who owns these stores?"

"People." Velnikov shrugged. "Companies, individuals, chains, families."

"Uh—not the government?"

"Of course not. The government is a police force and a law court, no more. Pretentious phrase, but 'Governments should be heard and not seen.' "

Jeff stopped. He gazed up at a tall building, then at the passing people—there were no vehicles here at ground level. He saw many Nehru suits, which he assumed were business attire. They embraced a very wide assortment of colors and combinations, all with three-quarter sleeves. Sensible; they stayed out of the way without being turned up. And odd-necked shirts and short skirts and shorts and blouses and tunics; people seemed to wear what they pleased, although there were no long skirts. (Fashion, Jeff assumed; women had not yet conquered Woman.) There were no neckties. And the only hairless faces were the women's: Men were again playing the role of men, with full sexual adornment. He noticed they'd stopped wearing wedding rings, too. They looked happy, and independence radiated. Independence? Paradox?

"Come along," Velnikov urged. "We'll be run over by pedestrians if we stand still. Besides, we have only two hours; this is Tuesday."

"Tuesday?"

"Oh, sorry." Velnikov walked on; Jeff paced him. "It rains on Tuesdays. After lunch. It's a damned nuisance." He sighed, shaking his head. "Last week some idiot started it two minutes early."

A woman dodged violently sidewise to avoid running into a rubbernecking Jeff Bellamy. She gave him a vicious look.

"Careful," Jim Velnikov said. "We don't touch, remember. The reason is behind us, but the custom remains. Besides, she was carrying a MedComp card; that means she's Fulfilled."

"Fulfilled?"

"She's got an OK for inoculation to reverse the contracep shot all females receive at birth. She's probably waited a long time, and now she's going to have her child. She'll receive another shot at delivery, just as her baby will, if it's a girl. Permanent infertility, correctible only by another shot—if and when she Passes."

Jeff nodded. Life insurance rates had been reduced again in '76; greater life expectancy. And the President had ordered them to decrease again in '80. Death was under some control, but birth was not, despite the more and more frequent debates in Washington. Man was growing old, as always, without growing up. Evidently he had. But . . . instituting the program Velnikov mentioned must have been riotous.

"Can you define 'fascism,' Jeff?"

"Mussolini . . . totalitarian . . . not exactly, no. A form of socialism, with one boss."

Velnikov chuckled. "Interesting paradox, isn't it? Contradiction in terms: socialism, with one boss. But fascism is simply defined as privately-owned enterprise with government control."

Jeff nodded. "I see. The stores . . . you're telling me they're privately owned but government-controlled. Well, that's an improvement over communism, anyhow."

Velnikov glanced nervously around. "I forgot—no one can understand you. You could be attacked, talking that way. Fascism is NOT an improvement over communism, although communism is a little more honest and does have the advantage of failing faster. YOUR government was fascist, Jeff: private enterprise with government control. Contradiction in terms." He waved a hand and made a hurried ritual of apology to a passerby. "THIS is capitalism."

"Doct—uh, Jim; look, you're confusing me. You're telling me this country was conquered by Russia and is now capitalist?" He watched the other man nod, his beard wriggling as he smiled. Jeff shook his head in perplexity. "And the government?"

"A democracy, of course. Capitalism *is* democracy, which is not democracy without freedom of trade."

"I think I need to sit down."

"Taxi!"

A light flashed on a nearby tube. A door slid open, revealing a grille. Jeff was reminded of an elevator. Then the grille slid back and he was looking into the small interior of an idling vehicle, tube-shaped. It rested in the larger tube, hissing, without touching any of its curved surface. There was no driver. They climbed in.

Velnikov took a little metallic plate from his breast

pocket—Jeff hadn't known the coat possessed one—
and held it briefly before a yellow light on a panel. The
light went out.

"Atlanta," he said, leaning back. Jeff felt the acceler-
ation (about which Velnikov complained). They sat
side by side, with a shoulder-high barrier between them.
Bisecting the seat, it made the vehicle seem even
smaller. But it created individual compartments. It was
more than just the visual illusion of space these people
wanted, Jeff knew. He wasn't stupid; he should have
realized that what he saw was incompatible with socialism. Everything he saw was just the opposite, even the
no-touching custom. But too much had been thrown at
him too fast, and the shock remained: Russia!

"We've left Lexington."

"Uh—you knew I was coming here—I mean *now*,
Jim. Do I . . . do I return?"

Velnikov nods without looking at him. "Yes."

"No! I won't! Never! Taxes . . . hmp! Oh, you must
know . . . why?"

Velnikov stares straight ahead. "Can't tell you," he
said, and Jeff wondered if he meant "will not."

Jeff noticed his speech was becoming slangier; said
so.

"The translator, Jeff. It's connected to Central Com-
putry, and it absorbs everything you say, analyzes,
stores it, and corrects its banks." He shook his head.
"Pitifully slow! Jeff—you know what a chauvinist is?"

Jeff Bellamy nodded, then said "sure"; Velnikov was
still not looking at him. Soundlessly, the brightly lit
taxicar fled through the transcontinental tube—without
touching it.

"Chauvinism ended in 1986," Velnikov says quietly,
looking straight ahead. "And progress began."

Jeff hardly heard him. The seat was soft and comfortable. But—*Russia!*

2

He was careful, and it took him a month. A month

of furtive researching and tinkering and fine-tuning, when he wasn't meeting with experts from every division of James Velnikov's company to make tapes for them. Total capitalism—tit for tat. They made him wealthy, in 2078. But when he was sure, Jeff Bellamy slipped into the telephone-booth-like cage in which he'd come to this time. He closed the doors. He took a long, deep breath and activated the machine. He had decided on 1887, and he could now control his arrival at precise time and place. And he had a gun.

I'm a fanatic, he thought. A damned fanatical chauvinist, which Jim Velnikov would say is a redundancy. It's all lovely . . . but it's Russian! We'd have reached the dream of Jefferson and Tom Paine without the "help" of Russia, dammit! And . . . this will prove it.

The man from the twentieth century took careful aim with his twenty-first-century rifle at the shouting nineteenth-century revolutionary. His finger moved up to nudge the firing button.

He felt nothing. Heard nothing. But Vladimir Ilyitch Ulyanovasa, alias Nikolai Lenin, shimmered for an instant and then was dust. And the universe was not destroyed. And Jeff sent the timebooth back to 2078.

—and is greeted by a smiling, bearded man in a Nehru suit and high, gleaming boots of smooth leather, or plastic.

"Jefferson Bellamy? Welcome to 2078. I am James von Schlemmer."

Now there, Jeff Bellamy thinks, grinning as he steps forth, *is a good old American name! Give me those German and Irish patronyms every time!* He starts to put out his hand, then halts, letting it drop to his side. Do they touch each other, these good old *Americans* of 2078? He'll not risk embarrassing von Schlemmer— but wait till they learn what the greatest American hero of all time just did! *They'll touch me then,* Jeff Bellamy thinks joyously.

Which is when the door opens and a uniformed man with cropped blond hair and a 1910 moustache stomps in. He clacks his booted heels loudly together and makes a robotically stiff bow to von Schlemmer.

"Herr Doktor-Professor von Schlemmer," he says, and follows it with a string of growly German. Schlemmer replies, "Yes. Now leave us." As Jeff realizes that Schlemmer's translator lets him hear one thing while the soldier hears another, the man snaps "Ja, herr Doktor-Professor!" and clacks his booted heels again, about-faces with robotic precision and stomps out. Schlemmer mutters something. Then he turns to his guest.

"Where . . . where is this?"

"Lexingtucky, American Republic," James von Schlemmer says, and Jeff wonders if the man has a monocle secreted somewhere on his stiffly erect person.

"And the language is—German?"

"Of course. What else? But things are far different from your time, Jefferson Bellamy! When you left— clever of you, Herr Bellamy—America was a conquered nation, yes? And old man Hitler still rode his throne. Times were hard; Americans did not take well to socialism!" He shrugged. "Well. We have much to ask you, to get the precise picture. The *world* did not take to socialism, you see. It always fails. It is but a temporary sort of government, invariably replaced by capitalism, as the leaders must offer the people some inducement to work. We have come to a true democracy, Jeff Bellamy, although it took Hitler to bring it about. Inadvertently—by instituting socialism and showing that it will not work, and by saving America from the fascism that was threatening to engulf her." He smiles, although a little stiffly.

"But come, Jeff Bellamy of 1978! I have much to tell you—we have much to tell each other!"

Jeff shrinks from the extended hand, wondering how Hitler solved the population problem. He dives back into the timebooth.

In a place that is not a place and a time that is not

a time, a confused Jeff Bellamy returns in his mind to his first trip to 2078, to Jim Velnikov's world.

He'd asked if the ride would be paid for. Velnikov shrugged.

"You're going to have to accept the fact that robots are cheap, Jeff, and it costs more in book-keeping to charge for transportation than not. Four corporations just underwrite it. It's deductible."

"That means the government has to get the tax money from individuals. So this is socialized transport!"

Velnikov smiled, rather tightly. "It's still capitalism, Jeff. And good system can adjust. All *must* adjust to a cybernetic technology. We'll have to pay for lunch, though." Velnikov grinned. " 'Free capitalism'—which is redundant. What the socialists-without-knowing-it of your time called 'robber-baron capitalism.' Today it's unrestrained, and wedded with cybernetics. It is world-wide, save in Australia and the People's State of North Africa. They're going through their zoo phase."

"What?" Jeff frowned at him. "Zoo phase?"

"Socialism/communism. Samaritanism: putting someone else's interests on a par with or ahead of your own. In other words, brother's keeper, and keepers are for zoos. I don't know who first coined the phrase."

Jeff laughed loudly. In relief and joy. "You said zoo *phase*. Capitalism is inevitable?"

"If men are to be free, and men seem to prefer freedom. Those two countries will outgrow it, just as we did." Velnikov spread his hands. "We're men—not bees or ants. We're selfish—naturally. It took us long enough to admit it! First, everyone in the world had to try assorted forms of Samaritanism before they reached the inevitable conclusion: Man must be free. That means democratic process. He must be free of his fellow men, and that means Man-ism: Hominism. Man must also strive to further himself, as an individual. As what he is: self-interested man, another redundancy. Hominism again, and free trade."

Jeff was grinning. Broadly. Then he frowned. "But

the reverse of what you call Samaritanism . . . isn't that piracy?"

"Be serious. Forget selfishness and say 'enlightened self-interest,' if you like fancy euphemisms. Unite that with the 'Do unto others' concept and . . . what do you have?"

"Uh, democracy, capitalism, and hominism?"

James Velnikov laughed, looking almost as if he wished to touch the other man. "Of course. That's our biggest asset: deductive reasoning! Man denied it long enough! We staggered around under a load of guilt and self-denial, embarrassed by our own accomplishments. It took an outside force—Communism—to make us see it and throw it off. Man learned to rely on himself and take the credit himself. And the blame."

Success through communism? Jeff was frowning, wondering: Could the past be changed? What if he went back and shot Nikolai Lenin before he got started?

Jeff could not smile. "But Russia conquered America."

"Thereby saving the country. They needed each other in the Food Wars, and together they stopped China. But then America was completely welfare-under-totali-tarianism, and Russia was beginning to move—because it was forced to become more and more capitalistic. When the wars ended, the American economy naturally collapsed. It was destroyed by its government, although the wars had kept it shored up for decades. Russia merely leaned out of the saddle to catch up the reins and started trying to compete with the world's most outstandingly capitalist nation: Japan. Next came the birth situation. Starvation's a little more 'immoral' than controlling population. It was a bad time. But the Chauvy Rebels really did it; they showed everyone how horrible pure chauvinism was."

In a place that is not a place and a time that is not a time, Jeff Bellamy nodded. He was proud—had been then—that his country had reached what he now thought of as Velnikov's world. But . . . Russia!

So he had gone back and killed Lenin before he became Lenin, in an effort to prove that America could reach Jim's world without the distasteful help of Communist Russia. But Russia trembling under a Tsar was totally different from the Russia united under that bright initial glow of communism. Hitler gained them as an ally and won War Two.

My country came out essentially the same, Jeff thought. *But now—'now'—it's Germans. Worse!*

He had to try and undo what he had created by killing Lenin. Now there seemed only one way, and with the awful rifle of Velnikov's world (had the rifle been invented, in Schlemmer's world? Of course; Jeff had it!). He made the trip. Nudged up the rifle's firing stud. Watched as the young Adolph Schickelgruber shimmered for an instant and then was dust. Hitler was gone before his first *putsch.* And the universe was not destroyed. And Jeff Bellamy, with a sigh of relief and satisfied accomplishment, returned to 2078.

3

The two black-uniformed men seize him the moment he opens the timebooth's hatch. They hustle him a few steps to a chair beside a desk that very much resembles James Velnikov's desk. And the letters on the books and on the door are Kyrillic. But the man is not Velnikov. The insignia on the drapery behind him is a strange one: a pair of vicious-looking eagles, back to back. Or perhaps it is one eagle with two opposite-facing heads, like the Roman Janus.

"You are Jefferson Bellamy, come here from 1978?"

"Yes!" And, he thinks, *they have the translator. But . . . well, the eagle has always represented America. . . .*

"I am Andrei Velnikov, Major, His Imperial Majesty's Intelligence. You were wanted in 1978, Jeff Bellamy. You cannot escape one hundred years into the future! We know all about your stealing from His government its greatest invention." He points a gold-braided arm dramatically. "That timebooth. You left a record,

you see: the setting was for 2078. We have been waiting. Unfortunately, history cannot be changed, Jefferson
Bellamy, so that we cannot send you back. But justice
will be served, even though it is a hundred years late!"
His eyes snap past Jeff's head.

"Take him away. Only the Imperial historians are
to be allowed access to him, and only with a pass from
me. Is that understood?"

The translator's power does not extend to the two
soldiers, but the "Da!" is not difficult for Jeff to understand. He is dragged to his feet and hurried from the
room.

As they hustle him along a dark, windowless corridor, the stone walls ringing with the sound of their
boots, Jeff twists his head. "I'll walk! You can stop
trying to crush my arms!"

One of them snaps something he does not understand
before they shove him into a small cell and demonstrate
the force-field across the doorway. Then they step out,
and Jeff collapses onto the bunk—it is made of plass
—and thrusts his face into the security of his cupped
hands.

He knows what he has done even before the berobed
—and bewigged—historian comes in with a recorder
and a guard with a face like a slab of smokehouse pork.
But Jeff asks anyhow.

"Who heads the government?"

"His Imperial Majesty Aleksander VII, by the grace
of god Tsar of Russia and all the world!"

And Jeff is slapped for failure to show proper respect
for Baron Alexei Grigorivitch Mosshechkov, Chief Historian by appointment of His Imperial Majesty.

After two months the kindly Stiva Goremykin, Third
Psychohistorian, succeeded in getting the valuable State
Prisoner One removed from the dark little cell and installed in a two-room suite adjacent to the History Center. He iterated and reiterated the man's story of having
"created" this world by assassinating a German leader

who would have duped Tsar Aleksander IV and conquered the world. It was reported that His Imperial Majesty grew fulminous of mien when he heard the word "assassinated." He became enraged at the suggestion that his illustrious ancestor, he who had conquered the perfidious Germans in 1947, could have been taken in by any Deutschlander. When the dead German's identity as an ignoble paper-hanger was revealed, Aleksander the Seventh rose, folded his sussurant robes around himself, and stepped without a word through the draperies behind his throne. Stepan Goremykin returned to Jeff Bellamy, downcast and dolorous.

"I was just able to prevent your being returned to your cell," he reported. "You've sealed your fate, my friend. Aleksander is convinced you are of no value, since you tell lies—treasonous lies. You will be tried: You will go into court and hear charges and sentence read out without pause for breath. Then it is a question only of whether you will be executed or imprisoned for life."

Staring at the floor, Jeff Bellamy nodded.

"You have an appointment with Colonel Velnikov on Tuesday next."

"It always rains on Tuesday," Jeff said. "After lunch," he added morosely, and, "in Camelot." He raised his head to turn dead eyes on the shortish, full-bearded psychohistorian. "*Colonel* Velnikov? He introduced himself as a major, Stiva."

Stiva nodded. "I need not tell you for what glorious service he was promoted and given lands in Wales," he said.

"No. What does that misplaced Gestapo bastard want to talk with me about?"

"Remind me to ask meanings of 'Gestapo' and 'Camelot,'" Stiva advised his recorder. The quiet little man nodded and made a note. "He wishes to discuss the machine with you, the one in which you came. We cannot explain it. How was it invented? You have spoken of other things we have not yet discovered. But how were the people of a hundred years ago able to develop a time-traveling device?"

"It had to be invented, Stiva. After all, I was in it, and I left from 2078 to go back and create *this* 2078, all by killing that slimy little psychopath. It had to be invented." *After all, as you idiots keep telling me, history can't be changed!*

Stepan Goremykin gazed at him, frowning. "I am forced to believe you, Jeff. But—my telling it to His I. M. merely imperiled us both. We have extended life-expectancy to eighty years, but I would not wager much that ours—yours and mine—is anything approaching that."

Lifting his head slowly, Jeff stared at him.

"What's your life expectancy, Jim?" he had asked another man named Velnikov, seated beside him in a tube within a tube, hurtling across the country at a speed far greater than the Tsar's world had achieved.

"One-o-six," Jim Velnikov had answered. "Not enough, after 30 years in school. We have some diseases you never heard of, Jeff. They keep popping up. By-products of civilization—and medical science ,of course. We haven't been able to stop cell degeneration totally, either." He shook his head. "And thermostats go on the hip. Two centuries won't be enough either, when we achieve it. And then we'll have to go even further on population control. We have to find a better fuel-system; gravity still remains unconquered. Property's too high. We haven't got to the stars. Kids are still brats, and in the really big cities, worse. And naturally we do have genuine robber-barons—like Morgan and Rockefeller. No system is perfect, or we haven't found it yet. We're trying."

"I thought Rockefeller was a good guy. Dimes to kids and all that."

"Press-agentry. Study further. He was a real rough-shodder. His descendants were liberal types, philanthropists, public servants: guilt-feelings, of course. Last year a senator talked for two hours, demanding a law

to control 'certain crass roughshodders,' etcetera. He
was aiming at one man, and everyone knew it: Josephson Varenukha, of Varenukha Tool Company. A man
with no morals."

"Did he get the law?"

"He got retired. The senator's constituents held a by-
election within three weeks. He's back where he belongs, running his plankton ranch and relearning what
he forgot about free enterprise during twenty years in
Washington."

Jeff was smiling. "I like that! How about Josephson
whatsisname?"

"A jury of his peers got him—businessmen, in the
marketplace. In eleven days he went from three billions
and thirty-one companies to three millions and two
companies. That is justice—not jail or a fine to enrich
a welfare government."

"But that's only a slap with a velvet glove!"

Jim Velnikov crossed a leg—carefully, not touching
his companion—and smiled. "Not to a Josephson
Varenukha, it isn't. Besides, geniuses shouldn't be destroyed. It's just that when their genius puts them so
far ahead that they start stepping on hands and heads,
it's time to remind 'em of what free trade is. And that
job is up to competitors, peers—not a blackmailer hiding behind the phrase 'federal government.' " He
chuckled. "He'll be back, and it will be harder to teach
him next time if he hasn't learned his lesson. You have
his kind in any society."

*But despite all that, Jeff had set out on his chauvin-
istic course of action.*

*He had killed Lenin, the results of which had forced
him to kill Hitler, the results of which made him a prisoner of an America dominated by a Russian feudalism
far behind James Velnikov's—Camelot. Russian or not,
it was apparently the best of all worlds, and Jeff wanted
now only one more change. It was a good world, and it
was his country, right or wrong.*

It was not too difficult, really. The guards wore side-arms in flapped holsters. They stood by the door, flaps buttoned. Colonel Andrei Valnikov stood beside his desk, posing beneath the Imperial two-headed eagle. The two scientists and the recorder kept a respectful distance; they could not go closer to the timebooth than Colonel-Baron Velnikov. They were filming, while the recorder took down Jeff's every word. He gave them plenty: mostly gabble. Talking, expounding donnishly, he paced for five minutes or so, waving his hands. Then, when he'd got himself close enough to the smugfaced Velnikov, he gave the twenty-first-century Intelligence colonel a mouthful of knuckles and kept on spinning with the movement. Three fast steps. He jerked the hatch behind him, dogging it with one hand while he reached for the timebooth's controls with the other. They couldn't kill him; he'd created their miserable world!

And he'd damnwell uncreate it. Nine weeks in their captivity had given him an abundance of time for thinking. He made the setting and pushed home the starter control. He glanced at the door. Some idiot was banging on it with a big gloved fist.

The banging stops. The room with the double-edged standard and the bloody-lipped colonel and the Imperial Hussars is somewhen else; 2078 will be somewhen else. He is out of time again, and he sets to work quickly, making the careful settings. He remembers the old ones, and this time he makes a one-minute adjustment. Just that: one minute. He draws a deep breath and pushes the starter. Then he pulls loose the plate he had unscrewed and replaced on his last timetrip. Yes; the gun from Velnikov's world—JAMES Velnikov's world—is still there. He draws it out and checks it.

There is probably another way. Probably some means of eliminating the problems and the opposition so that America, right or wrong, will arrive at the world of that first arrival, without its being Velnikov's world rather than . . . Smith's . . . or Bellamy's. There is probably another way, Jeff Bellamy thinks, whipping backward through years and decades. But he is through trying to find it. Velnikov's world is good enough. Perfect, save for the means of its coming about. The solution to correct the monstrous variations he wrought —will wreak?—seems simple enough. Strange, he thinks, and no doubt distasteful. But—the one sure way. And he is running scared now. Another change might result in a Chinese America of 2078, or a Johnsonian one, or . . . the destruction of the universe.

Everything must be returned to the way it was before he left Jim Velnikov's world that first time.

1887. December 17. The University of Kazan. The law school. The student demonstration. Yes, there was young Ulyanovasa-Lenin, haranguing and waving his arms. Jeff waited, his eyes snapping about for the first sign, the first flicker. He is across the compound from where he had rested briefly on his previous visit to this time and this place. He is waiting for his own arrival, unnoticed by the wide-eyed students whose rapt attention is on their wild-eyed leader.

You're a good guy after all, Nikolai Lenin. Your way was the only way to destroy Tsarism, apparently. Without you, Hitler conquered. Without Hitler, the Tsars did, and remained in the past of feudal absolutism. It's up to you to rescue the Russian peasant from the Tsars. Up to your successors—the murdering Stalin and Khrushchev and then Kosygin and Andropov and whoever came/comes next—to rescue America from fascism and dictatorship and revolution.

And up to me to save you. From me.

He stiffened, then breathed deeply, to relax. There it was. A flicker in the air. Then the steel telephone booth, a shimmery thing. He watched the hatch open. Saw himself—himself as he appeared in photographs, not in the mirror—glance around, then spot Lenin and lift the rifle.

Carefully Jeff Bellamy raised the rifle and sighted on Jeff Bellamy, who was raising a rifle. Carefully he held his breath and made certain his sighting would be perfect. Then his finger moved upward. The knuckle pushed the small round button. It depressed. Across the compound, his target, the Jeff Bellamy who was just sighting on young Lenin, shimmered for a moment and was dust.

Well, so much for the time-paradox he feared; he'd just killed himself, and he and the universe are still here. He sighs. Moves again through time. Sights Jeff Bellamy about to kill Adolph Hitler, ne Shickelgruber. And again Jeff kills Jeff, and the universe is not destroyed. And he returns/returned/will return to 2078. It's a good world, he thinks. Better than 1978, with all those damned taxes and welfare and fascism and Vietnam and—

But it isn't there. That is, James Velnikov isn't there; 2078 is, of course. First Jeff falls into the hands of the Consies, who control most of the South and East as far north as old Ohio and Virginia. After three days he escaped. Two days later he was in the hands of the Libs, in control of the thirteen states *they* call America. This time it will take him a week to escape, wondering what happened; some catalytic action that resulted in the unity of Velnikov's world is missing. He returns to his haven/womb, and after much thinking he sets the dials. And he went home.

He will stop it. He will fight. Through him, through the nationalism he will instill in his countrymen, America will wake up. One man has changed the history of the world before, he muses, lips and jaws clamped tight. *I will.*

There will still be a Camelot in 2080, but it won't be Velnikov's world. It will be Bellamy's world, he thinks, stepping out of the time machine in 1978. The clock on the wall advises that four minutes have elapsed since he departed for Velnikov's world, so long ago. To learn his destiny. Now he strode into the night to fulfill that destiny.

He did.

He had two years before the Russian takeover, and

then five more years of underground action.

Jeff Bellamy became the worst terrorist since Jenghis Khan. And Velnikov's world came about because of the unified reaction to the horror of the Chauvy Rebels of the 1980's. The Chauvy Rebels led by Maddog Bellamy, hanged in 1986.

Such was his destiny. It is a good future—the best—and it is his country, after all, right or wrong.

We were talking about blurb-writing, remember?

Here's another example: "This story is so God-awful good, it'll make your teeth ache."

Which still tells you absolutely nothing about the writer or the story. If the story is that God-awful good, you'll find it out for yourself when you read it. And if, God forbid, it isn't that good—well, then you'll know the editor for the liar he is.

But with a story like this one it's awfully hard not to write: "This story is so God-awful good, etc." Precisely because this story is that good.

At which point, the really slippery blurb-writer slips into instant analysis (in a weasely effort to prove himself at least the equal of the writer). Witness: "Pg Wyal has combined the unlikely elements of 1956 B-picture (The Amazing Colossal Man), scream-of-consciousness new-wave multi-adjectived sado-masochistic descriptive techniques, and heavy-handed political satire to produce the 1970 model Kong—the psychological fairy tale that pegs our society for where it is and for what it's at. His savage juxtaposition of the black colossus and the spider thing atop the Los Angeles City Hall succeeds where similar (Godzilla vs. Mothra) attempts at massive involvement into radical attitudes fail. . . ."

You get the idea. After reading the blurb, why read the story?

Back to lesson one: introduce the writer and interest the reader in the story.

The writer: Pg Wyal. (Followed by big blank.) Where to begin?

Do I dare call him mad?

Letters from Wyal are oft cryptic, containing only the semblance of sense. Badly typed, they are covered with illegible scribblings that seem to hint at genius but more often (upon examination) reveal only the deranged ravings of a depraved mind. Pg Wyal is a product of the times—a child of tomorrow, thoroughly disgusted by the behavioral sink of New York, yet unable to tear himself away from its sweat-stained shoving masses and fallout-covered elite. If Pg Wyal were to cut off his left ear and send it to me, I would be shocked only by the unimaginativeness of the effort.

Does that interest you in this writer?

It should. Especially because all of it is true.

Yet the above kind of hyper-cute analysis can be just as big a cheat as the earlier examples given on how not to write a blurb.

For one thing, it implies that I have Wyal pegged, right down to the last buttonhole. (And I don't. Hell, I don't even understand him most of the time.) For another, it implies that I am so perceptive a person and so effective a writer that I can reduce the sum total of this human being to a few choice images. (I can't. I don't think anybody can.)

I know Pg Wyal from his correspondence and from one in-person meeting. I know two different Pg Wyals. The in-print Wyal is vastly different from the in-person Wyal.

From his letters one would expect him to be a raving maniac. When I arrived at the offices of Crawdaddy (the Rock Magazine) one foul New York November afternoon, I expected to find him swinging one-armed from a trapeze mounted above the fortieth floor, from which he would hurl firebombs and confetti down upon the unsuspecting passersby. That's what I expected.

What I found was a quiet-voiced (dare I say "sensitive-looking"?) thoughtful individual who displayed no sign whatever of incipient insanity. He submitted that he wasn't (yet) the writer he'd like to be. He admitted to not having the discipline that the rest of us full-time writers brag about. Worst of all (or maybe best), he admitted that he hates to rewrite and avoids it with an almost religious passion.

I wasn't surprised at the latter. I already knew that Jerry wasn't a rewrite man. If you're going to get a good story out of Wyal, it's going to be first draft—or as close to that as possible.

Where I might rework a tale five, six, a dozen times, Pg does it twice. Period. End of sentence, paragraph and story.

Fortunately, and to my great and ill-concealed delight, much of what he writes that way is pure trash and utterly unsaleable. (Otherwise he would be a menace to lesser talents everywhere.) Unfortunately, every so often he pulls off something like "Side Effect" and leaves me chewing the ceiling, wondering how he did it.

I consider myself a lucky editor to get this story. In my opinion, it's one of the best in the book. It's certainly one of the best written. But that's only my opinion.

I'll get out of your way now.

SIDE EFFECT
(the monster that devoured Los Angeles)

Pg Wyal

No more a child:
Suddenly he realized he had stopped growing. After a lifetime of change—the cells exploding, bones stretching and twisting, balance and poise rocking back and forth on a fulcrum of time—he felt an ineluctable command in his body: stop!

He was complete.

It came as a tangible shock. One night, wallowing in the timeless reality of dream, his sleep was shattered and he jerked up in the unfocused dark with eyebrows knotted at the foreign perception. It was as if a cup had been clamped over a geyser, a physical command against the pressure to shoot upward. All freedom was lost. Both body and brain became strangely slow, dull. Lethargy laid down the law.

Adulthood.

Art ran bony fingers through thinning brown hair. He set the cup down hard on the saucer; coffee slopped over the rim of the cup. He didn't notice. Pushing the cup and saucer out of the way, Art spread the paper out flat on the breakfast table and surveyed it methodically, like a coroner with a good corpse.

CARDIAC CURE SEEN AS LONGEVITY A-GENT! The headline was in 72-point caps, as big as the *Times* had ever used. Idly, Art thought how *The*

News would have phrased it: FOUNTAIN OF YOUTH!!! But *The News* was always in bad taste. Lower class, he sniffed.

He scanned the article in increasing excitement: Below the big caps were smaller capital italics, reading: *ARTERIOSCLEROSIS SERUM EXTENDS HUMAN LIFESPAN INDEFINITELY.*

And then:

Physiologists at the Harvard College of Medicine have announced a general cure for the primary cause of heart disease. The doctors added that this cure for arteriosclerosis, or "hardening of the arteries," also appears to extend drastically—perhaps indefinitely—the normal lifespan. Dr. S. P. Thimbylquyst, spokesman for the University, stated in an exclusive *Times* interview that rats to whom the serum was administered enjoyed complete rejuvenation and were apparently immortalized. The rats that received the serum were all two years old or more—equivalent to a human age of ninety. All the rats used in Dr. Thimbylquyst's experiments survived, and ninety percent were rejuvenated. The rats were destroyed when the experiments were completed because, as Doctor Thimbylquyst explained, "We wouldn't want a race of immortal rats running around." Authorities at the University were reluctant to speculate as to the possible introduction of the treatment into general medical practice. However, Dr. A. P. Feinschmaltz hinted that this might occur much sooner than one would expect. "The experiments were at a very advanced stage when we announced them," he explained, "and FDA certification might come at any time." He refused to elaborate.

According to Dr. Thimbylquyst, Emeritus Professor of mammalian physiology, the "youth-serum" effect is due to the cleansing effect of 3-5-7-11-13-17 Lipidocreatinalymasimperatinose-III on the capillaries, those trillions of tiny blood cells that feed oxygen and nutrients directly into the cells. As Dr.

Thimbylquyst explained, the capillaries become coated and clogged with fatty deposits. 3-5-7-11-13-17 Lipidocreatinalymasimperatinose-III, a complex enzyme, oxidizes these deposits away, to be filtered out by the kidneys and subsequently passed out of the body in the urine. These deposits ordinarily tend to reduce, then completely throttle, normal capillary permeability. (Permeability is the ability of a membrane or tissue to allow diffusion of molecules from one fluid to another. Membranes may be *semi*-permeable, selectively passing and filtering chemicals in solution.) As one ages, Dr. Thimbylquyst added, the capillaries' permeability gradually diminishes, owing to the accumulating arteriosclerotic deposits, eventually causing cellular starvation and the death of entire tissues. When cells cannot adequately replenish their nutrients and oxygen needs, or flush out their own wastes, they strangle and starve, just as the entire body can die from lack of food or oxygen or the yellow ravages of uremia. Dr. Thimbylquyst found this gradual occlusion of the capillaries to be the major cause of aging in mammals. He continued to explain eatoinshrdlueatoin—

Art tried to find the rest of the article, but the newspaper's printer had chopped it off in the middle of its most interesting sentence. Thankful that nothing had been printed in Chinese at least, Art Noone folded the paper, pushed away from the table, and made breathless haste toward the wall phone. He approached the instrument with some of the same breathless urgency normally lavished on the BMT to Manhattan. With hands atremble and mind askew, he dialed his private physician, a kindly man who kept up on the latest developments and never missed a bet to try something new and interesting. Anything, Art mumbled with what desperation his starved neurons were capable of, to scramble the routine. Dying is the most tedious routine.

". . . As a matter of fact," said the nasal telephone voice of Mort Blaum, M.D., routinely, "I know somebody who knows somebody, and if you're game, I'm game. . . ."

"Game" is something you hunt.

A little prick in the arm—a tiny scratch and a chemical squirt. Then the stink of alcohol to wash off the pain, and he forgot about it. Dr. Blaum made a tiny mark on a big chart, and held high hopes. The nurse wiggled her arse and smiled smugly, the syringe in her white, soft hand dripping with traces of Art's gore. Art didn't worry about the pain; he patted his little paunch and strode out the door into bright sunlight and happy throngs (happy except for the junkies, bums and winos, and who notices them?). He whistled down the subway stairs, into the train, and out to Maimonides Avenue.

Gee, thought Art, it will really be nice to live forever. The slop in his veins began to dissolve from sagging vericose blood-vessels and flow into his kidneys. Gee, thought Art, won't it be nice to live to be a thousand? His cells began to absorb increased amounts of sugar, protein, essences of biochemistry. Gee, babbled Art Noone in the first sexual flush of a new adolescence, I wonder what Mars is like? He opened his front door; cells began splitting where fission had long ago fused. Gee, plopping down in his sofa with his shoes off and his spirits lofty, I wonder if I should get married? Or quit my lousy job with Shitz, O'Brien, Blab and Schlong? A million opportunities, hundreds of unlimited dreams, unfolded like pale orchids in his mind. Presently his dreams melted into sleep.

With the passage of weeks (weeks which seemed to grow longer, as if his appreciation of time had deepened), Art Noone lost weight, gained confidence, sold his house, let his hair grow long and tangled, quit his pointless job as a law clerk, and began to glisten with youth and health. At thirty-five, Art Noone looked, felt, and physiologically *was* like a man of eighteen. Baby of face, hero of loins, monster of appetites, glutton of experience—Art was a renewed soul. His stilted life, the dull daily snail's-furrow between dull house, dull office, dull TV set and dull sleep had been smashed, as if someone had tromped on the snail. He dug it.

"Dr. Blaum," he yelled excitedly (lately he was always excited) into the receiver, "I'm sorry, but I'm going to leave New York."

At the other end of the line there was a choked gasp. "But—what about the Experiment? What about all I've done for you, Art? You can't just pull up your roots and sail away like this! What a dandelion you are. A man of your age—"

"I dig you, but I don't dig you. I mean, I know what you mean, and I know what a crock of shit the thing is that you mean. Dig you later!"

Click.

Art, full of enthusiasm, hitchhiked to California: Long, tedious days of thumbing through Jersey, Pennsylvania, the long road through Ohio, Illinois, and Missouri. In Missouri he caught a ride on a truck, shot straight down the barrel of Route 66 (less glamorous than on TV) through the Missouri hills, out to the endless flat ocean-bed of Kansas (just a little tip of Kansas, but quite enough—it all looks the same); brown dead corner of Nebraska; Oklahoma nowhere with adobe hovels sitting in the stark Indian gasoline-pump redblown mesa, weird and alien, fascinating if you don't look too long and turn petrified gray from sagebrush sterility monotonous boredom (but food is cheap); down across the seemingly unfathomed depths of ho-hum Texas, the most sparklingly dull people in captivity—see the live puff-adder two bits, panhandle misery—throwing up in Amarillo (gravel gutter, bright gray pebbles, and the natives saying drawlwise, Yep, another hippy); losing the truckdriver to a series of bewitching neon bars—TEXAS LIL'S CREMATORIUM SPECIAL—he puked in Art's lap and said Sorry there; and thumb stuck in the dry plains breeze for five-

and-a-half hours—cars full of blond crewcut kids all
looking at you like you were a green vampire (blood—
you get thirsty and the dust is in your throat like rusty
Mexican plumbing with dysentery), don't pick up the
hitchhikers, they screw dogs or something and they'll
rob you of virtue and leave you full of sin—and finally
getting a lift from this hillbilly, he's going to the Golden
State, he's heard they got places there where the streets
really are paved with gold, Art wonders if they are
(they said so in Bronx), and this cat drives his 1931
Essex (they're both left over from the Depression—
derelict dreams, this dry teardrop keeps talking about
Roosevelt), it's a Mig 21 with bad suspension, no license—would you drive a spell?—oh, sure, be glad to
—sirens in the fading afternoon—the cop says you're
lucky the judge ain't in today, you can just pay me the
fine that'll be fifty dollars thankyou *sir* . . . and you
careen (what's that clanking noise? just where the
driveshaft come loose, nothin' t'worry about son) like
late for Hell through New Mexico, throw up from the
altitude in Albuquerque (*look* at that pig, Martha!),
throw up from the altitude again in Flagstaff (map
says we mus' be gettin' close), throw up just for
kicks in navigating thrilling curve on the long golden
stairway down the killer Sierras, rattle coughing and
vomiting blood into holy asshole Nevada stateline,
caught in the groin by the worst duststorm outside
Syrtis, Las Vegas 22 miles—hold on son, let's take a
ding at this, and what the hell—stranded geometrically
in nowhere, your feet beginning to smoulder from the
pavement, and along drives this chick in a brand new
Buick-8—would you like a lift? O, yesmam—and
climbing in spot a corpse in the back seat—oh! it's not
a corpse! it's her husband, who sees your hand slid-
ing protectively into her nymphomania, sorry buddy,
ride's over . . . and awaking to a sudden dawn of
sirens, you find your wristwatch—the one gramma
schwartz gave you for your twelfth birthday—has somehow vanished from your wrist, and half-unconscious

voices whisper that something has gone wrong with time, maybe Las Vegas wasn't such a bad idea? but that's urine under the bush, because here comes a businessman in a new Olds—he says, How are you fixed for blades? and you say What? and he says, Spades! (some esoteric meaning there), and you say How? and he says super-stainless double-pole double-throw or single-shot injector? and you still don't get it, and say Don't dig you, and he fatherly puts his arm over your shoulder asking fondly, Are you glad? and 42nd street is everywhere—this is not new, you say wearily, I'm alright—and he kisses you so gently and bites your little pink earlobe, and the message finally penetrates and you puke on his saber, which he scabbords immediately (he has no scars), and not even slowing down he pushes you out of the car (an eight-cylinder swish of potency), and landing disgruntled with the whole idea on glitering desert-shining rock you state screams, & logic of pain declaim, when a nice policeman comes up and puts you in splints saying the lulling curses of Law, and welcome to California. And it doesn't rain, really.

The bones knitted nicely, and fast, to the amazement of everybody in Cunnilingus Pass Hospital. He tried to explain his age to nurses (young man), doctors (son), orderlies (kid) who wiped his bottom, but none would heed. Alas, he'd burned his draft card at a Unitarian Church sit-in. According to California Law, a minor under 21 who defenestrates himself from the warm crotch of Security must serve not less than ninety or more than 364 days in an appropriate penal institution. "Teaches 'em a lesson"—and it *does*, too.

Suspect Arthur Noone (no identification), Age: 18 (?). Height: 6′1″. Weight: 180 lbs—

"Whoa, there!" cried the suspect, confused. "I'm only 5′11″, 35 years of age, and I don't weigh any 180 lbs. I'm the original 145 pound spaz, and don't hassle me about it!"

They hassled him into Chino, a nice boy's resort in the Cuyomacas. Most unlike catskill Jew tennis courts. At Chino Rehabilitation Center for Wayward Kiddies, Art learned how to hoe weeds, pick fruit, grovel for potatoes, hunker for the guards' kicks, build a wood Rehabilitation Rack out of fine mahogany, file a steel spoon into a beautifully crafted knifeblade, kick those smaller and be kicked by those larger (a pecking-order function manifest in Brooklyn only by baseball game attendees), bludgeon a guard so it didn't show, slash a prisoner so it did, and finally how to use a file at three A.M. to abrade away one's ball and chain, leaping thence two stories bunkerwise to freedom—and the open highway.

At dawn, five miles down the road at a rest-point carved bloody out of the mountainside's living flanks, Art got a ride from a sharp-looking kid in a Mustang, a car aerodynamically, mechanically, and sexually unsound. The Mustang had rotten suspension, the rear end kept trying to lurch into space whenever the car cornered (5,000 feet to freedom), and the kid didn't know fecalwise about driving shoddy detroit metal. At fifty mph, Art drew a finely-crafted spoon *cum* shiv on the Pepsi Kid and put it to him: "Slow down and fly right, or I'll gut you like a sturgeon in lake Titti-Ha-Nitti-gritti!"

The youth complied with enthusiastic alacrity, though the geographical simile was obscure. Donated later a full complement of colorful, ill-fitting rags to our hero, who in bad grace neglected to thank him a whit. Los Angeles came looming like San Bernardino out of the white perpetual fog, and trembling youth and rattling steed were deserted in favor of a telephone booth. Ah, San Gabriel, thy natives bask in the sun, yet hide in their stucco caves like so many guilty troglodytes; when they must speak, it is through the safe, vicarious anonymity of the telephone. Let us see Art drop dime, lift receiver, and speak across the miles and months:

"Hello—Doc Blaum? No this isn't a house call, it

ain't any advice for two bucks, and it ain't for kicks. This is Art——*Noone!* Stupid schlemiel doctor doesn't think of his patients, just his overstuffed wallet. Look ——I'm in California——fergodsakes, don't ask how I got here or what took so long, I ain't got time. I need dough, dig? Our experiment is hungry—and look, the *law* is looking for a guy of approximately my description—only, dig, it ain't the same description I had when I left Brooklyn——I *know* you know that, goddammit, just lemme finish, willya? Look, I got sucked up by the fuzz in Cunnilingus City——for hitchhiking without a license, if you wanna know. And they patched me up——I was a little banged up when this queer pushed me outta his car—and when they weighed and measured me they found out . . . well, I'd *gained* a little.——Yeah, I know you said to expect it—only I've *grown!* I'm six-one.——Yeah, yeah, I know all about that.——And that too. But screw *that,* because it just ain't so. I am now two inches taller than I was three months ago and I've got a funny suntan—and I wanna know why. So wire some bread to the San Gabriel American Express, and I'll get an apartment and fix you up with my number.——A lotta bread; this place takes *wheels,* since there ain't any train.—— Yeah, I think it's a drag too."

Click.

Half an hour later, Art Noone clenched twenty hundred-dollar travellers cheques in his hand (a nice muscular hand, profoundly brown from sun of California labor camp), and a map of the land's lay snuggled in his hip pocket. The Californians, a race of blond, tan supermen, tolerant of everything but the unfamiliar, directed Art to one of millions of stucco prefab courtyard apartments that dotted the basin like dixie-cups on a drive-in parking lot. For ninety dollars, Art received a brand new apartment in a brand new building; the walls were spidered with hundreds of tiny cracks, and a few really profound fissures and crevasses where seams had been scotch-taped together. The apartment house, like everything else in California, was settling quickly into the ground. In three or four months it would collapse into fine powder and be replaced by another, exactly similar. "Progress," the natives called it. "Planned obsolescence," scoffed critics—who, naturally, were not indigenous to God's Sunny Paradise.

"This is Art Noone again," said Art over the telephone. "I got me a little California trap, and I'm waiting for the jaws to snap. Any instructions?"

Dr. Blaum was cautious, medical. "First go get a complete physical—weight, height, blood pressure, heart-rate, urinalysis, crapometry—"

"—I dig, I dig. Enough technical junk; I can let the local doc worry about that. Any suggestions about the Man?"

"Try Feldman Steinbartz. He runs a chiropractic/obstetrical clinic in Glendale—across the street from the Ultimate Galaxy Shopping Center, Inc. Tell him Mort sent you—meanwhile I'll give him a buzz, filling him in on the details."

Art hung up the phone and bounced out into the smog-glazed sunlight. At first, he tried to hail a taxi— but after the tenth yellow Chevvy tried to run him down, he gave up. Apparently taxies were verboten, a foreign locust not to be plagued. He tried to buttonhole a passerby:

"Pardon me, but is there a bus to Glendale?"

A fat woman wearing a GREASY RONNIE FOR PRESIDENT button looked him over from head to heel. "What kind of filthy question is that?"

"Huh? I just asked—"

"Do you believe in Free Enterprise?"

"Huh?"

"Don't you know busses are *socialism?* Don't you know that public transportation is one of Karl Marx's most nefarious methods of infiltrating and subverting our Democratic Way of Life? Don't you know that busses can lead to communism?" She shook a white-gloved finger at him. "Many's the time our Mayor Sam

has warned us against these radical proposals to social-
ize transportation! Look around you—all you see is the
product of Free Enterprise! Would you demolish all
that for—*busses?!* Filthy beatnik kook! Rapscallion!
Hoodlum!" She spat eloquently upon the ground and
waddled away, her fat buttocks waggling like haughty
laundry bags.

Art, defeated, crossed the boulevard to a used-car
lot, which filled the area under a 600 foot geodesic
dome. The proprieter and his salesmen were doing a
TV commercial. . . .

The Star was a fat man with a nasal country accent.
He ejaculated "dang" with hypnotic frequency, punctu-
ating his enticements by slapping larded hands on polished fenders. His foot thumped tires with the predicta-
bility of a metronome.

". . . And now back to *Riders of the Flaming Cross*,"
the hawker said with a flourish. The TV lens went
blind.

"Pardon me," said Art, "but I need a good used car."

"How much bread?" the dealer oozed.

"Oh, a grand or two," Art replied.

The dealer whistled, a loud Arkansas shriek. "Roy,
get him the Olds—the one we got from the Police Department—not that one idiot! Yeah— the reconditioned
job." A slight trail of saliva began to dribble down his
puffy sunburnt chin.

Roy drove up the Olds. "How's this baby?" demanded the dealer.

"Well, I don't know—"

"Why not go for a little test drive?"

"Okay, but—"

Varrooom.

"Just listen to that engine. What a beauty."

Cough, sputter, clank, fart, thud.

"I guess I gave her a little too much throttle," the
dealer said. "Now just get in—say, you're a big guy
too! Need a big car. Now this baby, this little diamond,
this perfect rosebud of fine engineering—hey! *Hey!*

Come back with that thing you lousy foreigner! Hey!
. . ." The unctuous voice drained into the high background decibels of traffic noise.

Art hurtled down the boulevard, knotted himself into
a cloverleaf, and zoomed away on the freeway. GLEN-
DALE—NEXT TURNOFF beaconed a sign. Braking furiously, Art decelerated from seventy miles an
hour to thirty and successfully negotiated the narrow
exit channel. When he'd slowed down enough to shake
the freeway blur from his eyes, he saw a huge sign
stretching across the four-lane sidestreet: ULTIMATE
GALAXY SHOPPING CENTER, INC.—OPEN TILL
NINE PM EVERY NIGHT—PARKING SPACE
FOR 700,000 CARS, BUT NEW SPACE IS UNDER
CONSTRUCTION. The shopping center, a chrome,
glass and plastic behemoth of eyestrain, loomed to the
right, erupting and devouring huge hordes of brightly
dressed Californians. To the left, sedate and pompous,
modestly sporting a sign no more than three blocks in
length, was a structure whiter than Mayor Sam, and,
shadow-wise, twice as long: B'NAI B'RITH CENTER
FOR CLINICAL STUDIES, INC. Art pulled in.

The receptionist made him exhibit his circumcision
scar before he was allowed to see Dr. Steinbartz. "Just
a security measure," she explained in a plastic-smooth
voice. "We don't want Outsiders getting inside." She
smiled big regular teeth. "They might steal some of the
secrets."

Down a thousand antiseptic corridors, Dr. Steinbartz sat at his lavish ironwood desk, whose rich surface was marred by a single tiny square of paper. "Tell
me, boy, have you ever contracted any, ah, social
disease?"

"No, sir."

"Ahem."

"Beg pardon?"

"Hem." The doctor fiddled with the lonely piece of
paper. "This is an unusual problem. Your tests have
shown that you are six feet three inches tall, weigh 185

pounds, and have absolutely astounding stamina, strength, and vitality. You have a beautiful body . . . beautiful." Big hungry Jew eyes. "Furthermore, you are not even a native of Los Angeles—which fact suggests, in conjunction with your abnormal physical condition, nothing short of a superman—a true superman." He shook his head. "I can't make anything of it. You have no abnormal hormonal tendencies—no genetic diseases, no traces of disease of any sort. And you display all the physical signs of a man of eighteen—a person at his very peak of intelligence and vigor—even though your records, your personal physician, claim your actual age as thirty-five. Incredible." He looked up at Noone. "Do you feel any sort of physical distress, discomfort?"

Art shook his head. "I feel just great—I haven't felt like this since I was six years old. I sleep like an infant, wake up feeling totally alive and alert; I can run all day, screw all night, eat all I want—this is heaven!"

"Harrumph," croaked the doctor. "Umph. Pardon me. Indigestion. Have to stay away from Russian Lake Caviar." He rubbed a blue-veined hand over a red, blotchy forehead—puzzled, acutely uncomfortable. "We'll take more tests."

So they took more tests—excellent, carefully observed and conducted tests—all of which showed zero, zero, zero. Art Noone was healthy. Healthier than any 35-year-old had ever been before. Rejuvenation means far more than a sleek face: His body was a citadel—impenetrable to disease, impervious to infection, healing broken bones in short weeks, running like a shiny new Rolls, no rough edges. And of his mind, one may stutter only muddy similes. Think of light filling a cavern in loud sunbursts, the jangle of time-clogged mysteries in blood-bright flushes. All color, all sound, all nerves filed hard and sharp.

But he was growing, and the curve was smooth—a perfect parabola.

"Check in every two weeks."

There is a fact that only stupid people can ignore: You live in an ecology. A rat on the other limb of the world can destroy you. The past and the future are interlocked; from one proceeds the other, at a junction called Now. Just as there is an ecology of *life,* there is also and ecology of *time.* The tensions, balances, forces and strains of our dymaxion cosmos bend and flex our lives as struts in a great geodesic dome. All mass creates all life; all life sustains itself—through eternal and unstopping interaction. Universal tension. And, of course, the strains of *one* are distributed throughout the structure of *all.* Just as *all* reflects in the individual. The ultimate expression of a society is found in each individual—the strains of Totality are manifested in the Particular.

Ecology.

And nobody said the ecology had to be perfect.

Art, a great strapping monster by now, seven feet tall and puberty years young, found himself stranded in an alien landscape, a great bewildering flight from ecological reality. Naturally, this refugee from one insanity into another was an upsetting factor, a disastrous link in the big fat chain of society. Naturally, the local children of Paradise sensed this deeply in their cells, an ineluctable NAY! springing from their stunted California souls like semen out of a rutting bull. Naturally, Art Noone was (immortal and Pepsigeneration Superman though he be—the theoretical South C. Ideal) a bladderstone in the Great Urethra of Happiness that is LA. Oh, naturally. And what do you do with bladderstones?

Surgery:

Knock knock!

"Who's there?"

"Deputy."

"Deputy who?"

"Deputy Sheriff, you beatnick prick! Open the door!"

(Door opens.)

Knock knock!

(Cut to jail cell.)

"Mr. Noone, I'm very sorry to admit it, but your claims seem to be honest—completely straightforward. I think they should take you out in the desert and make you dig your own grave and then blow your head off, but after all, I am your attorney, appointed by Judge Glans himself, and I have to defend you (you bastard) in court. The charges are: (1) Obstructing an officer in the line of duty."

"My head got in the way of his pistol-butt."

"Precisely. (2) Escaping from a California Penal Institution, and endangering the morals of our Sovereign State's youth in the process. (3) Violation of Article 568 of the Censorship Act, which forbids using naughty words in private, public, or auto-conversation; and Article 569 of same code prohibiting cross-eyed glances at an Officer of the Law. (4) Being a menace to the public sensibilities."

Art injected: "Pardon me, but what is the definition of 'Public Sensibilities'?"

"That's for the Judge to decide, young man. If I were you, I'd leave the Law up to the lawyers, like God and our Founding Fathers intended."

"I see. I used to be a Law Clerk, you know."

"How nice."

(Exit lawyer.)

Why, wondered Art, must youth, even apparent youth, be persecuted? Could it be jealousy? Sex—a pederophobic sadism? The callous insensitivity and sloth timidity of the aged? An inborn desire to do hurt to the helpless? Glandular deficiency—progressive cretinism throughout the race? Plain malice? Or all of them, in various ratios and parts, according to individual cruelty or stupidity? Art was amazed by the increased sensitivity to pain he felt—how all sensations seemed magnified. Thinking about it as he squatted on the toilet listening to short efforts of urine trickle and tinkle into the water that had been stolen from Sacramento and Arizona, he conjectured (not altogether idly) that nerve cells must receive more oxygen and nutrient in the very young; that as one ages, and the capillaries fill with timely sludges and sediments, the nervous system starves and becomes more and more slow to respond—and responds weakly, with feeble electricities of pain or pleasure. How else to account for the diminishing discomforts (the decreasing notice of them) that follows age in its rusty tracks? What other truth could explain why a child will scream at a needleprick, and an adult merely mutter at evisceration. It's no wonder the old can accept death; by the time of old-age, you're barely even alive. Pain, like sight, fails as you age.

(Enter police officer, carrying bludgeon of titanium-clad lead.)

"Sonnyboy, git off that can. Ah'm gonna teach you a lesson."

"Yes, sir." Art stood, pulling his pants up.

"Just bend over so I can hit yore head a little."

"Yessir, baby."

The cop, a hundred kilos of sinew-webbed fat and bone-buttressed brain, swung his mace in a skull-devastating arc of hatred. Art, blur-fast, pranced aside. The cop's ugly rod sailed on past Art's head's former position, burying itself in the cop's foot like an infant trying to sink back into the womb. Howls of rage and revenge rang down the sterile metal corridors. Oaths were cast like heavy stones. On one clumsy foot, the drooling savage swung again at Art's head. But youth carried the sun-dripping day, and the billy smashed the cop's shin. Bone splintered; tongue swore; jaws worked and saliva gushed. "Cocksucker!" screamed the Law sagely. "Fucking commie pervert punk scum!" He hurled the bludgeon at Art's neck. Art, flicking his hand as if to ward off a gnat, deflected the ominous object from its righteous path. More screams from Good. Evil leaps on Good's back, rips off gray fuzz trousers, tears keys out of legalized Revenge's pocket. Kick in imbecile

head silences the forces of Right . . . and Wrong leaps
liberated out of cell, dashes in kangaroo leaps down jail
hall, past skeletons leering at him from behind silver
bars, rattles open another lock—

SIRENS SCREAM IN THE ULTIMATE HUNT-
ING NIGHT!

Cellblock door swings open, pursuit hot ahead. Art,
seven feet of rubbery iron flesh, leaps through a window (bars just spread like labia), falls two stories to
courtyard, sprints madly (arclight pinpoints evil, a
giant running grave) toward wall. . . . Guard screams,
"HALT OR I'LL SHOOT YOU MOTHERFUCKING
PIECE OF SHIT!" and looks surprised as a massive
hand slaps the machinegun equalizer out of his hand
and crushes his neck. Dark blood pools on the pale
ground. A tremendous twelve-foot leap, and Hero is
atop glass-toothed concrete wall, giving the Penal Authorities an unprintable suggestive gesture. Then Art
vanishes into the glowing suburban night, false prey in
a false dark.

Next Day:

" . . . No, no, I only killed a guard. They're dirt.
But I need some more money——MONEY!—and a
good place to hide.——Who?——*him?* Don't be a
boor. That Steinbartz gives me the willies. He's a faggot—a Jew faggot to boot.——Sorry about that.
Somma my best—hell.——Oh, hell, if you say so.
Those Jews don't screw around, I know—if they say
they got Security, and enough dough to bribe Mayor
Sam, then I gotta admit it. That goddamn hospital was
like a frigging fortress——whaddya mean, it *is* a fortress? Hello? Crap!"

Click.

Down his thousand white corridors, Feldman G.
Steinbartz huddled over precious notes. "Hummph," he
hummphed, "ha-hummph. You are a problem-boy. A
real nudnick. I only wish my little Ruth were alive to
see *this.*" He held up a graph. "Just look at you—
growing like nuclear proliferation! You are an anomaly

—a freak. Your crazy cardiac cure has been banned by the FDA because it causes overt sexual stimulation in the Borneo Crotch Bat—a totally damning sign. No drug that fails that test can reach the open market. You must've obtained it through—" peering over crafty glasses, "—quasi-legal sources."

A pregnant question requiring natal answers. "Dr. Blaum got it for me. He never said where."

"Well, young man, you are in deep trouble."

"They said that in jail. Just before I busted out."

"You are in *ecological* trouble." Semitic nose-rubbing. "Your biological ecology—your homeostasis—has been upset. Because of your little 'experiment,' your cells are undergoing a population explosion. I am certain that your case proves one thing: Growth is partly controlled by aging. The aging process in your case has been reversed—halted and then obliterated, through a poorly understood chemical agent. Now that your cells are receiving the oxygen and protein of brand new—infant—cells, your body is reacting as if you had actually *become* an infant again. You are therefore growing like a baby, will continue to grow until the arteriosclerotic deposits reach their previous level of corruption."

Art looked worried; he looked scared. "When will it stop? I can't go around twenty feet tall!"

"I beg your ridiculous pardon. An infant at birth is approximately one thirtieth his adult weight. A six-pound baby grows up to be a 180-pound man. At the time the drug was administered, your weight was 145 flabby pounds. Thus, when growth is completed—in about eighteen years—you will weigh about 3800 pounds and stand about eighteen feet tall. This estimate is based on your debilitated physical state at the time of the drug's administration. I notice you've improved a little since then—probably due to the cleansing out of the civilized poisons, a reduction to noble savagery—so that you are statistically optimum. The projected figures in that case are a weight of 5,400 pounds and a height of twenty-five feet. That's just as tall as Tyrannosaurus Rex at his glorious prime!"

"Lucky me," mumbled Art.

"Of course, your merely human body is not constructed to support such tremendous weight—your joints would collapse under the pressure—so you'll either spend the rest of your life supine, in a circus tent, or submerged in water, for support. You'll reach the limits of bipedal posture—it may even kill you. Really, medicine is a privilege, not a right; I think you're getting what you deserve for abusing that privilege."

Art stomped out, through the thousand clean corridors, into the luminous California air. The tiny, bright figures of men scuttled around his waist. Children pointed and giggled. Blond-bleached housewives pointed and speculated unladylike among themselves. Blond, muscular lads with surfboards tied to the roofs of their million autos honked and jeered. Thousands of strangers became a little more strange.

Freakishness set in.

It was wonderful to destroy. Picking up a suntanned midget in a black LA Gestapo uniform, Art snapped the doll's back—

Crack!

Art found himself lying in bed, legs and head high, rump low. The bed, eleven feet long, had snapped its wooden spine. Art twisted himself out of the ruins and surveyed the carnage: one super-hollywood wreckage. Prognosis: 100% medically, clinically, biologically dead. The yellow sun leered through his window like a manic, grotesque fruit. Sounds of randy automobile horns whistled through the air; the omnipresent highway coughed carcinogenous soot and sighs into his blackened lungs, boils and cankers studding his bronchial tubes. Everything, within his whitewashed apartment or without, was shrouded in thick white haze. Whites upon whites—color eluded him. He groped his way to the bathroom—sterile white porcelain—and washed his face in limp water. Staring into the glossy, flawless pane of uncritical mirror, he recognized a malignant growth.

But organized, orchestrated. A coherent cancer.

Still growing.

The floor (two inches of styrofoam and fiberglass) groaned under mammoth feet. Elephantine arms (trunks of tissue) fumbled with the electric minutiae of the kitchen and managed to snap off the toaster handle. *No toast.* The thought was clear as cut diamond, as solid and substantial as any childhood perception. Reality intruded on the unreal adult world. Youth's famished fires rekindled.

Clomp, clomp, clomp. Out into sunny (light! forever!) bedlam. (But, like the cancer of his body, an organized bedlam. Bedlam with rules. Bedlam sanctified and dressed in the flamboyant drag of Law.) Kiddy-cars beeped epithets at his waist. Volkswagen sarcasms hooted nimbly. Witty motorcycle bronx cheers drove him paranoid.

Stomp, stomp, stomp. Twenty long blocks to the Hypermarket. Ten pounds of parsley, twenty of salt (for the shaker), fifty of spare-ribs, a hundred of potatoes—

Andsoforth.

Tramp, tramp, tramp. He gargantuaed up the stairs, behemothed open the door, squeezed in, godzillaed across the living room, return-of-godzillaed into the kitchen, dropped three hundred pounds of groceries (two-day supply) on shiny linoleum floor, and wrapped king kong hairy fist around petite fay wray princess telephone—

"Hello, Dr. Blaum's office? No, this isn't an emergency. No, miss, I'm not calling for advice. No, I won't call back in half an hour he's busy. He's sitting on his arse filling out phony prescriptions for his pillhead friends, I oughtta know. Get him on the line—

"Blaum? Art Noone. Look, you lousy quack, you

got me into this—don't give me that crap!—and you're
gonna get me out. I want fast, fast, fast relief, or I'll
. . . Oh. Oh, you do . . . well, I didn't know that. Gee
doc, I'm sorry I called you that, really—"

Click.

"Hello? Hello?! Lousy sonofabitch!"

Thud, thud, thud. Ooze blobly into car. Drive them-
wise over rambling, rumbling concrete tapeworm, the
parasite in the pristine guts of Man. Endless road, the
shimmering heat-devils belly-dancing in the white glare,
till—

(Dr. Steinbartz, down thousand sterile corridors.)

"What may I do for you, my boy?" He looked up,
way up, into a shadow, at the sunshine superman.

"I don't want to be big." Art's burned graphite face
(hanging like cascade Gardens of Babylon in fleshy
folds) scowled; the not-so-delusive hysteria of Persecu-
tion was active in his brain.

"My boy, medicine is a privilege, not a right. You
cannot evade your responsibilities—your ecological responsibilities. You have tampered with Mother Nature;
now you must pay dearly. If you want, I can prescribe
a sedative. Or aspirin. However, I cannot, will not,
alleviate your condition."

A subsonic groan: "Why not?"

"You aren't Jewish. That will be five dollars, thank
you."

"Urrr-ggh-hh!" growled Art, maniac in his brain, out-
cast in his world, monster in his body. 7,000 pounds
of overfed meat, thriving on the sunlight, honey, and
rich organic wilderness of synthetic air—three and one-
half tons of slightly mad revenge.

"Arr-gghh-hh!!" he announced, and leaped at Doctor Feldman Steinbartz, MD, PhD.

"Yeea-agghh!" screamed Feldman, covering his eyes
with skinny old arms. Art picked him up in Beast-from-
20,000 Fathoms bone/thew tentacles, held the frail old
head in one giant hand and spindly, varicose legs in the
other—and splintered the doctor's brittle back. Blood

jetted out of the old man's mouth and dribbled into his blind, terror-wide eyes. Art threw him down, a used-up rag, and lurched insanely down a thousand screaming corridors.

The City of Angels gibbered, a whimper of raw cowardice. It was a town without a single speck of self-honesty—a sick town, made by sick people; the cycle was absurd, for sick people are generated by sick societies. Hot yellow sun on their sweating brows, the natives of Paradise fed okies to the Slime God in an attempt to assuage the angry fates. The Slime God (Mayor Sam himself, the puppet police-chief on his right arm) screamed *Sedition!,* bellowed *Subversion!,* raved *Anarchy!,* howled *Treason!,* bit his official Mayorial carpet in froths of righteous fear.

Governor Ronnie called on the telephone:

"What's this 'Monster' shit I keep hearing about on TV?"

Oily, oily, Sam soothed: "Now, Ronnieboy, don't worry your slick little head. The dye might run or something. We can settle this without outside interference. You just sit there in Sacramento and take care of your little problems, and we'll take care of ours. We don't need a thing here; we have it all."

Click.

The Slime God turned to his apprentice, spick/span young confident Dick Peck. Said Dick: "Clean out this fungus. Wipe this decomposing excreta from our sensitive bottom. Spray the insect with a Black Flag of purity and Public Decency."

"How," said Mayor Sam, "how so?" His turtle forehead was furrowed with worry.

"Call out the Militia," Dick Peck ejaculated. "Expunge this violence with violence beyond."

Delight erased the wrinkles and lighted the beady eyes. Up was picked a telephone, dialed was a number.

Forth marched the armies, Gideon trumpeting ecstatioally.

". . . So, kiddies," lisped Skipper Fagg, "send in all your little dimes, and we'll be able to finance the struggle for the White Race against the hideous menace stalking us all. Remember, send ten cents (or more) to Skipper Fagg's Faery Funhouse, 1776 Ventura Boulevard, and we'll send you a free SKIPPER FAGG'S FREEDOM FITE button of your very own. If you send in twenty-five cents, you'll get a free NIGGER NOONE dartboard and twelve barbed darts. Now remember—"

A tremendous crash. Dust and sudden pulverized clouds of billowing stucco. Plaster shaken from the roof. Screams, disembodied and terrible. The screen goes dark. We float in aimless darkness and silence for a few seconds. . . . Then, abruptly, we are injected back into glaring chaos. Skipper Fagg's mangled body lies sprawled across the big Fun Fallus clubhouse roof. Behind this is a terrible, ominous shape. . . . We focus . . . and see the revolting hulk of NIGGER NOONE, sunburnt black by the ubiquitous light, gesturing obscenely at our captive camera. "Noone takes no shit, kiddies. Skipper Fagg—look at him. He tried to give Noone shit. Skipper Fagg—you! behind the camera! get a closeup of that or I'll tear you apart!—now look at him. His neck is broken. His teeth got smashed down his throat. I tore off his nuts. Now, kids, that *hurts!* Hurts like hell. That's *pain,* kids. You ain't been alive till you felt *pain.* That's the trouble with this place—nobody feels any pain. It's all vanilla ice-cream and pepsi-cola. Well, listen: All that is changing right now. Art Noone—you remember that name—is running the show now. You kids do what I tell you—or you'll wind up like Skipper Fagg. I'll sneak up on you when you're sleeping and—"

A flash, concussion, schrapnel, then numb darkness.

(Cut to Sunset Strip.)

Rockets arced through the air spewing tails of incandescent yellow vapor. Striking the ground, they exploded into incandescence a thousandfold more brilliant, followed by shards of shrapnel and skull-shattering concussion. Bombs fell like a clashing of teeth. Art, trapped in the dichotomy of necessity and hatred, leaped from crater to crater in desperate fury, throwing stolen hand-grenades, mortar bombs, and occasional bullet-bursts at the avenging forces of oppression. The cops, all white, clad like night in cellophane shadows, blasted obscenities at him over loudspeakers, trying to shatter his spirit.

"ALL RIGHT, YOU COMMY BASTARD, PUT UP YOUR HANDS AND THROW DOWN YOUR MACHINE GUN, AND WE WON'T HARM YOU. YOU NIGGER PRICK."

Art huddled briefly in the ruins of a nightclub. His feet, slabs of tissue as large as pigs, sank deeply into a pile of cigarette papers and burnt-out roaches. The time-dried bones of a boy leered up at him, a distant white skull grinning with clean porcelain teeth. *Giant!,* the skull to accuse; *freak!*

Rock crumbled as a mortar round landed twenty meters away.

The rumble of heavy trucks.

Art peeped over the broken wall. A convoy of trucks —*Army* trucks. . . . ?

(Cut to Slime God, in sterile office.)

"No—no! We don't want any outside interference. Governor Ronnie, we don't *need* any. None! What do you mean—what? President Lynberg? You didn't! He called out the National Guard? Ronnie, this is terrible! How can we ever contain Whatts if we bring in outside agitation? Remember, it's only enclosed by barbed wire and machine-gun nests. . . . Those fucking black hordes could come spilling out of the Camp at any provocation. . . . I know that. Fine. But still, we don't need any outside interference—oh, go to hell!"

Click.

The Slime God (disguised as mild-minded Mayor Sam) probed thin, sneaky fingers through oily kidstuff hair. The television set in the corner of the office winked commercials at him like enticements to sodomy

—poopy-poop-poop music and Fab-grab-blab lyrics. Somehow, the whole thing seemed pointless, hollow. Mayor Sam's plastic and sunshine world crumbled into schizophrenic horror.

"Governor Ronnie can't help me," he subvocalized. "President Lynberg won't help things, the bumbler—*he* will cause this city to disappear in the stink of Black Revolution. This is a white town, and I aim to keep it that way." Issues were obscured in his foggy brain; bad decisions were arrived at.

"This," he said to himself at last, in the final throes of identity annihilation, "looks like a job for—*SLIME GOD!!*"

Alone in the empty office, he put on new skins.

The masses (black, in silver chains) rioted. Bricks were tossed at police cars, first; then bullets.

A surge of black flesh, death reveling in its ranks, gushed through the barbed-wire borders of Whatts Detention Camp and spread out across the hot summer streets like a million warrior ants in tropical torpor, frenzied dream. In anguished hatred, they hunted the parasite-pale white man, his racial HAVE like blood to the black sharks' ravenous HAVE NOT.

The white maggots shuddered.

Like an ebony Pharoah in the trembling mucous sunlight towered Art Noone. Jew millions at his feet were crushed. He swept through the truck convoy from behind, like ghost Indians shrieking down upon a phantom video wagon-train of European bandits, reclaiming the land for the landless. Machine guns rattled like a dying man's throat, but Art's hide was armor, his bones steel, and his appearance the embodiment of terror. White soldiers died as their truck was lifted in hands the size of fate and smashed to the ground, flaming graveyards, gasoline cocktails in the gullet of fear. Screams of fat, frail suburbanites wailed weakly and died after little struggling. Truck after truck was crushed, upset, picked up whole and strewn across the desert landscape in burning bits of metal and thumb-nail gouges of dismembered flesh. Cannons bellowed, rockets whistled, human throats roared and were torn open—jugular sorrow and spinal tears.

The convoy lay in piles of burning garbage.

Art stood high in the streaming light—naked onyx monstrosity with eyes redder than ruby laser-beams—and beat his chest. Some primal brutality had filled his soul, drained intelligence out of his mind, ignited the basic spark of the killer into a blazing pyre of death-hungry insanity. In triumphant ten-meter strides, he began smashing and ravaging his way towards the far-off white spire of City Hall, which glinted in the unend-ing light like some proud sexual beacon, a sacred white needle of superiority and power.

(Cut to Slime God.)

The Mayor of Los Angeles waited behind City Hall. His face was a slavering green vegetable, the drooling insides of a green pepper. White fangs peeped out of a slash of mouth, a red wound cut half across the green mask. His eyes were tiny, vicious embers of bigotry; yellow cataracts protected the small retinae from undue perceptions. His hands were malignant tumors of muscle, jagged with barbed claws, splintered-glass scales, horny protuberances, and a long black poison-ous switchblade spur hidden in each thumb. Four em-erald snakes coiled out of his sides, rib-crushing ten-tacles that could hold populations in their maniac grasp. His loins were swollen, impotent bags of rotting tissue, the necrosis of love; shame, or some hidden corruption, had flushed his genitals florid, red stoplights in the green golight afternoon. His legs were foul green stumps of putrescent flesh—pillars of plastic snot, gelatinous hunks of gangrene—with anemone-studded boils flow-ering explosions of decomposing ichor, rivers of pus flowing down to forked, split feet, each toe capped with lizard claws, gleaming knives of sinister black enamel. He hooked his claws through a fifth floor window, and waited.

(Cut to NIGGER NOONE.)

Pommeled by the fist-reality of heightened senses, Art's mind crumbled like charcoal into thalamal bestiality. The odor of urine blasted out of restaurants and hypermarkets; fecal smells drifted on latrine winds from the bars; women stank like dead fish, decomposing garbage. The world was a repository of filth, waste life's reward. The sun glowered like a sentinel of hell over the battlefield, a demon in lifeless space awaiting souls to collect by millions and damn. The noxious farts of ten million autos choked his lungs, rose before his red-rimmed eyes like thick steam, obscuring everything, diffusing the light until the objects in this shimmering landscape glowed, blurs of dulled color surrounded by multiple diffraction rings; spectra melted together, red through yellow and green into violet, actinic pain scorching the eyes into dead insensitivity, total blindness. His skin was blistered by chemical catastrophe, charred into blackness by a futile attempt at society in shit. Ecologies were violated—nothing lives in waste, nothing but the damned.

The giant soul of Art Noone crossed the last bridge, leaving concrete footprints three feet long, and entered Paradise's final, innermost citadel. Inside Paradise, like a worm in a brain, is Hell.

A bridal train of negro crime followed Art into Heaven. A million black refugees from insanity, finding themselves still unfree, converged behind a racial hero upon Los Angeles City Hall . . . and, Crusaders, did battle unto their Reward.

The only reward is death.

Art Noone stood still in the zenith sun and screamed. "All right, you scum, come out and fight!"

Not a voice peeped; the city was silent. A hot wind rustled concrete leaves, whistled through asphalt forests. Art called again, but no one called back. The City Hall building wavered in the light, a gleaming white fang. Silence.

Art trudged closer. He walked up to a wall and pounded on it. Fifty windows cracked; bird droppings, dust from time, billowed in white clouds into white air and dissipated. He pounded again. Still silence. He started to walk around the building.

The west wall yielded as much as the south. Silence, falling shards of glass, and bird-dropping snow. He yelled again, and walked around to the north side.

Something sank steel knives into his back.

Sirens.

Flame from sudden tanks.

Incendiary bombs, napalm, poison gas. The negro mob suddenly melted, black skin peeling back to show red blood, boiling under napalm fires to turn soot-black and blow away in a desert wind. Beneath the negro skin, the human blood, muscles writhed in mass agony; screams—the screams of a hundred thousand dying; human flesh blistering and burning in the long city afternoon.

Art tore the thing off his back and threw it against the white building. It was green, pocked, horrible. Its mouth—razor white teeth in a festering sore. Eyes—like puddles of leukemia-riddled blood. The thing scrambled off its haunches, and with a mindless scream *(NIGGER-R-R-R!)* threw itself at Art's corded black throat. Art swatted at it with his fist, crunching monstrous encysted bone under green blasphemy flesh. The animal fell back with a muffled grunt, and immediately lunged at him again. Machine-gun bullets, like impotent hornets, stung his thighs, but he ignored them. A mortar-round burst ten feet away, deafening him for an instant. The Slime God attacked—but then stood immobile as Art fixed it with burning diamond eyes.

Art and the Slime God peered into each others' souls—and quivered at the alien perception. In the Slime God, Art saw himself, as once he was. In Art, the Slime God saw how he might have been—born under a different star.

They spoke, and there was no other voice in the city.

"How did we come to this meeting?" said Slime God.

"Through the tangled highways of Fate," Art rumbled.

"Why are we thus?" said Slime God wonderingly.

"You're trapped inside of you, I'm trapped inside of me. That's just how it is—and neither of us seems able to live with it."

Understanding gave Art power over the twisted weir-shape of Mayor Sam. Fear lanced from Art's eyes into the other's bowels, and the Slime God turned to flee.

Scuttling up the white tower's slick sides.

Art leaped up after him. Five floors up, Art caught Slime God's oily leg and tried to pull him loose. But Slime God reached wildly through a window, locked steel claws around an office safe, hurled it down upon Noone. It struck him on the shoulder, and fell to the street. Art moaned—the shoulder was cracked. Slime God snarled down at him. A ghost of mirth began to spread across the bureaucratic abomination's face. Art quickly crawled up after him. He had the advantage and was not going to lose it.

Slime God shrieked. He felt his life draining away as he crawled away from the gutter, the sewers, all the life-sustaining fuel of politicians. The higher he climbed, the weaker he became. Art swiped at the monster's leg, barely missing, at the tenth floor. Ten floors above, the obelisk was capped by a flag spire, impaling the sky like a hypodermic needle. The sky was sickly, pocked with sores (clouds like purple hearts). Art craned his head towards it, taking fateful aim. Slime God looked up at it in abject terror, and wailed thinly. He reached a supplicating hand out to the sun; Sol sat demon in hollow space and ignored him. Death favors no man.

Slime God, defeated as he struggled, started to climb.

Behind in blind pursuit, the last Black hero strived towards annihilation.

At the top, they grappled. Slime God scratched his way to the tower's pinnacle, and clung out of breath to the quivering mast. Art Noone pulled himself to the edge, put his foot through a window for a foothold, and thrust himself up toward Slime God.

Slime God urinated on him. "Piss on all the black races!" he shrieked. Art, filled with masochistic hatred, tried to grab the Mayor's slippery ankle. Slime God slashed Noone's forearm with the shiv of his toe. Noone howled in pain and rage. His eyes were red welts of hatred. Slime God lashed out at him again—and Noone grabbed the two-toed foot in fury. It slipped out of his clutch, oily with unction and lies. Art, bitter and frustrated, filled with the hellishness of hate, leaped the last thirty feet. His bulk came down on the roof wth enough force to knock a chunk of stone into space. Slime God watched it spin slowly, suspended for an instant by some trickery of vision, and drift 250 feet to the ground. It shattered as it hit. Slime God saw his own skull collapse in the debris.

Noone grasped the flag-tower in one enormous black fist, and smashed at Slime God with the other. Sam lashed at the black incarnation with whip-fast tentacles. The blows made the whole building shudder, dislodging plaster from the ceilings, windows from their sills, sending stone and riot's rubble crashing to the awed streets below. Crowds, grown brave with isolation, gathered to watch the two avatars tear the life from each other. Oblivious to the mobs, Slime God clawed Noone with his poison switchblade claws, raking them across the black face. Thick red furrows appeared; blood flowed out of the furrows like crimson waterfalls. It ran down the building's sides, staining the white symbol red.

"Give up, Slime God," Noone screamed. His voice echoed through the flatland streets. "You're defeated already. You can't stop NIGGER NOONE!" With one mighty hand, Noone deftly ripped the great Flag from its staff; he tied it around his neck in a blur of fingers. The impromptu cape rippled and snapped in the high winds, a gaudy vestige of power in subdued flight.

"Go to hell, Nigger Noone," bellowed Slime God, lacerating Noone's chest with a lightning rake of his talons. "I'll never give up! *Never!*"

"Then you'll die, fascist scum!" Noone kicked with his free foot. The foot landed in Slime God's swollen green belly, knocking him clear around the erect flagpole; the monster grunted in pain, but held on.

"You haven't got me yet, Noone!" He, in turn, kicked out at the Black Avenger. The black god's thigh splattered blood in furious spurts over the monolith's white glans. Noone howled in agony.

"Thought you could get rid of Slime God that easily, did you Noone?" roared Slime God in false triumph. He relaxed his grip to deliver the death bite with ice-sickle fangs of cold death.

Colder death came hunting.

Art let go of the pole with one hand, and wrenched at Slime God's loose forearm with his crack-shouldered right hand. The pain throbbed, like the throbbing of orgasm. Vice-fingers clamped down over Slime God's nerve-laced flesh. White fire shot through the Mayor's feeble brain. The green hand relaxed on the spire completely; Noone held a screaming Slime God, kicking and clawing, upside-down over empty space.

"Look down, look down, look at what holds you up, Slime God!" The Mayor stared wild-eyed down at nothing, and let out a shrill peal of fear, the shriek of a million sirens in sober pursuit of death.

"Die, scum!" roared NIGGER NOONE, whipping Slime God over his black head, twirling him like a hollow-boned bird, then flinging the money-green apparition into space.

Mayor Sam sailed twenty floors to the sidewalk—and spattered in sprays of yellow blood.

Art screamed in victory; his voice mumbled across the entire basin like powerful, distant thunder.

"This is what happens to those who defy NIGGER

NOONE! Beware the Black Giant! The rape of the Slave is the rape of the World!"

All the ears were closed, deaf.

Bright steel birds flickered in the white sky. Art snapped his head around—and saw a shining metal wing swoop not fifty yards from the flag-tower. The roar of jet exhaust drowned his hysterical voice. The screams of the white mob below drowned even the jet.

He broke off the top of the flagpole, prepared to defend himself and his land against the planes. Now a whole squadron of them appeared—Messerschmidts, with L.A. POLICE DEPT. stenciled across the wings and fusilage. Some Nazi treachery had equipped the cops with the most vicious fighting machines ever built. Art swatted hopelessly at the flying sabers.

Machine-guns chattered in the pale sunlight. Granite chips jumped into the air. Art bellowed, and swiped at a plane. He hit a slow-moving wing, and it broke off. He could hear the black-helmeted pilot's scream as the plane veered into a nearby parking-lot and exploded. Then concussion.

But the wing had severed all the fingers on Art's left hand. The stumps glistened red and white in the sun's fading rays. Blood gushed out of severed arteries.

Copper-jacketed lightning shattered bones in Art's right shin. The foot dangled on ligament and sinew; muscles twitched futilely. "If this is the end," he screamed, "let me die like a man!"

Art stood up, on one foot chained and one foot ruined, at the summit of Los Angeles, and defied the planes roaring around him. He beat his chest in rage and apish hatred. His eyes glowed bloody, weeping incarnadine tears of impossible lust for murder. All the deaths of Earth's most violent species shouted in his brain. *Kill, kill, kill, kill,* screamed the warrior genes. "Death," whispered the Conquerer Past, a goad of the inevitable, and the argument was utterly convincing

Machine-gun bullet-bursts stuttered through his chest; the blood drained out of his brain. His glorious cape was torn from his neck; it fell in shreds to dishonor and oblivion. His body went limp. He fainted. Without a whimper, the black giant relaxed his last grip and fell from the climax of the white monolith in a slow, shallow arc twenty stories to the shimmering street. His skull was smashed to featureless pulp as he struck the pavement. Blood splattered clear across the plaza.

The body of Art Noone lay motionless and silent.

Amazed, frightened, white crowds gathered.

A few hours later, when curiosity had been sated and all the blood drunk into all the fat bellies, a garbage truck came and removed the bodies of Art Noone and the Slime God, Mayor Sam dead and naked. They were carried five miles to the La Brea Tar Pits and dumped uncermoniously in. Mammoths and ground sloths jostled for space. In minutes, the oily black tar had covered both bodies, had added another monster cipher to the pages of the past.

Everything went back to normal. Patrols of militia and vigilantes resumed their nocturnal prowls, sustaining order and spraying aerosol lies over the stink of the decomposing dead. The gutters filled wtih blood; the sewers overflowed with lymph and pus. The city throbbed again in a quiet pulse of commerce and greed. The nightmare had been only a flutter, a social fibrillation.

Across the street from the deserted City Hall, eating hamburgers in nervous bolts, the last reporter sat talking to a survivor of the purge.

The little spade sat mopping his brow with both manacled hands in the shade of the drive-in awning, looking patiently at the reporter. The white reporter was puzzled. The day's events had baffled him; he thought they were beyond understanding.

A grin flashed white in the obsidian face.

"This here America," the little burr-head said smiling, relaxed, "this is all a *mirage*. We all just on *vacation* here. Pretty soon, now, we all gonna pack up our things, put all our sanity in an overnight bag, and catch the train back to *reality,* where we come from in the *first* place!" He laughed.

In the glare and heat, the reporter shivered.

The tarpits bubbled.

*The first in a series
of superb science fiction short stories.*

ALPHA ONE

Edited by
Robert Silverberg

*ALPHA TWO soon to be available from
Ballantine Books*

From the old pro's to the new wave—the best
science fiction of the best science fiction writers.

Brian W. Aldiss	Damon Knight
J. G. Ballard	R. A. Lafferty
Alfred Bester	Fritz Leiber
James Blish	Barry Malzburg
Larry Eisenberg	Ted Thomas
Charles L. Harness	Jack Vance
C. M. Kornbluth	Roger Zelazny

The variety of subjects in this collection is matched
only by the richness and diversity of their handling
—brilliant, frightening, clever, bizarre, powerful,
witty, funny—and several steps in-between.

Wonderful reading by any standards—and a positive feast for science fiction cognoscenti.

To order by mail, send $1.00 to Dept. CS, Bal-
lantine Books, 36 West 20th Street, New York,
N.Y. 10003

**Winner of the HUGO Award for the
Best Science Fiction Novel**

STAND ON ZANZIBAR
John Brunner

". . . Brunner conducts himself brilliantly."
—Judith Merril

". . . far from conventional science fiction-
fantasy."

—*Publisher's Weekly*

A Giant of a Book

650 pages! $1.65